THE CHEATER'S GAME

GLASS AND STEELE, #7

C.J. ARCHER

CHAPTER 1

LONDON, SUMMER 1890

*T*he American Wild West was precisely how I imagined it would be. The hot sun beat down on the dry earth, horses' hooves kicked up dust as cowboys chased off the Indians, and characters I'd only read about in Willie's dime novels whooped and hollered. Willie didn't appear to be enjoying the show as much as me, however. I did my best to ignore her and concentrate on the ATTACK ON AN EMIGRANT TRAIN BY INDIANS, AND REPULSE BY THE COWBOYS, the fifth act on the program.

"Their hollering really carries," I said. "I can hear them clearly even from here. Although we do have good seats."

Matt had secured tickets two rows from the front in the grand arena at the Earls Court Exhibition Grounds for Buffalo Bill's Wild West show. I'd not been interested in attending at first when I discovered the date, but now I was rather grateful for the distraction. Sheriff Payne's execution was scheduled for today. Watching the cowboys, sharp-shooters, Indians, and other performers for a few hours was better than sitting at home, watching the clock. Not only would it stop me thinking about our role in ending his life, it

1

would also stop me worrying about Patience's wedding to Lord Cox. Ever since they announced their engagement two weeks ago, I'd had a niggling doubt it wouldn't go ahead. My blackmail of Lord Cox had worked very well and he'd agreed to marry her, thereby freeing Matt from his obligation, yet I'd expected the baron to renege every day since. Even now, two days after the wedding had hopefully taken place at Rycroft Hall, my stomach was knotted with anxiety. A distraction in the form of grand entertainment was certainly welcome. When Matt purchased two tickets, I thought he and I would go for his birthday last week, but he'd insisted Willie accompany me. Duke and Cyclops had flatly refused. I couldn't think why. The show was marvelous.

"Oh look, the cowboys are coming to the rescue," I said, sitting up straighter.

Willie snorted.

"Look at that riding," I said. "They're going terribly fast and only holding on with one hand. It's very skillful."

She snorted again.

"The Indians are riding bareback," I went on. "Even you must concede that's very well done."

She finally bit. "Riding bareback ain't hard to do, India." She emitted another snort as she crossed her arms over her chest. "Most of us learned to ride that way before we were knee high to a fly."

"Yes, but at those speeds? With only one hand on the reins while someone is shooting at you?"

"The cowboys ain't really shooting at them. There ain't no real danger."

"They're in danger of falling off."

"No, they ain't," she said forcefully. "You're so gullible, India."

I rounded on her. "And you're jealous of Annie Oakley

getting all the attention." I turned back to the show, determined not to miss more than a moment and equally determined not to be drawn into Willie's moroseness.

"Jealous?" she cried. "Of *actors* making fools of themselves in a ridiculous show?"

The woman in front of us turned and probably meant to hush Willie, but the sight of a woman dressed as a man seemed to shock her into silence.

"What?" Willie snapped at her. "This is what a lady sharpshooter really looks like. Not *that*." She waved a hand at the arena where a few minutes ago, Annie Oakley's bullets had split a card held edge-on and hit coins tossed in the air. I'd been in awe. Willie had sniffed and slouched in her seat.

The woman turned back to the performance without uttering a word.

"Are you saying you're as good as Annie Oakley?" I asked Willie.

"Put a cigarette in your mouth and let's see if I can shoot it in half."

I lowered my gaze to her waist, hidden beneath a masculine jacket and waistcoat. "Please tell me you left your gun at home."

"Call me jealous again and you'll find out."

I rolled my eyes and turned back to the show. When Willie got like this, there was no talking to her.

Unfortunately she wasn't in the mood to be ignored either. "Annie Oakely ain't bad," Willie conceded. "But this..." She pointed her chin at the cowboy and Indian theatrical. "This is just a play. It ain't real. It ain't even close to being real."

"It seems to me the riders are really riding, and the Indians look real from here. The program says the wagons are even the same ones used years ago."

"It's a cliché."

"Clichés start out as original. Besides, that doesn't mean it's inaccurate."

"The true Wild West ain't like that."

"Perhaps not anymore, but it must have been years ago, before your time."

She swore under her breath. "It's overdone, India, created for folk like you who're wet behind the ears."

"Does it matter? It's entertaining and interesting. Now be quiet, you're ruining it for me."

"And for me," the woman in front piped up.

Thankfully Willie obliged. She even climbed out of her sour mood to watch the re-enactment of a buffalo hunt, complete with sixteen real buffalos. It seemed she'd finally grasped the enormous scale of the production and appreciated how difficult it must have been to bring so many people and animals to England.

"Buffalo Bill is an incredible man," I said after the final applause faded and people rose to leave.

"Pfft. I know dozens who can shoot like him," she said.

"I mean to organize a show like this. You have to admire him for it."

"I s'pose I do. Can we get a drink now? I'm as thirsty as a lizard in the desert."

I wanted to see the rest of the exhibition first but it was easier to keep Willie satisfied by obliging. We left the arena, stopping at the first refreshment bar we came across. Unfortunately, so did many other spectators who'd been watching the Wild West show.

"There's too many people," Willie whined.

"I can't do anything about that," I said, joining the end of the queue.

Willie, however, walked off. It would seem she wasn't too thirsty after all. We crossed the bridge over the railway line and entered the main building. It was filling up quickly with ticket-holders who'd come from the arena after the show. I wanted to take my time and look at the displays of American products, but Willie wasn't interested. She walked right past the whirring sewing machines and didn't even glance at the noisy printing presses. I, however, paused at the paper making equipment. Mr. Hendry the paper magician had created his paper by hand, using the traditional method of soaking rags until pulpy. Of course, he improved the quality of his paper by infusing magic through it. This paper felt thinner, the quality poorer.

"Isn't it great?" asked the salesman.

"Very nice," I said, moving on.

Willie had disappeared. She couldn't have got very far, but I could no longer see her amid the crush of people. I might look for her all day and not find her. When I did find her, I'd wring her neck. She was as bad as Matt's aunt, Miss Glass. No, she was worse. At least Miss Glass had the excuse of her age and mental infirmity; Willie had no excuse. She was simply selfish.

We must have stumbled into the machinery section of the exhibition. The clanking, stamping, and grinding of American ingenuity filled every stall as well as my head. I was surrounded by noise. I forged on until I came to the end of the aisle. Up ahead were two pavilions. The sign out the front of the right one said Art Gallery, and the left Dining Saloon. Willie was no art lover.

I pushed open the door to the saloon and spotted her sitting at a table with two men. Somehow, in the short period of time we'd been separated, she'd found someone to play cards with. She'd never leave now, going by the gleam in her eye.

"There you are," I said, joining her.

"Shhh. I'm thinking." She pushed up the brim of her hat

and studied her cards. She had a poor hand but spent a long time considering her options.

Her two companions studied me as they waited. "Good afternoon," one said in an American accent. "You been to see the show?"

"I have," I said. "It was marvelous. Are you part of the exhibition? Do you have a stall in here?"

"We're in the show, ma'am." The man had an impressive moustache that drooped past his chin. It was thick and darker than the hair on his head, and threaded with gray. His friend was younger, about thirty as opposed to forty, with dimples and boyish good looks that would have made my heart flutter at fifteen years of age. He gave me a cursory glance before returning to the game.

"How exciting," I said. "Are you one of the riders?"

"Riders and sharpshooters, both of us."

"I was very impressed with your skill. The way you scooped up those flags without falling off looked extremely difficult. You're very talented."

"Stop gushing, India," Willie said, discarding three cards. "It ain't becoming for a lady in your situation."

I gave her a tight smile. "I wasn't gushing."

Willie grabbed my hand and showed the men the ring on my finger. "She's marrying my cousin."

The mustachioed man laughed and picked up his glass. "We were just talking."

His friend smirked and discarded two cards from his hand. "Leave her be, Emmett, and play. I got to win back my wages or my wife'll skin me."

I snatched my hand away. "You look set to stay here a while, Willie. I'll be back in an hour."

I left them to their poker and wandered past the kiosks. There was so much to see, from American-grown food to American-made everything. I inspected coaches and tools, woods and precious metals, weapons, medical apparatus, jewelry, musical and scientific instruments, and several stalls dedicated to the finer arts. An hour wasn't long enough. I gave up touching objects when I realized I couldn't see everything in that time. I'd not felt magical heat once.

Magicians wouldn't exhibit at an extravagant fair anyway. It was too risky to display their wares, particularly now that speculation about magic was still rife, despite newspaper articles on the subject having ceased. The speculation had reached America, so Oscar Barratt told me. His article from *The Weekly Gazette* had been republished overseas, but only in a small regional newspaper in Ohio. The existence of magic was hotly debated here, but it had not reached the same heights there.

I wasn't sure if that was a good thing or not.

I returned to the saloon to find Willie sitting with the same two men. I tried getting her attention from across the room but she didn't look up. She was focused on the game. By the look of the stack of coins in front of her, she was winning.

"Ready?" I asked her.

"The hour ain't up yet," she said.

"Yes it is."

The mustachioed man—Emmett—pulled out a gold chronograph and perpetual calendar watch from his waistcoat pocket. It looked like a LeCoultre we'd fixed in our shop two years ago. LeCoultre watches were expensive. "Your friend's right, Miss Johnson. You better go with her." He threw his cards on the table, face down.

The younger man slid them back to Emmett. "*We* don't have to stop playing."

"It ain't no fun with just two." The impressive mustache twitched with Emmett's smile and his dark brown eyes sparkled. "Miss Johnson brings class to the table. It's no surprise she's winning."

Class? Good lord, if he was going to flirt with her, he should at least make it believable.

The only sign Willie gave that she'd heard him was the pinking of her cheeks. "Let's finish this round, gen'lemen, then I better go before steam rises from India's ears."

Emmett picked up his cards. Both men lost and Willie won the round. She pocketed her winnings and rose.

"Real pleasure," she said, tugging on her hat brim. "Maybe we can do this again some time while you're in London."

"How 'bout tonight?" Emmett asked, also rising. The younger man lurched to his feet too, as if he just remembered Willie were a woman and a man should stand when a woman did. He picked up his glass but noticed it was empty and put it down again with a sigh.

"Sure," Willie said. "Where?"

"The Prince of Wales, a saloon near here. A pub, as the English say. The cast often go there after a show. Bring your fiancé, ma'am," he said to me.

"He's away. But can we bring two of our friends? They're homesick Americans and will be delighted to meet you."

"Delighted," he mimicked in a terrible English accent.

I laughed. He laughed too and kissed my hand before turning his attention to Willie and repeating the action. She was stunned into speechlessness.

"See you tonight," I said, taking her arm.

"Bring your friend," she said with a nod at the younger man.

Emmett clapped him on the shoulder. "I will if his old lady lets him."

"She ain't the boss of me," the man mumbled.

Willie and Emmett exchanged grins.

"Come on, Emmett," the young man said as we walked off. "Let's keep playing."

"You better stop while you've still got something left, otherwise your old lady'll use you for target practice," Emmett said.

"His wife's a sharpshooter in the show," Willie told me when we were out of earshot.

I gasped. "Annie Oakley?"

"The other one."

"Isn't it marvelous that there are two female sharpshooters? It just goes to show, doesn't it?"

"Show what?"

"That women can be as good as men at an activity dominated by men."

"I s'pose. Ain't never thought about it before."

"Ha! You can't fool me, Willie. It's all you think about."

"Not all," she said, lightly. "Right now, I'm thinking about big mustaches and what it says about a man."

"What does it say about them?"

"That they're hairy *everywhere*."

I couldn't tell if she thought that was a good thing or bad.

A LETTER from Matt was waiting for me when we arrived home. It simply said he missed me and couldn't wait to see me the following day upon his return. He and his aunt had traveled to Rycroft Hall for the wedding three days ago. He'd not wanted to go, particularly since I wasn't invited, but I'd urged him to attend. Patience was his cousin, but more than that, someone needed to be on hand in case Lord Cox got cold feet.

The note hadn't mentioned that Matt's powers of

persuasion had been called on, but no doubt I would receive a full report the following day.

I tucked the note into my reticule and was about to head up the stairs when Duke emerged from the library, a grim set to his mouth.

"It's done," was all he said.

I drew in a deep breath and let it out slowly. Willie put her arm around me and gave me a welcome hug. I hadn't thought I'd be so shaken by Payne's execution, yet I felt a little ill. He'd tried to kill Matt, he'd succeeded in killing our coachman, and kidnapped Gabe Seaford and me. He was a monster, a madman obsessed with destroying Matt. I should be glad it was finally over. I *was* glad. This strange feeling would pass, in time, but for now, I was relieved to have my friends with me, although I missed Matt terribly.

"Shall I bring tea into the library, Miss Steele?" Bristow asked.

"We'll help ourselves to something stronger from the sideboard," Willie said.

"Tea will be fine," I told them both. "It's too early for liquor."

"Speak for yourself."

A newspaper was spread out on the table in the library with Duke's boots underneath, the toe of one touching the heel of the other. He waited for me to sit then resumed his seat at the table. Willie helped herself to the decanter of whiskey.

"Where's Cyclops?" I asked.

"Out," Duke said.

"Out where?"

Duke shrugged. "He didn't say."

"Hope he gets back before tonight," Willie said, saluting us with her glass. "We're going to The Prince of Wales, in Chelsea."

"Celebrating?" Duke shifted in the chair, a pained look on his face. "I hated the sheriff, but I ain't going to dance on his grave, Willie. It ain't right."

"Not a celebration, you idiot." She sat in one of the deep armchairs by the fireplace and stretched her legs toward the hearth even though the fire wasn't lit. "We're playing poker with some of the cast from the show. We met two of 'em in a saloon. One was a real sucker, Duke, and he'll be there tonight. As innocent as a newborn babe, he was." She jangled the coins in her pocket and chuckled into her glass.

"Let me guess, the sucker lost almost every round, but not all," he said. "He seemed surprised when he did win, and was desperate to keep going, thinking his bad luck would end soon."

"You sound as if you were there," I said.

Willie sank into the chair. "He was a genuine fool, Duke, I'm telling you. Come along tonight and see for yourself. If I get in too deep, you have my permission to get me out before I lose my Colt."

"Can I throw you over my shoulder and carry you out?"

"Just try it, Duke, and find out."

He grinned and picked up the newspaper. "There's a review of the Wild West show in here. It says it's spectacular, like nothing else seen in London before. What'd you both think?"

"It was spectacular," I said, as Bristow brought in a tray of tea things. "You should have come, Duke."

"And watch some actors pretend to catch Indians and ride around shooting off their guns?" He straightened the newspaper with a flick of his wrist. "I got better things to do."

"They're not actors. The Indians are real Indians, the riders can ride like they were born on horseback, and the sharpshooters didn't miss. You should have seen Annie

11

Oakley and Buffalo Bill. They were amazing. Tell him, Willie. You enjoyed it by the end, I know you did."

She sniffed. "It was all right. Weren't nothing special, Duke, but it made me think of home. In a good way, mind."

"Mrs. Bristow and I saw it on our day off," Bristow said, handing me a cup. "We thoroughly enjoyed it."

It was difficult to keep a straight face as I pictured the very upright butler and housekeeper gasping in awe at the feats of American cowboys and Indians. Sometimes he seemed more proper than Miss Glass.

"It ain't my thing," Duke said. "But poker tonight will be good. Actors or not, they're American and I could do with some good old home-grown company."

"What about me and Cyclops?" Willie cried.

"I said *good* company."

Willie removed her boot and threw it at him, hitting his shoulder. Duke just smiled.

* * *

THE PRINCE of Wales was filled with Americans, mostly men, none of them with an Indian or Mexican heritage. One of the few women present eyed me with a narrowed gaze, as if I were an oddity. She was about to turn back to her companions, standing around a table, but caught sight of Willie. One corner of her mouth lifted in a smirk.

Willie didn't notice. She was looking for Emmett. We found him seated in a cloud of cigar smoke at the back of the pub, playing cards with two other men. He beamed upon seeing us.

"Glad you came." He shook her hand, then took mine and kissed the back of it. "And this must be your two friends."

Willie introduced Cyclops and Duke, and Emmett shook their hands too.

"Where are you from?" Emmett asked.

"California, mostly," Duke said, "but we've been all over."

"You're a sharpshooter?" Cyclops asked.

Emmett smoothed his mustache with his thumb and forefinger. "Sure am, but I can't give you a demonstration. You'll have to come and see the show for that." He laughed and clapped Cyclops on the shoulder. "Bill Cody don't give away nothing for free."

"Where are you from?"

"All over, like you."

"What else do you do?" Duke asked.

Emmett balked. "Nothing. The show takes up all my time."

"What did you used to do, before you became a sharp-shooter for Buffalo Bill's show?"

Emmett's gaze flicked between Cyclops and Duke and back again. "What's this, an interrogation? Are you lawmen? Because I've got nothing to hide. Ask me anything."

Cyclops put up his hands in surrender. "Just curious about how a man gets into this line of work."

Emmett's shoulders relaxed. "He buys William F. Cody a drink and chews his ear off about how he can shoot a tobacco tin off a log at sixty paces until Cody can't stand it no more and gives him a chance."

"Is he here?" I asked, looking around, only to find that several of the men were staring at me. I moved a little closer to Cyclops.

"Bill's too important to drink with us." Emmett patted the empty chair beside him. "Sit down, Miss Johnson, and play poker. Let's see if you can keep that lucky streak going. You remember Danny, don't you? Danny Draper?"

The younger man from earlier in the day looked as if

he'd had too many drinks already. A modest stack of coins piled up in front of him as he hunkered over a deck of cards. "Five card draw," he said as he shuffled. "That all right with you, Miss?" He set the deck in front of Willie.

She cut the deck, tapped the top for good luck, and smiled. "Fine with me."

One of the men at a neighboring table offered me his chair and I reluctantly took it. I would have preferred to stand to see more of the room, particularly the woman I'd seen upon entering. She had a familiar look about her, but I didn't recognize her face.

Duke and Cyclops stood behind me. Neither had been asked to join the game. After the first round, Duke ordered ales for himself and Cyclops, and a sherry for me.

"The Prince of Wales came to see our show," Emmett said as he inspected his cards. Unlike Danny Draper, he didn't seem to mind conversation while playing. It certainly wasn't affecting his game, going by the winnings piled up in front of him. "He spoke to us. He seemed like a nice fellow but his accent was real funny. Like he had a mouth full of marbles. 'How do you do,'" he mimicked in a terrible version of the upper class English accent. "'Nice to meet you. You Americans are the most intriguing characters.'" Emmett chuckled and threw down a card. "No offence, Miss..."

"Steele," I said.

"No offence, Miss Steele, but you English are real strange."

"Amen," Willie said.

Emmett glanced at his replacement cards and pushed some coins into the middle of the table. "It's not just the accent. Everyone's so polite all the time. Just yesterday, a boy picks my pocket and apologizes to me before running off."

I almost believed him until he threw his head back and guffawed. Several people turned around, shook their heads and looked away again. The woman I'd seen earlier strode toward us, scowling.

"You making a nuisance of yourself again, Emmett?" she asked.

Emmett signaled her to come closer but she stayed put. "Annie thinks it's the weather here that affects the English, don't you, Annie?"

Annie? Was *she* Annie Oakley? It explained why she looked a little familiar. I'd seen her perform in the show. I couldn't see her face from the grandstand but this woman was petite like Annie Oakley. I was too shy to ask, however.

"Why the weather?" Cyclops said.

"The cold makes everyone stiff," she said.

He laughed softly.

"Watch out for Emmett," she said to Willie. "He's got a knack for winning."

Did she mean he cheats? Cyclops and Duke must have thought the same because they eyed one another and then turned to Annie. She walked off and the crowd soon swallowed her.

"Ignore her," Emmett said. "She thinks I cheat, but I swear, I'm just lucky. You can check my pockets if you want." He stood up to show us he hadn't slipped a card beneath him then turned out his pockets. All empty. Duke even checked under the chair. There were no spare cards stuck to the bottom.

"Sit down," Danny growled. "He don't always win," he said to Willie. "He's just on a lucky streak tonight."

Willie showed them her cards. Three of a kind. "Not anymore." She grinned as she raked in her money.

Danny groaned. Emmett merely chuckled. "I better start concentrating," he said.

They played a few more rounds and I grew increasingly bored. I spotted Annie Oakley by the bar, talking to the only other woman in the room, a pretty blonde who couldn't have been more than twenty. Annie looked about thirty with long brown hair that fell past her shoulders, and a short but trim figure.

I was considering how best to approach when she saw me and beckoned me over.

"Sorry to interrupt," I said, sounding like a breathless girl at her first dance. "I just wanted to say how much I admired your show today."

"You saw it?" Annie put her hand on her friend's shoulder. "Then you would have seen May. She's also a sharpshooter."

"Pleased to meet you," I said. "My name is India. India Steele."

The pretty blonde named May bobbed a curtsy.

"She ain't the queen," Annie said. "You don't have to curtsy to her."

May blushed. "It's the accent," she said. "I feel like I got to bow and scrape to everyone here then scrub their floors." She giggled and bit her lip.

"I'm just an ordinary Englishwoman," I said, and once again I realized that wouldn't be the case for much longer. I was about to marry the heir to a title. When Matt inherited it, I would be Lady Rycroft. It was so absurd that the first time I'd realized, I'd laughed until I cried. I no longer cried but I often wanted to laugh.

"Who're your friends?" Annie asked me.

"The big one is Nate, but everyone calls him Cyclops. The other is Duke."

"And the woman?"

"That's Willie."

"She dresses like a man," May said in a soft voice.

"She hates corsets and dresses," I said.

"So do I but I don't wear trousers."

"She can wear what she likes," I said, wanting to defend Willie. "She answers to no one but herself."

"Yes, but—"

"She's lucky," Annie cut in. "Not too many women can do as they please, unless they've got an understanding husband, like me." Her gaze drifted off to a group of men talking quietly around a table.

"You should take to wearing trousers then," May said with a smile and nudge of her elbow. "They'd look well on you. Or is he not *that* understanding?"

"He'd allow it, it's Bill who wouldn't. I can hear the old man's voice now: 'There ain't no point having a lady sharp-shooter in the show if no one knows she's a lady,'" she intoned in a deep voice.

May giggled again. "He'd still have me."

"You shot very well today too," I said.

"Not as well as Annie, but I ain't too bad."

"Willie's a good shot," I said. "So she tells me. They're all from the Wild West but have lived here for a few months. They're going to stay a little longer, although I suspect the winter might send them packing."

"Seems they like their poker," Annie said.

"They do. They taught me, but I don't find much enjoyment in it. I'm not very good."

"Don't tell Emmett and Danny that," Annie said, leaning closer. "They'll have you taking a seat and betting your savings away in no time."

"Annie!" May cried. "My husband's not like that, although you might be right about Emmett." She pointed at the poker players. "Danny's my husband." She suddenly stiffened. "Is he losing again? Christ, I'll wring his neck."

She went to storm off, but Annie caught her arm. "Let me offer some friendly advice, woman to woman."

May didn't look too pleased about lingering another

moment, but she settled for glaring daggers in her husband's direction. It was lost on him, however. He didn't look up from his hand as he teased his bottom lip.

"Don't march over there, all angry," Annie said. "You got to be womanly about it. Try convincing him to go home with you for a little treat." She winked. "If you demand he leave in front of everyone and create a scene, he'll dig his heels in."

May sighed. "You're right. Perhaps I'll leave him for a few more minutes to see if he wins it back."

"You're thinking like him," Annie said with a shake of her head. "Don't do that. It's how gamblers go broke."

May made a mewling sound and looked as if she'd burst into tears. "I don't know what to do. I hate how he plays with Emmett all the time. Emmett wins more than he loses. Much more."

"He's got the luck of the devil, that's for sure."

Duke joined us, shaking his head. "We're going soon, India. Willie's almost lost it all."

"She never learns," I said on a sigh.

"At least she only gambles what she can afford to lose now."

He was right. Willie was better than she used to be, stopping herself when she reached her limit. She used to keep going until someone dragged her away or until she lost everything. Still, I wished she wouldn't gamble at all. She'd be in a terrible mood all night.

"Go on, then," Annie said to May. "You know what you got to do. And you two," she said to Duke and me, "take your friend home before she ends up like Danny, owing Emmett more than he can afford."

Duke didn't need to be told twice. Perhaps that was why he'd come over, to get permission to stop the game. It would seem Annie Oakley's permission was all he needed.

"Come on, Danny," May was saying when I reached the

group of players. "That's enough now, let's go home." She stroked his cheek and pressed herself against him.

"Just one more round," he said, circling his arm around her waist and lowering her onto his lap. He nuzzled her neck. "One more, I promise."

She pulled away and shoved him in the arm. "It's always one more with you."

"The game's ending now," Duke said. "Willie, come on. We got to go."

Cyclops rose but Willie merely sighed as she stared at her hand of cards.

Emmett touched her arm. "Not yet, Miss Johnson. Stay a while longer. It's still early and we're having fun. Your luck will turn any minute now, I know it will."

"We have a big day tomorrow," I reminded her. "Matt's coming home."

"Then you go," Emmett snapped at me.

I blinked. "Pardon?"

"You heard me," he snarled. "You go home, Miss Steele. Miss Johnson can make up her own mind. I can see she's not the sort who takes orders from anyone, let alone the likes of you."

"The likes of me?" I echoed. I would have asked what he meant but I was too stunned to think clearly. Where had this ugly side come from, and so quickly too? He had a stack of coins in front of him, so he couldn't be worried about winning back any losses.

"Don't talk to India like that," Duke said, squaring up to Emmett.

Cyclops stood at his back, his one eye drilling into Emmett, a formidable presence that few would argue with.

Emmett stood slowly. Sitting down, he didn't seem all that big, but now he was standing, he was easily as tall as

Cyclops, although not as broad. "Like what?" Emmett sneered. "Like she's a prissy school mistress?"

Willie shot to her feet and poked her finger into Emmett's chest. "Don't you talk to my friend like that. Take it back."

Emmett grinned, revealing yellowing teeth beneath his moustache. "You going, Miss Johnson? Without even a fight? Come on, stay and play with me. I got a feeling your luck's going to turn."

"I ain't got no more money."

"Sure you do. A resourceful woman can always find more."

"What's that supposed to mean?" Duke spat.

Willie didn't need Duke to defend her honor. She was quite capable of tearing Emmett to shreds with a few select words. She poked her finger at him again. "The only reason I'd stay is so I can work out how you're cheating and expose you."

Hell.

The room silenced. The only movement came from the cigar smoke, swirling languidly up to the rafters.

Emmett slowly cocked his head to the side, like an automaton winding up. "I ain't a cheater."

Willie angled herself between Duke and Emmett, a fearless little figure. Or a stupid one. "I don't know how you do it, but I know you're cheating."

Annie came forward and caught Willie's arm. "Come away. Don't rile him."

Emmett laughed, a hollow, brittle sound. "Or maybe I'm just good."

"No one's that good or that lucky," Willie said.

"Come away now," Annie said, louder.

I took Willie's other arm and together we managed to get

her out of Emmett's reach, although I felt her resistance with each step.

"If you were a man..." Emmett looked her up and down. "You've got balls, I'll give you that, but—"

Duke's punch slammed into Emmett's jaw so hard, Emmett fell back across the table and rolled onto the floor. Duke shook out his hand. "You're done insulting my friends."

Some of the men advanced, perhaps to get a better look or to help Emmett to his feet. Or perhaps to even the score. It was hard to tell. Cyclops took no chances. He grabbed Duke by the shoulders and ushered him toward the door. Willie and I followed. We passed a beautiful blonde woman of middle age, watching on with a wicked smile. She saluted Duke with her sherry glass.

I glanced back at the pub as we raced across the road, and almost turned around and went back in. I'd seen a face in the window. The face of someone I'd not expected to associate with a traveling troupe of American cowboys.

$\mathcal{M}$att returned home the same way he'd left it a few days earlier—with a big smile and an embrace that lifted me off my feet. His aunt's response was more understated but enthusiastic in her own way.

"Do try not to be so vulgar, Matthew," she said. "The servants are watching."

Bristow didn't raise an eyebrow as he held the door open for the footman to bring in the luggage.

Matt settled his hands at my waist. "I missed you," he purred in my ear.

"I missed you too." I linked my arms behind his head and kissed him lightly on the lips.

I caught sight of Miss Glass pinching the fingertips of her glove with brisk precision and a scowl. I kissed Matt again, lingering this time.

"Thought we heard someone," Duke said, coming down the stairs, Cyclops at his heels. They both shook Matt's hand and greeted Miss Glass politely. She offered them her hand. Duke took it and held it a moment, but Cyclops kissed the back. She smiled at him.

"It's lovely to be home," she said. "Bristow, bring tea to the drawing room. I'm in dire need of Mrs. Bristow's brew. The tea at the last inn tasted like pig swill."

"Matt!" Willie cried, trotting down the stairs. She flung her arms around him then gave Miss Glass an equally fierce hug.

"You haven't changed," Miss Glass said.

"You expected me to become a lady in four days?"

"One can always hope for a miracle." Miss Glass held out her hand to me. "India, accompany me to the drawing room. Tell me everything that happened in our absence."

We headed into the drawing room, the others following. "So they're really married?" I asked.

"They are," Miss Glass said. "It was a small, simple affair, after all the drama of the engagement."

Drama didn't quite describe the anxious days we'd spent trying to find a way to free Matt from his obligation to marry his cousin, Patience. In the end, it had taken scandalous information about Lord Cox to bribe him into proposing. A scandal I still hardly believed. How Lord Coyle had discovered it, I couldn't say, but if he had not, we would have been in a difficult predicament. I tried not to think about the debt I owed him. Tried not to think about all the things he could ask me to do to pay back that debt. One thing was certain—it would involve using my magic in some way.

Miss Glass sat on the sofa and indicated I should join her. Matt sat opposite, still smiling. He was certainly happy. The wedding must have gone well.

"What's the estate like?" Willie asked Matt. "Is the house big? Is there a forest and can we go hunting in it?"

"Both house and estate are big," Matt said. "There are woods and they sometimes go fox hunting and shooting. We did none of that while we were there, though."

"India, you must have freesias and gardenias in your nosegay," Miss Glass said.

"Why? Because Patience had them in hers?"

"No, because she didn't. She couldn't. They're for purity and innocence and that girl is neither. You are quite entitled. And the wedding feast must be six courses or more. They only had five." She shook her head. "It was positively sparse."

I refrained from rolling my eyes but caught sight of Matt rolling his. I smiled.

"You say the wedding was small, Aunt," he said, "but it seemed grand to this simple American."

"It was small by our standards." She patted the gray curls at the nape of her neck. "When a baron's daughter weds, it's usually an elaborate affair with more guests than servants. Richard didn't even invite a hundred."

"I don't know a hundred people in England," Matt said.

"You don't have to *know* the guests. Not when you have a barony or are the heir to one."

Wisely, Matt changed the topic. "How was everything here in our absence?"

"Fine," Duke said quickly. "Nothing happened."

"And yesterday?" Matt asked as Bristow steered a tea trolley into the room.

"I told you, nothing happened."

Matt arched a brow. "Payne was executed. That's not nothing."

"Right. Sure." Duke cleared his throat. "He's dead."

"I know that, but..." Matt sighed and turned to me. "Are you all right, India?" He looked at me with sympathy. Of everyone, he would know that my feelings on the matter were complex.

"I am," I said, pouring the tea. "The show was a welcome distraction."

He gave me a small smile. "So you liked it?"

"Very much." I handed Willie a teacup. "Even Willie enjoyed it, didn't you?"

"It gave us something to do," was all she said.

I described the show to Matt and Miss Glass from the opening announcements to the singing of the national anthem at the conclusion. Miss Glass wrinkled her nose when I told her about the female sharpshooters.

"I suppose you enjoyed that part," she said to Willie.

Willie merely lifted a shoulder and sipped her tea.

"What about the rest of the exhibition?" Matt asked. "Did the Americans dazzle you with their ingenuity?"

"We didn't stay long," Willie said before I could answer. "We looked at some stalls then left. Didn't we, India?"

I glanced from her to Duke to Cyclops. It would seem they weren't going to mention meeting the show's crew afterward or last night. I didn't like lying to Matt, even if it were only a lie of omission, but I didn't want them to be upset with me for tattling.

"How is your dress coming along, India?" Miss Glass asked, saving me from making a decision.

"My wedding dress?"

"Yes, dear, of course I mean your wedding dress."

"Fine, I think."

"You ought to see the dressmaker and ask how she's progressing. You can't let these people think you've forgotten about them or they take too long."

"She's hardly going to think I've forgotten about my wedding dress," I said. "Now, tell us about the ceremony. Did Patience look happy?"

"Did Cox?" Willie muttered into her teacup.

"She looked radiant," Matt said.

"She looked well," his aunt countered. "As well as a plain girl can look. He seemed content enough. It's hard to tell with him."

"Ain't that how the English lords like it?" Cyclops asked. "All stiff and formal so no one knows when they're happy?"

"That's somewhat of an exaggeration," I said. "But perhaps not so much for Lord Cox. He does have a reserved way about him." It was probably because he felt he had to live up to a higher standard than most, to avoid scandal. I wondered if that was just his way or if he was like that because he shouldn't be a lord at all. The half-brother he'd never met should have inherited their father's title, but having never known his father, he'd been cut off from his birthright without even being aware of it.

"Thankfully not all the English are like that," Duke said. "Ain't that right, Cyclops?"

Cyclops's eye narrowed. "I suppose," he said carefully.

Duke smirked. "Some are real friendly. Real friendly indeed."

Cyclops lowered his teacup. It looked dainty with his big hand wrapped around it and the handle sticking out away from him. "What are you getting at?"

Duke smirked. "You came home smelling like violets yesterday."

Cyclops grunted. "You don't even know what violets smell like."

"They smell like a woman and that's what I smelled on you when you came home."

"Are you courting someone?" Miss Glass asked. "Is it Catherine Mason?"

Cyclops set his teacup down in the saucer. "Duke got into a fight last night."

Miss Glass gasped. "Over Catherine Mason?"

"No," I said, taking her hand. "Perhaps you should rest. You must be tired after the journey."

"I am tired, but now I want to hear about the fight. Are you hurt, Duke?"

"I'm fine," he said with a pointed glare for Cyclops. "And I only got into a fight because he insulted India and Willie."

"Mostly Willie," I said.

"Ain't nothing I've never heard before," she said. "But you know how Duke gets, Matt."

"What happened?" Matt asked.

"We were at a pub," Duke said. "And it weren't a fight, just one punch to shut his damned mouth. It was one of them Americans from the show."

Willie finally told the story of how we met them after the show and then again at The Prince of Wales. "I'm sure he cheated," she said, "but damned if I know how."

"It doesn't matter now," I said. "At least you walked away when you did."

"I don't like being cheated, India. I ain't green nor a fool."

"Nobody thinks you are."

"*He* does! They all do, even that idiot, Danny Draper."

"Sounds to me like he was in on it," Matt said.

"I don't know," Willie said. "He seemed genuine."

Cyclops nodded. "If he were in on it, then his wife wasn't aware. She got real worried he'd lose more than he could afford."

"I don't understand," Miss Glass said. "How could the second man be involved if it were all a trick carried out by the other one, Emmett?"

"It starts with the first game, played at the show ground pavilion," Matt said. "Danny loses on purpose so Willie thinks he's a hopeless player. Emmett wins some and loses some in a normal pattern that doesn't raise alarm bells. That's just to entice Willie back later to play again. That's when Emmett cheats. He wins everything from Willie and Danny, and hopes to drag Willie in for even more. Or perhaps so she'll return the following night, hoping to win back what she lost. With Danny losing so easily, she thinks she can at least win some of the time. It also makes the game seem authentic because a man's not supposed to cheat a friend."

"Emmett gives Danny some of the winnings later," Cyclops added. "So Danny never really loses."

"Diabolical." Miss Glass cast Willie a sympathetic look. "Don't feel ashamed that you fell for such an elaborate trick, Willemina. They sound very clever, very organized."

Willie sank further into the chair. "I wanted to work out how Emmett cheated. I could have stopped earlier if I wanted to."

Not a single one of us believed that, but nobody wanted to say so.

Miss Glass retired to her room to rest before dinner. Matt took her place beside me on the sofa, close enough so that he sat on my skirt. He grasped my hand and rested it on his thigh.

"Now that she's gone we don't have to drink tea," Willie announced. "Who wants a brandy?"

"There's brandy in the library," Matt said.

Willie pointed at the sideboard. "There's brandy right here, too."

"They want to be alone," Duke told her.

"And miss out on our excellent company? I don't think so."

Everyone stared at her.

"It were a joke," she said. "Come on, you two big lugs. Let's get drunk before dinner to remind Miss Glass what she's been missing."

"There's something else we need to tell you, Matt," Cyclops said. "Something India saw last night."

"It was some*one*, actually," I said. "And I'm not even sure what it means, or if it means anything at all."

"Go on," Matt prompted.

"I saw Sir Charles Whittacker in the pub. It was odd considering it was filled with Americans from the show."

"Was he alone?"

"I think so, but it was hard to tell."

"It might be nothing," he said, deep in thought.

"He saw us too," I said. "At least I think he did. He quickly looked away."

"Could just be a coincidence," Willie said. "He might want to mingle with the cast and crew of the show. He might be half in love with Annie Oakley. Most folk are."

"Are you?" Duke asked.

"I got better things to do with my time than make cow eyes at a married actress."

"She ain't an actress, she's a sharpshooter. And what have you got to do that's more important than meeting her? Ah, right, I remember. Losing at poker."

Willie thumped his arm. "You're a turd."

He chuckled and led them out of the drawing room.

"Are you worried about seeing Whittacker again?" Matt asked when we were alone.

"Merely curious," I said. "I'm sure I saw him at the bareknuckle fights that night but he denied being there. And now he turns up at The Prince of Wales on the same night we're there. If I see him a third time in an unexpected place, I'll start thinking he's following me."

"I'll confront him."

"No, Matt, don't. I was joking. He isn't following me."

"He might be. Perhaps he's spying on you for Coyle. Coyle wants your magical services, and the only way to do that is to find out something about you that you don't want made public, or don't want me to know about." His lips curved into a slow, delicious smile. "He doesn't realize I know everything about you."

I swallowed the panic rising up my throat. Coyle already

had something on me. If Matt found out I'd gone to Coyle for information about Lord Cox... I didn't want to think what would happen.

Matt leaned in and kissed the flesh beneath my ear. "Or almost everything," he murmured.

I closed my eyes and let all thoughts of Whittaker and Coyle drift away as Matt kissed my throat, my cheek, my chin and finally my mouth. He scooped me onto his lap and splayed his hand at the small of my back. There was tenderness in the kiss, and heat too, the combination proving to be a very real threat to my morality. I forgot we were in the drawing room, where anyone could walk in on us, and pressed myself into him, wanting his hands all over me—and his lips.

Matt smiled against my mouth. "The sooner we marry, the better."

"I agree," I said, drawing in a deep breath and the scent of him. "Two weeks. Not a day more."

He stole another kiss. "Did I mention how much I missed you?"

"You did, but you can mention it again."

"I missed you terribly, Miss India Steele," he murmured. "It wasn't right being there and not having you with me, and I told my uncle so. You're my fiancée, and you should have been invited."

"Even if I had, I would have found an excuse not to attend. It would have been too awkward."

"It was," he muttered. "People I've never met kept looking at me. They all seemed to know who I was."

"Or they could have been admiring the most handsome man in the room." I toyed with his hair, wrapping a dark strand around my finger. It was so short it only wound around once. "My only reason for going would have been to keep an eye on you." At his confused expression, I added,

"Your health." I pressed my palm to his chest and could just detect his strong heartbeat through his waistcoat and shirt.

He lay his hand over mine. "The watch is working perfectly. I haven't felt unnaturally tired or needed to use it once since you and Gabe combined your magic in it."

"Not once? That is a relief."

"It's working as it should."

I folded him in my arms and pressed my lips to his forehead. I took a moment to capture the feeling and store it away. It was what happiness felt like, and I never wanted to forget it.

* * *

THE HEADLINE SAID IT ALL:

AMERICAN SHARPSHOOTER ROBBED AND KILLED.

"It's Emmett!" I said, peering over Matt's shoulder at the newspaper. I pointed to the picture. It was clearly Emmett, in all his mustachioed glory. "I can't believe it."

"What about him?" Cyclops asked, taking his seat opposite at the breakfast table with a single boiled egg and a slice of bacon on a plate.

"He's dead." Matt passed him the newspaper. "Shot through the chest."

Duke and Willie leaned toward Cyclops and read the headline .

"It was a bungled robbery, according to this." Cyclops tapped the paper then set it aside. "Tragic."

Willie picked up the paper and scanned the article. "Couldn't happen to a nicer fellow."

"Willie!" I cried.

"I wish I'd worked out how he cheated before he died."

"Let's not talk ill of the dead," I said, pouring myself a cup of tea at the sideboard.

"Why not? He was a cheater, I'm sure of it. Being dead don't change that fact."

I let the matter go. There was no point asking her to speak nicely about Emmett, but at least Miss Glass wasn't present to hear it.

Cyclops pushed his plate away. He'd only eaten the egg. "So now you're back, Matt, what are we doing today?"

It was a good question, and one I'd been contemplating since we'd decided to stay in London. In America, Matt had helped the law to bring gangs to justice. Sometimes he'd infiltrated those gangs, and other times, he'd investigated them using other means. In London, he had some invest-ments to manage, but his man of business and lawyer usually took care of that. He was at a loose end. They all were. I worried to think what it might mean for London in general and our household in particular. Willie was already sinking back into her gambling ways. What would be next? And what would a bored Cyclops and Duke get up to?

"You going to eat that?" Willie asked Cyclops.

"No." He pushed the plate toward her.

Willie picked up the bacon, tipped her head back and slipped it into her mouth like a large lizard swallowing a smaller one. Duke watched on, impressed.

"Aren't you feeling well?" I asked Cyclops.

Cyclops clasped his hands over his stomach. "I *feel* fine. I look fat."

"You're not fat. You're simply a bigger man."

"He's fat," Willie said around the mouthful of bacon. "London life's been too good to him."

"I'm not ordinarily so idle," he said with a shrug. "I'm carrying a few extra pounds."

Duke mopped up the egg yolk on his plate with a piece

of toast. "He wants to make sure he looks good for a certain pretty blonde."

"Shut it," Cyclops growled.

"Catherine?" I asked. "Are you two seeing one another?"

"No!"

"But he wants to," Duke teased. "He's getting ready, just in case she stops by. Last time she came for tea, he'd just come in from the stables and he was all dirty. Time before that, he had a bruise from when I punched him."

Willie chuckled. "And the time before that—"

"I'm leaving." Cyclops shoved his chair back. "The children are annoying."

"Stay away from the lilac water this time," Duke said, laughing.

"Next time I invite Catherine over, I'll give you advance notice," I said to Cyclops. "In fact, I haven't seen her in a few days. I'll invite her today."

"Don't bother," he muttered. "There ain't nothing between us and never will be." He smacked a snickering Duke on the back of the head as he walked out.

Willie laughed harder.

"Don't tease him," I scolded them. "He's heartsick."

"Then he should do something about it," she said.

"Like you?" Duke grunted. "You're just as bad, pining over that nurse. Go and speak to her."

Willie snatched up the last piece of bacon from Duke's plate, also smacked him on the back of the head, and strode out without another word.

"You were supposed to speak to the nurse, India," Duke whispered across the table.

"I'd rather not," I said. "It's none of my business."

"Agreed," Matt said.

Duke sat back and tapped his finger on the table. I knew that look and didn't quite trust it, but if he wanted to interfere, then it wasn't my place to tell him not to. I doubted Willie would appreciate it, but that was Duke's risk to take.

"What do you think about helping out the sisters at the convent again?" Matt asked him.

Duke shrugged. "Sure. That place is held together by prayer and cobwebs. They can't pay us."

"I'll pay you."

"You won't get nothing for it."

"I'll get the three of you out of my hair. India, what are you doing today?"

"Going over the wedding menu one final time with Mrs. Bristow," I said. "And I'd better see how the dress is coming along, just to appease your aunt." I had a list of things to accomplish before the wedding, but none were urgent. All the plans had been set in motion already, and there was little to do now until the wedding itself.

Bristow entered and announced a visitor. "Detective Inspector Brockwell is here," he said. "He says it's urgent."

"I'll be right down," Matt said, rising.

"He's not here for you, sir. It's Mr. Duke he wishes to see."

Duke met Matt's gaze. "I think I know what this is about."

We greeted the inspector in the entrance hall where he stood holding his hat in both hands by the brim. The firm set of his jaw was worrying, but the two constables standing at his back were alarming.

"My apologies for the early hour," Brockwell said, punching out his consonants.

"You wish to speak to me?" Duke asked.

"I do. Come to Scotland Yard to answer some questions."

"Can't I answer them here?"

"What is the nature of the questions?" Matt asked.

"It's in regard to Mr. Duke's argument with one Emmett Cocker, the night before last. Mr. Cocker was..." He glanced at me.

"Murdered," I finished for him. "The newspaper claimed a thief murdered him, probably by accident."

"That may be, but the newspapermen made that up before knowing all the details. They had a deadline."

"And you don't give out much information," Matt finished.

"You think Duke did it, don't you?" I murmured.

Brockwell's fingers tightened on the brim of his hat. "Just come to the station, Mr. Duke."

"No! He's not going anywhere with you." I moved between them and crossed my arms over my chest. "If he goes with you, you'll throw him in the holding cells. I know how this works."

"Step aside, Miss Steele. This is none of your concern." He appealed to Matt.

"At least have the decency to look me in the eye," I snapped.

Brockwell cleared his throat and his gaze momentarily lifted to mine before sliding away again. It would seem he was ashamed to even look at me, and that was most concerning of all.

It meant he thought Duke guilty.

CHAPTER 3

"*I* didn't kill him," Duke said.

"Just come to Scotland Yard, please." Detective Inspector Brockwell stepped aside and indicated the door and his constables standing in front of it.

"No," I said again.

Duke placed a hand at my back. "It's all right, India. I don't want a scene, not here. You'll wake Miss Glass."

I took his hand and clutched it between both of mine. I hadn't expected Brockwell to be so unreasonable. I could never quite decide if I liked him or not. He was thorough, which was certainly a good trait in a detective, yet he was a stickler for following rules. I suspected he wouldn't bend them, not even for the royal family let alone acquaintances like us, no matter how many times we'd helped him in the past.

"Come now," Matt said genially, "there's no need for formality, Inspector. We're old friends, and old friends help one another."

"We are not friends, Mr. Glass."

"Of course we are. You know more about me than almost anyone, and that makes our relationship unique."

"It's true that we've been through a lot together, and I've seen things I cannot easily forget, but I have orders to investigate this matter thoroughly, and I intend to do just that."

"I want you to be thorough too. I imagine there's enormous pressure to solve this case as quickly as possible. The murder of a cast member from Buffalo Bill's show will attract a lot of public attention." He glanced at the door. "Attention that I'm sure you would rather avoid. By taking Duke with you, you'll cause a stir."

"There are a lot of journalists waiting at Scotland Yard," Brockwell admitted. He glanced at one of his constables, standing like a statue by the door. "They didn't stop me this morning because they didn't know I was assigned to the case, but they will probably know by now."

"Your return will see them flock to you, and Duke's character will be maligned. I don't want that, Inspector, and I don't think you do either. Not after everything we've done for you."

The inspector huffed a short laugh. "Very good, Mr. Glass. Very smooth. I'm surprised you haven't mentioned the commissioner's name yet. You usually do to get your way."

"I don't need to mention his name." Matt smiled. "Come and join us for coffee, eggs and bacon and let's have a civil discussion."

"And sausages," I added. "Bring your men."

"They can stay here," Brockwell said. "Lead the way, Miss Steele."

"If I'd known the breakfast would have convinced you, I'd have mentioned it first," Matt said, smiling.

I headed back up the stairs to the dining room, the men following. Duke had gone utterly silent while Matt chatted with the inspector. Matt's charm was on full display as he made sure the conversation focused on the inspector and the confidence the commissioner had shown in his abilities by assigning him to this particular murder.

"Please sit, Inspector," I said, taking a leaf out of Matt's book. "What would you like? The bacon and sausages are still warm and there's quite a bit of everything left. Cyclops is on a diet."

"A little of everything would be excellent." The detective sat and asked Duke to sit opposite. "Once Mr. Glass and Miss Steele leave, we'll begin."

"They can stay," Duke said.

"No."

Matt didn't object. He served food and coffee for Brockwell then held the door open for me. "Come and see us before you leave, Inspector."

"I plan to. I want to speak to Miss Steele, too, and perhaps your cousin and your pirate friend, although I want to assure you they are not under suspicion."

"I shouldn't be either," Duke said tightly. "I didn't do it."

Matt lifted a finger, a small signal to Duke to remain calm, before he and I left.

"Shall we listen in?" I whispered.

"Duke will tell us everything. We'll wait in the drawing room."

He asked Peter the footman to find Willie and Cyclops. Willie arrived first, looking worried. "Fossett says Duke's been arrested!"

"Not arrested," Matt said. "Brockwell's questioning him now in the dining room."

She glanced at the door just as Cyclops entered.

"Duke's been arrested for murder?" he asked.

"Questioned," Matt said. "It seems someone told the police he punched Emmett Cocker the night before he was murdered."

I cast a glance at the door. "Poor Duke."

"He's got nothing to worry about," Matt said, taking my hand. "He didn't kill Cocker."

Willie snorted. "Innocent people get arrested all the time. You know that."

"Brockwell is a good man. He won't arrest anyone without evidence, and he won't find any evidence against Duke because Duke didn't do it." He lifted my hand to his lips. The warm kiss was a comfort but my concern remained.

The questioning took as long as it takes to eat two slices of bacon and two sausages. The inspector joined us with a satisfied look on his face and Duke seemed a little less worried too. I blew out a slow, measured breath.

"I'm glad to see the three of you here," the detective said. "There's no need to question you separately. I'd just like to ask for your version of events that night."

"Duke did nothing wrong," Willie snapped.

"He punched a man in a public place. That's assault, Miss Johnson."

"Emmett deserved it. He insulted me and India. Duke was just defending our honor."

"It's still assault."

Duke suddenly sat on a chair as if his legs could no longer hold him.

"A jury wouldn't convict him," Matt said. "Not when they learn about the insults."

Brockwell contemplated Matt's legal argument with pursed lips. "Miss Steele, in your own words, tell me what happened that evening."

I told him everything I could remember, and Willie and Cyclops agreed with my version of events.

"He got what he deserved," Willie added.

"Because of the insults?" Brockwell asked.

"Because he's a cheater."

That got Brockwell's attention. Up until then, he seemed to be going through the motions, not even writing in his little notebook, but now he set pencil to paper. "Why do you say that?"

"Because he cheated."

"We have no proof," Cyclops countered. "Willie just suspects."

"I don't *just* suspect. I know a cheater when I see one, and he had to be cheating. No one is that lucky."

Brockwell sighed and flipped his notebook closed. "Let me know if you think of anything else. And Mr. Duke, don't leave London. I may need to speak to you again, if new evidence comes to light."

"It won't," Willie said, "because he didn't do anything."

Duke shook the detective's hand. "I'll be here if you need me."

"What have you learned so far?" Matt asked. "Who have you questioned?"

Brockwell pocketed the notebook and pencil. "I can't give you that information, Glass. You know that."

Matt pushed up from the armchair. "I might visit the commissioner this morning and offer my services for the investigation."

"That won't be necessary. It's in hand."

"No it ain't," Willie shot back. "If it were, you wouldn't be here questioning Duke, you'd be out there, looking for the real murderer."

I linked my arm with hers and smiled at the inspector through gritted teeth. "Please forgive her passionate nature. She's American."

"They're not all as passionate as Miss Johnson," Brockwell said. "Not a single tear was shed when I broke the news to Mr. Cody and Mrs. Oakley. They're not even stopping the show today out of respect."

"There, see?" Willie said. "No one liked him. You should look among the other cast members for the killer. I'll even give you a name. A sharpshooter called Danny Draper lost a lot of money to him. Or he might have been a partner in his cheating game. I don't know, but it's worth questioning him. Ask if there were others who also got cheated. They might hate Emmett too, or owe him money. Talk to Danny's wife. She got real angry when she thought her husband was losing. What was her name again, India?"

"May," I said.

"I reckon there'll be a lot of folk who hated Emmett on account of his cheating. Look for someone who doesn't seem to have enough money."

I put my arm around her. "Let the inspector do his work now, Willie. He knows what he's doing."

"Look for someone with a temper," Willie went on. "That ain't Duke. He's as gentle and kind as can be. Sometimes too kind."

"He did hit the victim, Miss Johnson," Brockwell said. "He's not all that gentle."

"Only to defend my honor. Please, sir, it weren't him. Understand? It weren't. It couldn't have been."

Duke took her hand and squeezed. "You're going to get hoarse if you keep talking."

Willie sniffed and hugged Duke's arm.

Brockwell reached for his hat, but Matt got to it first.

"I *will* be speaking to the commissioner," Matt said.

"This is not your concern, sir," Brockwell said.

"I beg to differ. When one of my friends is questioned over his involvement in a murder, it is my concern." Matt handed him the hat. "Good day, Inspector. Fossett will show you out."

41

Matt opened the door and asked Peter to see the detective to the front door.

"Now what?" Cyclops asked as we all stood in the drawing room after Brockwell had left.

"Now we wait," Duke said.

We were all rather terrible at waiting. None of us could stand being in the house. Cyclops and Duke went to the convent to see if they needed any work done, while Willie and Miss Glass accompanied me to the dressmaker's. Willie was poor company, worried as she was, and Miss Glass was little better. She insisted I change the hem detail and when I refused, she had one of her turns. This time I was certain her mind was in perfect working order and she was simply doing it to get attention, but I took her home anyway. Matt was already back from his visit to Scotland Yard.

"Well?" I asked.

"Commissioner Munro refused my assistance," Matt said. "He only wants our help if it's a magical matter." He sighed and rubbed his temples.

I sat on the arm of his chair and massaged the back of his neck. "I don't think Brockwell believes Duke did it. He looked satisfied with our account when he left here."

"It's not always easy to tell with the inspector. He keeps his cards close to his chest."

"Speaking of cards, no doubt he'll find a few more suspects who think Emmett cheated. I assume Brockwell hasn't ruled out theft because Emmett's valuables were stolen, but his money could have been taken by someone Emmett beat at poker."

He nodded slowly. "It's a good theory. We'll see how it plays out, but if Brockwell questions Duke again, I'm going to insist Munro allow me to help clear his name."

"If Duke is a suspect, he won't allow any of us near the

inspector for fear of compromising the investigation." The truth of that stung us both into silence.

The following morning, we bought as many newspapers as we could and gleaned some new information about Emmett's murder. It was a popular topic, making the front page on every daily. According to the reports, Emmett was found in a laneway near The Prince of Wales with a gunshot wound to the chest. No gun was found at the scene and the bullet was lodged in the body. All newspapers still reported it as a robbery gone wrong and claimed the police had interviewed several suspects but not arrested anyone. Two of the papers had accompanying articles about the victim, his life in America, and his work as a sharpshooter. It read like an advertisement for the Wild West show.

"I bet Buffalo Bill himself wrote these," Willie said. "Or told the reporters what to write."

"Will they take the bullet out of the body?" I asked. "So they can check what type of gun fired it?"

"Most likely," Matt said. "That'll narrow down the type of weapon, but I suspect most of the cast from the show own a gun."

"The sharpshooters will own several," Duke said. "Annie Oakley uses smooth-bore rifles in the show but she'll have pistols and revolvers too."

Willie snatched up one of the newspapers and read through the article again. "Emmett's gun wasn't found." She slapped the paper with the back of her hand. "He's a sharpshooter, he wouldn't walk about the city without his gun. Maybe he was shot with his own gun, and if he was shot with his own gun, he let someone get close enough to him to take it. He knew his killer."

She looked so happy that I hated shooting down her theory. "If it was a robbery, the thief wouldn't leave behind a valuable weapon. And if the robbery was staged by the murderer, to make it look like a theft gone wrong, then they would have taken the gun with his other belongings for authenticity. In other words, the murderer could have shot him from a distance and removed Emmett's weapon afterward."

Willie threw the newspaper back onto the table and slouched into the armchair.

"So we're back where we started," Cyclops said heavily. "With no clues."

"This ain't going to get us anywhere," Duke said. "We'll leave it to the police. Brockwell will find out who did it."

"Sorry, Willie," I said. "Your theory might still be proven correct. I do like it."

"As do I," Matt said. "In fact, I like your theory better than the story about a theft and accidental shooting. For one thing, not many simple thieves carry guns. Country high-waymen who prey on moving vehicles do, but city criminals are more opportunistic. And for another, none of these reports mention missing clothing. Someone desperate enough to resort to thieving is probably not going to leave behind good shoes and a hat." He leaned forward and scanned one of the newspaper reports on the table. "This journalist specifically mentions the victim's fur-felt hat lying near the body."

"Fur-felt's good quality," Willie said, sounding enthusiastic again. "No thief would leave that behind. Seems it wasn't a stranger with their own gun who killed him after all."

Bristow appeared in the doorway and announced two visitors. "Mr. Barratt and Mr. Nash to see you."

"Professor," Nash corrected, as he passed Bristow. "Good morning. I hope we're not intruding."

Oscar eyed the newspapers spread out over the three occasional tables. "Has something happened?"

"There was a murder," Willie said.

"We met the victim," I clarified. "He was one of the sharpshooters from the Wild West show at Earls Court."

Oscar scanned one of the articles. "Is magic involved?"

"Shhh," Nash hissed, glancing at the doorway. "The servants."

"The servants know," Oscar told him. "They must, if they've been living under this roof."

"Magic isn't involved," I told them. "We're merely interested in the outcome. Please come in, sit down."

"Are you two here for a reason?" Matt asked. "Or simply to read my newspapers?"

Nash looked worried that he'd offended Matt. "Oh, no, of course not. It's a very good reason, as it happens. It's about a book."

Willie pushed herself up. "Then I'm leaving. Books make my eyes hurt."

"Oh? You should visit an optometrist. Spectacles can really help." Nash removed his spectacles, squinted in Willie's general direction, and put them back on again. "I visit a fellow near Trafalgar Square. I can give you his name if you like."

"I don't need no goggles." She strode out of the drawing room.

"But she thanks you anyway," Duke said and followed her.

Cyclops tapped his fingers on his thighs before he too rose. "I've got something to do."

"Was it something I said?" Nash asked, watching Cyclops leave.

"They don't like books?" Oscar offered.

"They don't like talking about books," Matt said.

"They might like talking about this one," Oscar said. "It's about magic."

I winced. "I have been meaning to return it to you, Professor, but I haven't finished it yet. I've been busy with wedding plans, you see."

"I understand and congratulations." Nash cleared his throat and his cheeks flushed. "Barratt told me of your engagement. I'm very happy for you. Congratulations," he said again.

I'd thought Matt was exaggerating when he claimed the professor liked me in that way, but if the blush was any indication, perhaps he was right. How sweet.

"Thank you," Matt said. "I'm a very lucky man."

"You are indeed. Miss Steele is very rare. That's what we've come to talk to you about, as it happens."

"Our wedding?" Matt prompted. "Your invitations are in the post."

I tried to glare at him but he wasn't looking my way. Indeed, I'd say he was purposefully not meeting my gaze so he didn't burst out laughing. He looked as if he could barely contain it.

To my surprise, it was Oscar who chuckled. "Let's not get ahead of ourselves, Gavin."

They were using first names? When did this close friendship begin? And why did it leave me with an uneasy feeling? Matt seemed worried, too. His amusement suddenly faded as his gaze flicked between the two of them.

"First of all, this isn't about the book Gavin loaned you, India," Oscar said.

"You can keep it for as long as you need it," Professor Nash added.

"Second of all, I wanted to offer my congratulations on your engagement in person. I know I sent a note after reading the announcement, but I should have come. We're friends, after all."

"Thank you," I said.

Matt simply gave him a flat smile.

"And finally, I wanted to apologize for my behavior the last time I saw you both, and the times before that. My brother always riles me. We haven't gotten along in years, and I'm afraid I can't control my temper around him. Nor can he, but I won't apologize on his behalf."

Their disagreements had been heated and sometimes violent. Although the latest problems seemed to stem from Oscar's articles about magic, I suspected the origins of their feud were much deeper. Isaac's wife's name, Cecilia, had come up more than once, and Oscar had hinted at the financial control his brother wielded over the family. The articles added fuel to an already burning fire.

"Is he still in London?" I asked.

"He returned home. He achieved what he wanted." Oscar waited, his head slightly tilted, as if he expected us to say something. "The private loan from the banker, Mr. Delancey," he added. "And my promise that I won't write any more articles."

"You promised that?" Matt asked.

Oscar settled into the chair and crossed his legs. "I did."

"It sounds like a promise you can keep, considering *The Weekly Gazette* is refusing to publish more articles on magic and other editors are refusing to buy them."

He simply smiled. "I've come up with a better idea. I'm going to write a book with Gavin."

"So that's what you meant," I said at the same time Matt said, "No."

"You don't have a say in the matter, Glass," Oscar said.

Matt stood and towered over Oscar. What did he intend to do? Intimidate him? "It's not a good idea. You know why."

"It's a very good idea. An entire book allows me to delve into the topic of magic more thoroughly. I'm going to include an entire two chapters on the history of magic and magicians." Oscar nodded at the professor. "That's where Gavin comes in. He's going to be an advisor, acknowledged, of course, if he wishes."

"You think this is a good idea, Professor?" Matt growled. "Have you lost your senses?"

The professor swallowed as Matt moved to stand in front of him, all hard features and flashing eyes. "I...I... That is..." Nash pushed his glasses up his nose. "I think it will be better than the articles. As Oscar says, it'll allow him more scope to really explore the topic and explain it sensitively and reasonably. It'll make magic less mystical and more real to the artless, thereby allaying fears."

"How will it allay fears? Artless craftsmen will still worry that magicians will take over their businesses. The guilds will tighten their requirements and some will begin a witch hunt. You know your history, Professor. I'm sure you're familiar with the Salem Witch Trials in America, and similar persecution here in England. Do you want that on your consciences?"

Nash swallowed again and leaned back a little.

"Matt," I said, "come and sit down." He obliged, albeit stiffly. He looked as if he would spring up and wring Oscar's neck at any moment. "Gentlemen, you must realize the danger you're courting by bringing the public's attention to magic all over again, just when it has started to fade. Magicians like your brother won't like the book, nor will the guilds."

"I know that," Oscar said. "It's unfortunate they can't see my side of it, but I do think most magicians want to get the word out. They don't want to live in the shadows anymore. I know you understand that, India. Don't try to deny it. I know you."

"You do not," Matt snarled.

I clasped my hands tightly in my lap and dared not look at either man.

"Not only are many magicians keen to have their magic in the open, the public is curious too," Oscar said. "If we can win them over to our side, then this current tension will all be worth it."

"Tension?" Matt exploded. "You think that's all this is? Tension? People's businesses are at stake. A lot of money could be gained and lost, and when that happens, there is always trouble. Another history lesson for you, Professor."

Nash sank even further into the chair.

Oscar scooted forward, perching on the edge of the seat. "We must break the guilds' stranglehold on our crafts, our businesses, our livelihoods. They should never have been allowed to get so strong. They're shutting out legitimate, hard-working magicians who only want to feed their families and practice their art in peace."

Matt threw his hands in the air. "Unbelievable," he muttered.

"How will you even get it published?" I asked. "The Stationer's Guild controls all the publishers and printers."

"I know of an independent printer working in Shoreditch," Oscar said. "He has agreed to print a thousand copies for me. If they all sell, he'll print more."

"By independent, you mean illegal," Matt said. "To operate without a license from the Stationer's Guild is against the law."

"That's why this must remain between us. Don't jeopardize this, Glass. It's not just the book and our work that you'll be destroying, but the printer's business. He'll be shut down and fined, perhaps jailed. The guild will come after him."

"I beg your pardon," I bit off. "Matt's not going to do

anything so cruel. If something happens to your printer, it won't be his fault. It'll be yours, for using his services."

"Of course, of course," Nash said quickly. "Mr. Glass would never do such a thing."

We all turned to Oscar. "I want you to promise, Glass," he said.

Matt held Oscar's gaze for a long time. "You must have come here knowing this would be my reaction," Matt said. "So why are you telling us this? I doubt it's just a courtesy call."

Nash cleared his throat and glanced at Oscar. Oscar suddenly looked less sure of himself with each passing moment as Matt's icy stare drilled into him.

"We will be using names of real magicians in the book," Oscar said. "Mine, of course, and—"

"No. You will not use her name."

"And other names of magicians who've given me permission."

"Other magicians have given you permission?" I asked.

"Two, so far, but I hope to get more."

"No," Matt said. "Absolutely not. You will not endanger her."

"It won't endanger her," Nash said, suddenly leaning forward too. Like Oscar, this book enthused him. It was difficult not to feel at least a little excited too. "It'll draw out other magicians," Nash went on. "When they realize what she can do with her magic, how she doesn't need a spell to make her watch move, other magicians will come out of hiding. I expect other powerful magicians will reveal themselves, if only to us and in secret."

"You're both mad," Matt said.

"What if we leave out her name, but just mention what her powers can do," Oscar said. "Then if someone approaches me and asks for her name, we can give it to them privately."

"And what if it's a guild master pretending to be a magician to learn where she lives?"

"We'll make them perform a test," Nash offered. "A magical test."

Matt shook his head, more in disgust than refusal. I said nothing; I simply watched on. As usual, the topic conflicted me. I wanted to live in the open. I wanted to practice magic. But the risk of persecution was very real. There was every reason to stay in hiding, and I agreed with Matt on that score—for now.

"We *have* to use her," Oscar said. He'd scooted so far forward I thought he might drop to his knees on the floor and beg.

Matt got to his feet. "Get out. Both of you. I've heard enough."

Oscar hesitated but Nash stood. He turned to me. "Let us know if you change your mind," he said.

"She won't," Matt said.

I bit down, grinding my back teeth.

Oscar rose and grasped my hand. "Think about it, India."

"Get. Out," Matt growled in a voice I'd never heard before. "Fossett! Make sure these gentlemen leave." He waited by the door until both men passed him.

I closed my eyes and squeezed the bridge of my nose. I felt the sofa cushion beside me sink.

"Are you all right?" Matt asked, voice normal again.

I opened my eyes to see his hand reaching up. He brushed my hair off my forehead, a gentle gesture that made my heart ache, not because it was tender but because of what I was about to say. He'd be hurt. "He was asking *me*, Matt, not you."

"I won't let him endanger you."

"It's my decision to make," I said, "not yours."

His fingers pulled back but his hand remained in the air between us; a sweet gesture interrupted, a moment, frozen in time, that could haunt me. "Don't, India," he said with quiet steel. "Don't make me say it."

I had to. If I didn't, it would trouble me and it would only rear its ugly head another day, and become even uglier. "Say what? That as my husband you can forbid me?"

He looked away.

"We're not married yet," I said.

I walked out of the drawing room, very aware that he did not follow.

CHAPTER 4

"*We* should go to Emmett's memorial," Willie said over breakfast.

"Why?" Cyclops asked. "Because we're American and he was American too?"

"Because it's a good opportunity to witness how his friends react to his death."

Cyclops plucked the eggshell out of the eggcup, tipped it upside down and shook it. Not a drop of yolk fell out. He sighed and cast a longing glance at the covered breakfast platters on the sideboard.

"I'm a suspect in his murder," Duke said, stabbing a rasher of bacon with his fork. "It ain't a good idea for me to go."

"Then stay here," she said. "The rest of us will go. What do you think, Matt?"

Matt hesitated. "I—" He broke off with a glance at me. "India? Do you think we should go?"

"I have no strong opinion on the matter," I said. "You decide."

I drained my teacup. Even though I wasn't looking at

Matt, I could feel his gaze on me. He'd been stealing glances at me all morning, quickly looking away when I caught him. Clearly my outburst yesterday troubled him. I, on the other hand, felt relieved to get it off my chest. Discussions like that had to be had before the wedding. There was no point letting them fester. It would only hurt more later.

"That's it." Willie threw her napkin on the table. "The air in here's thicker than a glutton's waist. What's going on with you two today?"

"Nothing," I said.

"Then why's Matt's face longer than a nag going to the knackery?"

"Don't, Willie," Matt said.

She looked from Matt to me then back again. "You two ain't leaving here 'til you've kissed and made up. Come on, Duke, Cyclops. Let's leave them alone."

Duke waved a piece of toast at her. "But I haven't finished my breakfast."

"Bring it with you."

Cyclops got up and left, but Duke lingered, blinking at his plate like it was his long lost love. Willie reached across the table, snatched up the plate, and headed out. Duke finally followed and shut the door.

"That was subtle," I said, getting up to refill my cup at the sideboard.

"India," Matt purred.

When he didn't go on, I said, "Yes?"

He was suddenly standing behind me, his hands lightly stroking my arms. "I'm sorry about yesterday." He kissed the top of my head. "Am I forgiven?"

I sighed and leaned back into him. "So you understand why I was cross?"

"You have a mind of your own. You're more than capable of thinking and speaking for yourself."

I turned and peered into his troubled eyes. His hands fell to his sides. "You've been thinking about that answer all night, haven't you?"

"Did it sound too rehearsed?"

I clasped his jaw and stood on my toes to kiss him. "Thank you for understanding," I murmured against his lips. "I was worried you wouldn't."

I felt his muscles relax against my palm. "It took me a few minutes to calm down and realize you weren't going to help Nash and Barratt with their book, and it wasn't about that. Also, my aunt pointed out you've been making your own decisions for years, and that I was being a petulant cowboy, storming in with guns blazing. Those are her words."

"I can hear her voice in them." I stretched my arms around his neck, coaxing a soft smile from lips. "She doesn't realize that I rather like cowboys."

"Should I wear my hat and holster?"

"Oh, Matt," I murmured against his mouth. "You do like to tease."

His lips stretched with his smile. "And I didn't even have to mention the boots."

Our kiss started with an explosive release of the tension we'd both been harboring since our argument. His arms wrapped around me, holding me so tightly my ribs hurt, and my fingers dug into his shoulders, clinging, trying to draw him closer when we were already as close as two clothed people could be. The kiss turned slow, sensual, a calmer yet no less passionate one. We finally broke apart when someone knocked.

"You two made up yet?" Willie shouted through the door.

Matt stroked his thumb along my lower lip. "I suppose we should rejoin the world."

"If we must." I took his hand and together we met with Willie, Cyclops and Duke.

"Have you decided?" Cyclops asked.

"Decided what?" Matt said.

Willie clicked her tongue. "The memorial service for Emmett. What have you two been discussing in there?"

"That ain't your business," Duke told her, cradling the plate of toast to his chest.

She looked as if she didn't agree but Matt spoke first. "I think it's a good idea to attend. We might learn something, and right now, the more evidence we can gather to point the finger at someone else, the more Brockwell will turn his attention away from Duke."

His mouth full, Duke hummed his agreement.

"It's settled then," I said. "But you're right, Duke, you shouldn't attend."

He swallowed. "Fine by me. I'm going out anyway."

Willie thrust her hands on her hips as he walked off. "Where are you going?"

"Ain't none of your business."

Cyclops clapped her on the shoulder. "Give him some peace. He never goes anywhere without us."

"That's because we're fun. Well, *I'm* fun. Lately you're a drag, Cyclops. You got to either do something about Catherine or stop thinking about her. And don't you mention the nurse to me." She poked him in the chest. "I ain't sitting around pining for her and eating like a bird to look my best for her. I'm getting on with life. Now come on, and let's get ready for the memorial."

Cyclops looked down at himself. "I am ready. Are you changing?"

"I'm getting my Colt. Ain't turning up to the memorial of a gunslinger without a weapon."

I watched her head up the stairs, wondering if she

meant wearing the gun was a tribute to Emmett or she was worried for her safety.

* * *

WE ARRIVED EARLY AT ST. Cuthbert's, a church not far from the Earls Court Exhibition ground. Emmett's body was going to be sent back to America for burial and a proper funeral, but the memorial service was meant for his fellow cast members. So it was surprising that few turned up.

We arrived early and stood at the back, watching the mourners as they entered and took their place. Indeed, the term mourners overstated it somewhat. Only May showed any sign of emotion.

Willie nudged me with her elbow. "There's Annie Oakley," she whispered. "She don't look too sad. I reckon we watch her."

"You think she's a suspect?" I whispered back. "Based on what information?"

"On her lack of emotion. You'd think she'd be sad to lose a friend."

"Nobody here looks particularly sad, except for May."

Willie craned her neck and scanned the other faces. "Remember the blonde eye-full from the pub? The one who looked pleased when Duke punched Emmett?"

"Is she here?" I asked, looking around.

"No, but I got the feeling she knew him. I expected her to be here. Maybe she was pleased about the punch because she hated him, maybe even enough to kill him. That makes two suspects now."

"Are you counting Annie Oakley?"

"Danny Draper, but we can count Annie Oakley if you want. She should be questioned anyway, on account of her being important to the show."

The other important person for the show, Bill Cody himself, sat in the front pew beside Annie Oakley. I recognized him from the show's posters, although the likeness had been made more youthful. Unlike the rest of the mourners, he left immediately after the service. He didn't stay to file past the open casket with the rest of us.

Most of the mourners hardly glanced at the dead man's face. Not even May. Her tears had dried too. I was beginning to wonder if she'd been acting earlier.

I peeped into the casket and meant to just pass by, but stopped instead. Emmett's hands lay flat over his chest, a spray of playing cards face down beneath the fingers as if he were keeping a winning hand close before he played them. It was a poignant gesture for the gambler, yet it wasn't the gesture that struck me. It was the compulsion I felt to touch those cards.

It was wrong, yet I couldn't ignore the need. I gathered my nerve and reached in, all too aware that the cards and gunmetal grey suit covered the fatal wound. My little finger brushed the cards and I gasped, pulling back. I curled my fingers into a fist and pressed it to my stomach. I searched along the line of mourners for Matt and our gazes connected. He frowned.

"Keep moving," the man behind me whispered. "We've got to get back to prepare for the show."

I spared a glance at Emmett, his face set into an expression that must have meant to look peaceful but instead looked unnatural. *So that's how you did it.*

"What is it, India?" Matt asked as he joined me by the front pew. "You've gone pale."

We walked out of the church where only a handful of mourners remained. My mind reeled and I must have sported an odd look on my face because Cyclops and Willie also asked if something was the matter.

"India?" Matt clasped my elbow. "Are you going to faint?"

I shook my head and indicated they should follow me out of earshot. "You were right, Willie," I said. "Emmett cheated, and I know how."

"How?" all three chorused.

"He was a paper magician. The cards on his chest were warm from magical heat. It was strong enough to feel through my glove."

They stared at me then, as if a dam burst, all spoke at once.

"You don't say," Cyclops muttered.

"I knew it," Willie spat. "That lying, cheating dog."

"Good," Matt said with decisiveness. "This means we have a reason to investigate. We'll inform the commissioner now."

Willie caught his sleeve as he went to walk off. "Look." She nodded at Annie Oakley, on the arm of a whiskered gentleman. "Want me to interrogate her?"

"We're not officially assigned to the case yet," Cyclops said.

"So? It ain't never stopped us before."

"What do you hope she can tell us?" Matt asked.

Willie shrugged. "All sorts of things."

"She could tell us who the blonde woman from the pub was," I said, looking at the remaining mourners. "There's May and Danny. Let's ask them."

"We ain't assigned yet," Cyclops said again.

"So?" I asked, echoing Willie.

Cyclops appealed to Matt, but Matt simply held up his hands. "As far as I'm aware, we're simply sharing memories about the deceased with fellow mourners."

We greeted May and Danny with kind words of sympathy. I introduced them to Matt and watched on as he employed his charm to full effect.

"I never met him," he said with a solemn air, "but Willie told me so much about him that I wanted to pay my respects today. She called him a masterful poker player, the best she'd ever come up against."

"She called him a cheater to his face," Danny sneered with an arched look for Willie.

"I call everyone who beats me a cheater," Willie said. "It don't mean anything. Emmett beat me, fair and square."

Danny held her gaze. "Your friend hit him."

May placed her hand over her husband's arm and Danny swallowed his next words. "It's lovely of y'all to come," she said. "Unfortunately, not many could."

"We saw Miss Oakley," Willie said, gazing off in the direction of the Earls Court exhibition grounds. "They were close?"

"Not particularly." May dabbed at the corner of her eye with her handkerchief and sniffed. "She had a run-in with Emmett."

"She lost to him at poker too?"

May nodded. Her husband's fingers tightened on her arm and she winced. "But not very much, I believe," she added. "Annie flared up then immediately calmed down again and forgot all about it, and about Emmett. She's like that."

"Me too," Willie said. "That's what happened the other night. Emmett beat me, I got all riled, but I got it out of my system. Hell, I wanted to play him again."

That perked Danny up. He displayed his dimples to full boyish effect. He really was quite beautiful when he smiled. "Come to The Prince of Wales tonight. I'll play you."

"Danny," May chided. "Not tonight. We should be honoring Emmett's memory."

"Playing poker will honor him. It was his favorite thing. He always had a deck of cards in his pocket," Emmett said to us. "Sometimes you'd see him wandering around, holding them, flipping them, doing tricks—sleight of hand, that sort of thing. It's like he was born with a deck. I was glad to see he'll be buried with them."

May gave him a wan smile. "You two got along, despite him always beating you. Very well, play a few rounds tonight in Emmett's memory, then no more. You lose too much."

"He beat you regularly, did he?" Matt asked Danny.

Danny bristled. "It weren't regular."

"It was quite regular," his wife said.

Danny fell into a broody silence.

"Maybe your luck'll change tonight," Willie said cheerfully. "I think I will come. To honor Emmett, of course. Win or lose, it doesn't matter."

I doubted a single one of us believed she meant it.

"There was a pretty blonde at the pub," I said. "She seemed pleased when Duke punched Emmett. Do you know who she is?"

"This here's the prettiest blonde," Danny said with a jerk of his head toward his wife.

"Stop, Danny, you're making me blush," May said, dipping her head coyly. "I've seen the woman you mean, but she's not one of us."

How mysterious. Before I could ask more questions, however, Matt changed topic. "What did Emmett do before he joined the troupe?"

"Don't know," Danny said, "but I've got a suspicion it weren't good or he would have mentioned it."

"It must have been a shock to hear of his passing."

"It was awful," May said, dabbing at her eyes again. "Bill told us all the morning after they found him."

"It was fortunate we weren't there when it happened,"

Danny added. "We left The Prince of Wales only a little while before."

Matt circled his arm around my waist and hugged me to his side. "I was worried when I heard about it. India said she'd been there only the night before and met Emmett." He stared into my eyes and spoke softly, as if he were speaking to me, not two strangers. The effect was mesmerizing and I was unable to look away. "Imagine if she'd gone that night too and stepped out of the pub at the wrong time. The thief could have attacked her. It doesn't bare thinking about." His arm tightened and his eyes turned dark, grim.

I blinked up at him, trying to play my part of self-assured woman yet finding myself sucked into his act.

May's sniff broke the spell. "Unless she entered the laneway, she would not have met a grim end at the point of the thief's gun."

"You think the thief used his own weapon and not Emmett's?" Matt asked.

The rapid change of pace left my head spinning. It threw May off guard too. She opened and closed her mouth several times before finally answering. "Isn't that what the newspapers say?"

"Aye, it is," Danny said, sounding distracted as he checked his watch, a simple open faced piece with a crack through the glass. "May, we have to be getting back. Nice to meet you, Mr. Glass. Miss Johnson, I hope to see you tonight. I feel like Emmett'll be watching over us, helping us both win."

"Then he'd better send a couple of unsuspecting greens our way," she said, touching the brim of her hat.

We watched them go then returned to the carriage.

"I had so many more questions for them," I said as Matt assisted me up the step.

"Too many questions," Willie said, getting in unaided.

"You'll scare them off. I know it's hard for you, India, but you got to try to be subtle."

I snapped my skirts out of her way as she sat beside me. "You want me to take subtlety cues from you?"

"That's the spirit. Speaking of subtle, who else thought they overdid it?"

"Overdid what?" I asked.

"Their performance."

"What performance?"

"Just now." Willie turned to me. "You mean you didn't notice? India, you are an innocent."

"I am not!"

"She's trusting," Matt said to Willie. "It's not a character flaw."

"Can you tell me what you're referring to?" I pressed. "Are you saying that May was *acting* sad?"

"She might have been," Matt said. "But we're referring to their efforts to get Willie to the pub tonight to play poker. Willie is supposed to believe that Danny was genuinely hopeless the other night and wasn't working with Emmett. They're relying on that perception to draw her back."

"He's working the swindle alone now," Cyclops said. "Risky."

We turned a corner a little too rapidly, sending Willie and I sliding along the bench seat. Matt and Cyclops hardly moved, however, their broad shoulders ensuring they were wedged together opposite us.

"No one's mentioned the obvious, yet," I said, resetting my skirts. "Emmett was a paper magician, and we already know a paper magician."

"You think Emmett and Hendry are related?" Cyclops asked.

"It's a possibility," Matt said. "It's worth asking Hendry if he knew Emmett."

We'd met Melville Hendry when investigating the death of the editor of *The Weekly Gazette*. He'd sent threatening letters to Oscar Barratt, urging him to stop writing his articles about magic. Fearful for his life, business and relationships, he'd not wanted attention drawn to himself. It was an angry former lover who'd committed the murder, to implicate and punish Mr. Hendry. Our involvement in unraveling the sordid mess had not endeared him to us, however.

Matt met with Commissioner Munro alone at Scotland Yard, leaving the three of us waiting on Victoria Embankment, watching the water craft pass by. Patience not being Willie's strong suit, she was the first to begin pacing up and down. Cyclops soon joined her, while I resorted to tapping my fingers on the embankment wall.

When Matt finally returned, he was smiling. "Brockwell will see us now."

"Munro agreed to let us investigate?" I asked.

"You sound like you doubted my powers of persuasion."

"Not for a moment."

"Liar." He grinned and offered me his arm to cross the road.

Without the threat of imminent death hanging over his head, Matt had returned to his more amenable self, and with that came the charm he possessed in spades. Some gentlemen thought being charming meant performing a slick routine, but it came naturally to Matt. It was that genuine charisma that won most people to his side.

A constable led us to Brockwell's office, hidden away in the bowels of the new building. Commissioner Munro must have informed him of Matt's visit because he appeared to be expecting us.

"I see you've brought your posse, as you Americans say," Brockwell said, shaking Matt's hand.

"Duke ain't here," Willie informed him, also offering her hand.

Brockwell hesitated before shaking it and Cyclops's too. He hesitated again, perhaps waiting for me to offer mine, but by the time I'd decided I should, he'd sat again.

"My apologies for the lack of chairs," he said, smoothing his hand over his tie which didn't remove a single crumple. "I rarely have so many visitors."

Cyclops and Matt remained standing, leaving the chairs for Willie and me, however Willie decided she preferred to stand with the men so I sat alone. Brockwell watched us with an amused gleam in his eye, mostly directed at Willie.

"The commissioner informs me that you have reason to suspect the victim was a paper magician," Brockwell said. "Why is that, Miss Steele?"

"I felt magical warmth on the cards placed beneath his hands in the casket. I accidentally brushed them," I clarified, lest he think I liked touching dead bodies. "Emmett also liked to play poker and won easily. So easily, in fact, that Willie here suspected him of cheating."

"Only I didn't know how he did it, at the time," she said.

"And how could magic help him cheat?" the inspector asked.

"We can't know for sure," Matt said. "Perhaps he simply felt the heat in certain cards that he himself placed there. Or perhaps he used a spell that allowed him to identify them. It's a question we'll ask Melville Hendry."

Brockwell's left eyebrow arched. "The other paper magician? Is interrogating him wise, considering his state of mind after the Baggley murder?"

"His state of mind is irrelevant," Matt said. "You know that."

Brockwell's lips flattened.

"We'll be delicate," I assured him. "It's our belief that

65

gentle questioning will be the only way to get him to talk to us."

"Agreed." He rested his elbows on the chair arms and steepled his fingers beneath his chin. "A woman's touch is needed. Perhaps the interview should be conducted without men present. Miss Steele, perhaps Miss Johnson can join you."

"Willie?" It burst out of me before I could control it. That and the spluttering laugh.

She crossed her arms. "Why not me?"

"Why not indeed," I said. "But let me do all the talking."

Her lack of agreement worried me. "We'll go today," was all she said.

"Report back immediately," Brockwell said. "Will that be all?"

"You're yet to inform us of what you've learned so far," Matt said, employing the same commanding tone as the inspector. "Munro made it clear we're to work together on this, and since my friend is a suspect, I can assure you I'll do everything I can to clear his name."

"Your loyalty is commendable."

"So he's still a suspect?" Willie asked.

"Until proven otherwise, yes."

She clicked her tongue and muttered something under her breath.

"Pardon?" Brockwell prompted. "Did you say something, Miss Johnson?"

She lifted her chin. "I called you a son of a—"

"Willie!" Matt snapped. "The inspector is only doing his job. You know that."

Willie looked away, her nose in the air. Brockwell's lips twitched ever-so slightly before settling into his usual dour expression.

"You were about to tell us what you've learned so far," Matt said.

Brockwell scratched his sideburns.

"Commissioner's orders," Cyclops reminded him.

"Very well. There are a few important things I've discovered. The first is the victim's weapon. It was found in his room when my men searched it."

"You sure it was his?" Willie asked.

"The handle was engraved with his initials and his colleagues confirmed it belonged to Cocker. He had others, too, which he used in the show, but this was his everyday one, the one he carried with him. Apparently he liked to walk around the city with it."

"So?" Willie said. "Lots of people do."

"No, Miss Johnson, they do not. Not here in England."

"That's because you English folk are strange. Where I come from, a man never leaves home without his gun. Some women, too. If it was his everyday gun, why didn't he have it on him that night?"

"That's a question I'd like to find the answer to."

"Did it shoot the bullet that killed him?" Matt asked.

"It's the right sort, but more tests need to be conducted."

"Where was he staying while in London?"

"The cast members have rented various lodgings near the exhibition grounds. The show's stars have houses on Philbeach Gardens, whereas the lesser known members rented rooms in houses located in less grand streets. Mr. Cocker was residing in the loft of a house in Childs Street along with three others, including a married couple." He searched through the papers on his desk, shifting torn scraps aside, making an even bigger mess of his already untidy paperwork. He eventually found what he was looking for and handed it to me. "The address."

"Your men have conducted a thorough search?" Matt asked.

"Of course. Excepting the gun, there was nothing else of note in Cocker's room. The other lodgers were questioned but all claimed to be asleep at two in the morning, which is when the coroner estimates time of death occurred. However, they'd seen him earlier that evening at The Prince of Wales where he liked to play poker, as Miss Johnson learned to her detriment, I believe."

"He cheated," she declared.

"So it seems. The married couple, a Mr. and Mrs. Draper, were among the last to see him."

"Danny Draper also cheats at cards," Willie said. "They were in it together, although he ain't a magician."

Matt told the inspector how we suspected Danny, and perhaps May, were involved in the duplicity and were most likely continuing to use the initial set-up to fleece unsuspecting players. "It's a ruse that can last only a little longer now that Emmett is dead. Without him and his magic, it'll be much harder to win all the time."

"Their acting skills ain't that good," Willie clarified.

"They're reasonably good," I said.

Brockwell nodded slowly in thought. "So they're unlikely to be suspects in the murder. It's in their interests to have Cocker alive to continue with their scheme."

"Perhaps that's why May was so upset at the memorial," I said. "She was lamenting the lost winnings Emmett would share with her husband for playing his part. If her tears were genuine, I mean."

"It's likely," Matt said. "Considering how many people Emmett cheated, the murderer can probably be found among their number."

"There's more." Brockwell searched his papers again, but this time found what he needed near the top. "I sent a telegraph to my American counterparts when I learned of the murder, and this morning I received a response. It seems Emmett Cocker was wise to come to England when he did." He passed the message to me.

"He was wanted by the law?" Willie asked, peering over my shoulder.

"No," I said. "But he was known to them. He was being hunted by a man known as Jack Krane."

"Krane!" Matt joined Willie in looking over my shoulder.

Willie swore. "Remember him, Cyclops?"

"I remember," Cyclops said darkly. "He ain't a man you want to cross. Did Emmett cheat him too?"

"It seems so," I said, passing the message back to Brockwell. "According to this, Krane is wanted by the law, along with members of his posse, for several crimes, including murder."

"Emmett was a dang fool to cheat him," Willie said.

"What do you know of this Krane?" Brockwell asked Matt.

"I've never met him, but I've heard of him," he said. "He and his posse are a menace."

"Do you think they'd cross the Atlantic to get their revenge?"

"It's doubtful, but not impossible. I don't know him well enough but if I had to guess, I'd say he's too busy in America to chase one man all the way over here."

"Depends how much Emmett cheated him out of," Willie said. "I've known men get obsessed with revenge. It don't matter how much it costs them, or how many lives have to be lost, if they can satisfy their lust for it, they will."

"'Specially if they've been humiliated," Cyclops added. "For some, that's worse than death."

"I won't rule Krane out then," Brockwell said.

"I think we'll notice if an outlaw posse come to London,"

I said. "Do you remember the Dark Rider?" Finding him had been our first investigation together. The outlaw had tried to hurt me to get to Matt, only to fail thanks to my watch saving me. My old watch. My new one had so far lain dormant in my reticule in times of danger.

"I remember," Matt said, laying a hand on my shoulder. "If Krane comes here alone, he will be harder to detect. I'll make some enquiries."

"That's all I have at this point in time," Brockwell said. "You have my permission to speak discreetly to Hendry and follow the magical line of inquiry. Thank you for the information about the cheating, and about the Drapers in particular."

"There's one other thing," I said. "There was a blonde woman at The Prince of Wales, that night we were there. She isn't part of the show, but she seemed to know Emmett and looked rather pleased when Duke punched him."

Brockwell scratched his sideburns again. "I'll see what I can find out about her."

"As will we." I rose and put out my hand. "Thank you, Inspector. Willie and I will report back after we've spoken to Mr. Hendry."

He came around to my side of the desk and shook my hand. "I look forward to it." He grasped Willie's hand next, even though she hadn't offered it. "Very much."

CHAPTER 5

*M*att refused to return home while Willie and I spoke to Mr. Hendry. He wanted to wait nearby, in case we needed him.

"Why would we need you?" Willie asked.

"He can make weapons from paper with the utterance of a spell," Matt reminded her.

"And India's watch will save her."

"We don't know that," I said. "Besides, if it does work, it will save me, not you."

The carriage deposited us around the corner from Hendry's Smithfield shop. The shop was empty but the *thump thump* of machinery from the workshop at the back told us where to find him. I pushed open the door and cleared my throat, but he couldn't hear me over the hammer pounding the pulp. I stepped up to him and waved my hand in front of his face.

He emitted a squeak, quickly followed by a scold. "It's rude to sneak up on a fellow, Miss Steele." The machine slowed to a halt as he rose. Despite the warm room, he looked as well dressed as ever in a gray and red striped waistcoat with a tie in the same hue of red. Not a single hair was out of place, even though he'd been leaning over his work. The thick steely locks remained swept off his high forehead—a forehead creased in a frown. "What do you want now?"

"It's rude to speak like that to a lady," Willie shot back. "'Specially one who cleared your name of murder."

Mr. Hendry had the decency to look sheepish. "You're right. I apologize. Welcome. Please step into my shop."

We returned to the shop where displays of paper, card stock, invitations and books were set out on the counter top and in glass cabinets. It was a small space but he didn't require anything larger. He rarely sold pre-made wares, preferring to make his wares to order according to his loyal customers' requirements.

He remained behind the counter and pulled out a ledger. "Are you here to order invitations? I read about your engagement. Congratulations."

"We don't need invitations," I said. "It'll be an intimate affair, and everyone we wish to be there has been personally informed."

From the look on his face, one would think I'd just told him I drowned a litter of kittens. "But...but...every wedding requires invitations. Even one hastily put together."

"It ain't like that," Willie said hotly. "They just want to get married straight away on account of all the fuss lately with his cousin."

"Of course, of course." He slid a piece of paper across the counter and handed me a pencil. "Write the details down, as well as the number required, and I'll have something made up. My regular calligrapher owes me a favor and will put the order through straight away."

"I don't know," I said.

"It'll be very elegant, very sophisticated." He pushed the pencil and paper closer to me.

Willie took the pencil and wrote the details down. "Send the account to Matt at the delivery address. Now, we want to ask you something."

He sighed. "Go on then."

"A man by the name of Emmett Cocker was murdered," I began. "He was an American sharpshooter in the Buffalo Bill show. Did you know him?"

"I don't know every murder victim in London, you know." He picked up the paper and read what Willie had written.

"He was a paper magician."

He lowered the paper. "Oh. Now I see why you're here."

"Are you sure you don't know him?" Willie asked.

He gave her a withering glare. "Of course I'm sure."

I wished I'd torn the article from the newspaper to show him Emmett's picture. "He didn't seek you out?"

"Why would he? It's not widely known that I'm a magician."

"He might have been aware of your existence," I said. "Perhaps through family stories. It's likely you came from different branches of the same magical lineage."

"That is a possibility. There are stories of some members of the family settling in America more than a hundred years ago. He could be one of their descendants, but I can't help you with any details. I'm sorry. Now, do you mind?" He waved the paper. "I have work to do."

"One more question. If you wanted to cheat at cards, could you use a spell to do so?"

"A spell to identify them only to the magician?" He shook his head. "I don't know any spells like that."

73

"But if you did know one...?"

"I told you, I don't."

I thanked him for his time and we left the shop. "Do you think he's lying?" I asked.

"He started getting hot under the collar when you pressed him about the spell," Willie said. "And he seemed to remember about the American branch of his family late, and not until after you mentioned it."

"Perhaps he'd forgotten."

"I don't like perhapses."

"Nor do I."

Cyclops was sitting on the driver's seat when we returned, chatting to the coachman, while Matt stood on the pavement, leaning against the carriage door, his ankles and arms crossed. It was a relaxed, confident stance and one that epitomized all the good things about him now his health had been restored. I couldn't help smiling.

"It seems you were successful," he said, smiling back.

"Not in the least. I just like looking at you."

Willie groaned. "Save me before I drown in the syrup, Cyclops."

Cyclops jumped down and joined us. "So what did he say about Emmett?"

"He never met him," Willie said. "Emmett never visited, so he claims."

"You don't believe him?"

"We're not sure," I said. "He admitted to having long lost family in America, and assumes Emmett belonged to that branch. That's all the information he offered. We both picked up an air of evasiveness, however."

Matt surveyed the street, lined with small shops and workshops operated by craftsmen of different persuasions. How many magicians took refuge behind their small operations? How many practiced their art in secret, like Mr. Hendry, or hid it altogether, like Mr. Gibbons the cartography magician? Very few turned their magical craft into a large scale operation like Isaac Barratt, the ink magician. People like Isaac would be the first to be brought down if the artless took a stand against their magical rivals, but these smaller craftsmen would be victimized too.

"We could ask the neighbors if they saw Emmett enter the shop," Matt said. "He wore distinctive clothes and had a distinctive accent so it's not quite as bad as searching for a needle in a haystack."

"Distinctive moustache too," Willie added.

"We'll ask around," Cyclops said. "Duke, Willie and me."

"After I report to Brockwell," Willie said. "No need for you to come, India. There weren't much to report anyway."

"It's settled then," I said. "What will we do, Matt?"

"Speak to Sir Charles Whittaker. I want to find out why he was there at the pub that night, what he knows about Emmett, and what the so-called Collectors' Club knows."

"What if he won't tell us anything?" I asked. "He pretended not to be at the bare knuckle fights."

Matt's lips simply curled into a curious smile that made me glad he wasn't about to interrogate me.

WE RETURNED HOME with Cyclops in tow but not Willie. We found Duke playing cards with Miss Glass in the sitting room, a plate of sandwiches on the side table next to them. Duke waved a sandwich at us in greeting, his mouth too full to speak. Miss Glass didn't look up from her cards.

"Can you beat that?" she asked, showing Duke her cards.

He sighed but did no not reveal his in return.

I tried to sneak a peek over his shoulder, but he placed the cards on top of the deck and shuffled them. Miss Glass added her winnings to her sizeable pile. I wondered if Duke would let her win with a pair of eights if they were playing for something more valuable than matchsticks.

"Where's Willie?" Duke asked, his sandwich finished.

"Speaking with Detective Inspector Brockwell," Cyclops said, taking a sandwich.

Duke snatched the plate away. "Ask Bristow for your own."

"He's bringing more," Matt said.

"Aren't you on a diet?" Duke asked Cyclops.

"I ain't stopping eating altogether," Cyclops said.

"You don't need to be on a diet, Cyclops dear," Miss Glass said. "You're perfect the way you are."

"Thank you."

"Miss Mason says so. I overheard her telling India once."

I couldn't remember Catherine saying it quite so baldly, but the gist was the same.

Cyclops looked as though he wanted to walk out of the room but changed his mind when Bristow entered carrying three more plates piled with sandwiches cut into triangles.

"Eat up," Cyclops told Duke. "We've got work to do when Willie returns."

Miss Glass made a face of protest. "If you're going to discuss murder, I'm leaving. It's quite an unsavory discussion for a lady." She rose and waited, but when I didn't rise too, she left, sighing so loudly and repeatedly I could hear her all the way to the staircase.

"What have you been doing this morning, Duke?" I asked, taking a sandwich.

"I went to hospital to visit a certain nurse."

"You did?"

He smiled around his sandwich.

"Willie'll kill you if she finds out," Cyclops said. "Make sure I'm here when you do."

"She won't kill me because she won't find out," Duke said. "I'm not going to tell her and neither are any of you."

"So?" I prompted. "Tell us how it went."

"She won't change her mind about Willie. That's definite."

"That is a shame. Did you list all her fine qualities?"

"She knows Willie's qualities, fine and otherwise. She didn't want to talk to me at first, when I told her who I was. But I gave her no choice."

Cyclops's eye widened. "You kidnapped her?"

"No! I dogged her every step."

"Right." Cyclops shoved a sandwich into his mouth with a shrug.

"She says she can't be with Willie," Duke went on. "She can't be with any woman. She's got a fiancé, a good man she doesn't want to hurt. She's got no brothers and sisters and says her parents will disown her if she doesn't marry."

"Willie would take care of her financially," I said. "And she has her work as a nurse."

"It's not just that, India. She loves her parents. She doesn't want to hurt them or cut herself off from them, not for something she described as a 'fleeting fancy.'"

"Oh."

"She ain't willing to give up her life and loved ones to indulge a passing whim. Them's also her words."

We sat in silence, eating and thinking. For my part, I tried to put myself in the nurse's shoes. I considered whether love was something I would give up everything for. I rather suspected it was. I'd been prepared to give up my life in England to be with Matt. But I had to admit that our situation was different. As difficult as our relationship had been, it wasn't taboo. Nor did either of us consider it a passing whim.

"It weren't a wasted trip altogether," Duke said. "I got to see what the nurse was like, to see what sort of person Willie would want."

"And?" I prompted. "What was she like?"

"Capable, efficient. She's respected by the other nurses."

Cyclops grunted. "She sounds like a laugh."

"He has a point," I said. "Those are all excellent traits in a nurse, but what of her character? Was she lively? Or reserved?"

Duke shrugged. "I didn't speak to her for long. She didn't like my questions."

"She stormed off, didn't she?" Matt asked, amused. "You do have a way with women, Duke."

"Most of what I learned about her came from the other nurses," Duke admitted.

I touched his hand. "You tried, and that's the main thing. You're a good friend, Duke."

"Yes, ma'am, I am."

Willie returned just as the rest of us were preparing to leave again. She regarded each of us in turn in the entrance hall, hats or gloves in hand, and told us we had no patience.

"You were gone an age," Duke said, slapping his hat on his head. "We waited a long time, but we can't wait all day."

"I had to wait for a hansom. And Jasper was busy when I got there."

"Jasper?" Matt and I both asked.

"Jasper Brockwell. You two been working with him all this time and didn't know his first name?" She clicked her tongue. "Wait for me. I'll be back down in three swishes of a bronco's tail."

We all stared after her as she took the stairs two at a time.

"Japser," Matt said, his tone somewhere between amused and bemused. "I would never have guessed."

* * *

Sir Charles Whittaker was not at home but his house-keeper expected him back mid-afternoon. Instead of returning home, Matt and I stopped for ices on Oxford Street and afterward he insisted we browse for home wares.

"Why?" I asked, as he steered me into Mortlock's china shop. "The house is fully furnished. It has everything we need."

"But does it have everything you *like*? It was furnished by my father, years ago, in his bachelor days. Not only is it masculine but some of the furnishings are dated. I thought you might like to put your own touch on it."

"I hadn't thought of that. I'm used to it the way it is." I'd never considered changing a thing.

"It's your home, India," he said quietly. "Change what-ever you want." He leaned closer as the shop assistant made her way toward us. "Money is no object and you don't have to buy anything here," Matt whispered. "But don't tell her that."

We spent some time looking at dinner sets, vases and other knick knacks in Mortlock's then wandered along Oxford Street, entering shops that sold soft furnishings and other such items. We even perused furniture catalogues. We settled on a dinner set we both liked and had it sent home, but I needed more time for the larger purchases.

"I'll ask your aunt for her help," I said as we left a draper's shop. "And perhaps Willie."

"Or you could look through some magazines."

"You really don't want me to seek their input, do you?"

"I want my fiancée to retain her sanity."

We returned to Sir Charles's house, and his housekeeper was in the process of telling us he hadn't yet returned when a hansom pulled up at the curb and deposited him outside.

"What a delightful surprise," Sir Charles said in his rich plummy accent. I'd originally thought him a wealthy man, judging by the accent and his well-tailored suits, but Hammersmith wasn't the best address in London, although it was far from the worst. "Come inside, out of this heat."

He asked his housekeeper to bring tea and led us into the sitting room. Like the man himself, the room was neat and furnished in a simple style, not at all cluttered as some homes could be. He quickly gathered the magazines scattered across two occasional tables but not before I noticed they were a mix of catalogues and magazines about horses and carriages.

"How can I help you?" he asked, settling on the chair, leaving the sofa for Matt and me.

"We want to know what you were doing at The Prince of Wales the other night," Matt said.

Whittaker's lower lip protruded as he thought, then he shook his head. "I don't recall being there. What night was it?"

"Don't play games," Matt said, matching Whittaker's idle tone. "We know you were there. We also know you were at the bare knuckle fights, yet you claim not to have been."

"Unless you have an identical twin, you were there," I said. "At both venues."

A look of resignation came over Whittaker's face. "You're right. I was there at the fights, and also at the pub. So?"

"Are you following me?" I asked.

"Of course not. Why would I?"

"To report my activities to Lord Coyle and the other members of the club." It had been a nagging thought that I couldn't shake, but now that I'd said it out loud, it sounded somewhat ridiculous. "I don't know."

"You lied to us about the fights," Matt said. "You must see that it makes you look suspicious."

The housekeeper brought in a tray with tea things and cake. We waited until she finished pouring before resuming the conversation. I think Whittaker was glad to have the time to think of what to say.

"I didn't like admitting I was at the fights because it's not the most seemly of pastimes," he said.

"You were ashamed?" Matt asked. "Of watching bare knuckle fights? Sir Charles, we were there as well. Our friends participated. Why would you be ashamed to admit your presence to us?"

"Your friends fought? I didn't know that." He sipped his tea. "Who knows why I said what I did? You caught me, and all I could think to do was deny it."

"And what about The Prince of Wales pub?" I asked.

He set his cup down on the saucer. "That's a different matter. I had heard about Emmett Cocker's talent for cards and thought it suspicious that he continued to win, time and time again. So I watched him to decide for myself if he used magic. Rest assured, I wasn't following *you*, Miss Steele. I know what you're capable of. I don't know what Emmett Cocker is—was—capable of."

"You heard that he was good at cards and came to the conclusion that he was a magician?" Matt scoffed. "Come now, you don't expect us to believe that, do you?"

Whittaker lifted one shoulder in an elegant shrug. "It's the truth. I suspected he might be a paper magician."

Matt contemplated his sponge cake but didn't eat any. I thought it was rather delicious and ate a whole slice as I considered what to make of Whittaker's claim.

"In your time of watching Cocker, did he visit Melville Hendry?" Matt asked.

"I don't know."

Matt smiled. "I think you meant to say that you didn't see him visit Hendry."

Whittaker smiled back. "I couldn't watch Cocker all the time. He may have visited Hendry when I wasn't looking. I'm just one man, Mr. Glass."

"Yet the club contains many."

Whittaker sipped.

Matt set down his cake uneaten and stood. "Thank you for the tea, Sir Charles."

"You're very welcome. Stop by any time, Miss Steele." He took my hand and patted it. "Always a pleasure."

Matt strode to the door and waited for me to exit ahead of him. "I don't like him," he muttered as he assisted me into the carriage. "He's lying."

"He certainly is," I said. "The question is, why?"

* * *

DUKE, Cyclops and Willie returned in time for dinner. At Miss Glass's insistence, they changed their attire, but only superficially. The men exchanged their neckerchiefs for clean ones and Willie changed her waistcoat and neckerchief. It was more than I expected her to do. She also did it without grumbling. She was in a good mood.

"Did you discover if any of Hendry's neighbors saw Emmett?" Matt asked after dinner had been served.

"Not now, Matthew," Miss Glass said on a sigh. "You ought to know that discussion of your investigations are not to occur over the dinner table."

He apologized, and I switched to talking about our shopping expedition and Matt's idea to redecorate. I watched

Miss Glass for signs that the suggestion to redecorate upset her, but she seemed quite amendable.

"Your father's taste was excellent," she told Matt. "But it's all rather old fashioned now. I have a lot of ideas, India. Shall we discuss them after dinner?"

"I'd loved to."

Willie looked at me as if I were mad.

"Would you like to help us?" I asked her.

"I'd rather pull all my teeth out, sober." She raised her glass of wine in salute. "But you enjoy yourself."

"I have magazines in my room," Miss Glass said. "Modern ones with modern ideas," she added with a pointed glare for Willie. "Then we can go shopping."

While Miss Glass didn't like discussing murder investigations over the dinner table, she had no such qualms once dinner had finished. We sat in the drawing room, she with a magazine on her lap and a stack on the table beside her, while I listened to Cyclops's report.

"Hendry's immediate neighbors on both sides of the shop didn't notice a customer matching Emmett's description," he said. "But two doors down, at the shoemaker, an American came in to have his spare pair of boots repaired."

"Did he match Emmett's description?" Matt asked.

"The shoemaker couldn't remember much about the fellow's looks, only his accent."

"It's not a certainty that it was Emmett then."

"It's a good chance," Willie said.

"I prefer certainties over chances. We need to find out for sure if it was Emmett."

"Ain't no use in asking the neighbors again," Duke said, rising. "Who's coming to The Prince of Wales to watch Willie play Danny?"

We all decided to go, much to Miss Glass's dismay. She'd wanted to talk about decorating. I asked her to make notes and gave her a pencil and paper to write down her ideas. She was busily flipping the pages of another magazine when we left.

The Prince of Wales was full of Americans again. Annie Oakley was there, having a drink with May. They were within sight of Danny, looking relaxed at a table, cards in hand. Each player had a modest pile of coins stacked in front of them.

"Mind if I join you?" Willie asked.

"Go right ahead." Danny pulled out a spare chair for her and beamed. "This here's Willie," he told the others. "She's a real good player."

I left them to their cards and joined May and Annie, seated on high stools. The evening was still early but the smell of ale and tobacco was so thick it was eye-watering.

"Is it wise to bring your friend?" Annie Oakley asked with a nod at Duke. "No one particularly liked Emmett but he was one of us."

The ripple of chatter had increased upon our entry but had since died down. Some of the men watched Duke but they didn't seem particularly hostile. Matt surveyed the room, his gaze sweeping back and forth, watchful.

"We'll leave if it looks like there'll be trouble," I assured her.

"That handsome fellow your fiancé?" Annie asked.

"He is. He's American too, on his mother's side."

"He dresses like an English toff."

I smiled. Matt would hate to know that others saw him as a toff. "He wanted to come tonight and meet all of you. He has taken quite an interest in poor Emmett's murder, as it happens."

"What kind of an interest?" May asked, staring at Matt with such intensity that it was a wonder he couldn't feel it.

"He's curious about the beautiful blonde woman we saw here the other night. Did you notice her, Miss Oakley?"

"Call me Annie," she said. "I ain't Miss Oakley anyway on account of I'm married and Oakley is a stage name. I did notice that woman. Who could miss her? She was real pretty. But I don't know who she is. An acquaintance of Emmett's, I suppose, but she didn't go up to him that night."

"Are you sure?" I asked.

"Course I'm sure. She sat over there." She pointed to a table near the door. "She was alone and wanted to stay on her own, although several of these deadbeats tried to buy her drinks. She wanted nothing to do with them." She chuckled into her beer.

"You hadn't seen her before?" I asked. "Perhaps back in America?"

"Nope."

"But you must meet a lot of people."

"I do, but I'd remember a face like hers. She was a real beauty."

May eyed her sideways.

"Did Emmett pay her any attention?" I asked.

"No, but maybe he didn't see her," Annie said. "When he's playing he focuses real hard on the cards. Doesn't he, May?"

May agreed. "The outside world ceases to exist for him."

"I've even seen him talking to himself, muttering away like he's lost his mind."

I leaned forward. "What did he say?"

Annie shrugged and looked to May. May shrugged too.

"Were the words in English?"

"Why wouldn't they be?" Annie asked.

"Of course they would be," I mumbled. "I wonder if that woman was from Emmett's past. Perhaps she was American too."

"She was," Annie said. "So says Big Joe over there." She nodded at a tall fellow with a thick black beard. "He tried to sweet talk her. She told him to jump off a cliff, but he says she had an American accent."

"You spoke to him about her?" May asked.

"So?" Annie drained her beer and beckoned one of the serving women over. "Three beers."

"I don't drink beer," I said.

"You do tonight." Annie threw some money on the serving woman's tray and turned back to us. "I reckon that blonde was Emmett's girl, someone he jilted back home. She must have followed him here."

May wagged a finger at her, her eyes bright. "Yes. Annie, I think you're right. I think *she* killed him."

"Whoa, slow down. It's a big jump from jilted lover to murderer."

"I don't think so. I think women are very capable of murder, given the right circumstances. I know some very vengeful women."

"So do I. 'Specially when their men have left them for another." Annie rubbed her jaw, much like a man would rub his whiskers as he thought. "Seems like a long way to come though, just to get revenge."

Revenge. The outlaw Jack Krane wanted to get his revenge on Emmett for cheating him at poker. Could the mysterious woman have been sent by Krane to keep an eye on him and perhaps report back? Or to murder him? It seemed so unlikely, yet I couldn't shake the thought.

"Have you seen her since Emmett's death?" I asked.

"Can't say I have," Annie said.

"If you do see her again, notify the police immediately. She might be important."

Annie saluted me. "Yes, ma'am."

I laughed. "You really ought to talk to my friend Willie. You're very similar."

"And I'd be glad to." She peered past me. "Seems she's winning."

"It's early yet," May said.

Matt had engaged two men in conversation. I suspected he was gathering information about Emmett too. Duke watched the card game over Willie's shoulder, and I spotted Cyclops winding his way back to them through the crowd, carrying several tankards.

"Do either of you know much about Emmett's past?" I asked.

"Nope," Annie said as the waitress deposited our beers on the table. "He came to Bill claiming he was a good shot. He proved it and he joined us."

"Just like that? No questions asked?"

"Why ask questions when you might not like the answers?" I must have looked shocked, because she laid a hand on my arm. "You seem like a nice girl, India. I bet you live an easy life, all protected from the world, nice parents, food on the table. That ain't a bad thing. It just means you don't understand people like me, people who've had it rough. Maybe Emmett had a rough time too and wanted to leave his past behind. He wouldn't be the first to join Bill Cody's show to escape."

May drained half her glass in one gulp then suppressed a belch. "I think I should keep an eye on my husband. I don't want him losing more than we can afford."

I waited for her to leave before sidling closer to Annie. "It seems Danny loses often. How can he afford it?"

She shrugged. "Don't know and I don't care. Ain't none of my business, and it ain't none of yours."

"But aren't you curious?"

She chucked me under the chin with her finger. "Let's go watch. I want to get to know this friend of yours."

We rejoined the game and watched Danny's losing streak continue. As the game wore on, his wife grew more and more interested. Her smiles remained, but they grew harder, and the fingers clutching Danny's shoulder turned white at the knuckles.

Danny lost every last penny. May stormed off without a word, pushing her way through the crowd. Danny raced after her, calling her name.

"You play well," Annie said to Willie.

Willie turned. Her jaw dropped when she realized who was talking to her. She nodded her thanks and a pitiful smile flirted with her lips before disappearing. She raked her winnings toward her, then attempted to stuff the money into her pockets. Several coins dropped on the floor and rolled away.

Annie laughed. Willie flushed scarlet which made Annie laugh more. She flung an arm around Willie's waist and squeezed. "How about you buy me a drink with them winnings? India says you and me would get along, and I want to see if she's judged me right. I drink beer. What about you?"

"Anything," Willie said, a little breathless.

Matt, Cyclops, Duke and I left the pub, although Duke cast a glance back at the door from the street. "Is it a good idea to leave those two alone?" he asked. "I got the feeling they could get into a whole lot of trouble in one night."

Cyclops slapped Duke on the shoulder and steered him toward our waiting carriage. "Just look forward to hearing the account in the morning."

I told them what I'd learned from Annie about the mysterious blonde on the way home. "I also asked about Emmett's past, but neither May nor Annie knew anything. I saw you two making inquiries," I said to Matt and Cyclops. "What did you learn?"

"Same as you," Cyclops said.

"Very little then."

Matt clasped my hand, placing it on his knee. "It seems Danny isn't capable of winning without Emmett's magic. He played badly tonight."

"I wonder if he knew about the magic," Duke said.

"We could ask," Cyclops said. "Or maybe we shouldn't. Not yet."

"Let's not mention magic unless we have no other recourse," Matt said.

I agreed. "May seemed very angry. She, at least, must have thought him capable of winning without Emmett. How disappointing for her to be proven wrong."

* * *

BEFORE WILLIE HAD EVEN RISEN the following morning, Matt and I received a note summoning us to Lord Coyle's house. He showed it to me over breakfast. I felt the blood drain from my face as I read.

I screwed it up and gave it to Bristow to throw away. "I don't think we should go."

"I tend to agree," Matt said.

I let out a breath, more relieved than I cared to admit. It wasn't that I thought Coyle would betray our secret arrangement to Matt—the arrangement that resulted in Matt being free to marry me. It was more that I worried that *I* would betray it. Thinking about the secret made me feel ill. I hated to keep anything from Matt. It felt like a betrayal.

It *was* a betrayal. That's how he would see it, even though I'd done it for us. He'd been adamant that we wouldn't ask for Coyle's help in forcing Lord Cox to marry

Patience. He'd been worried about the price Coyle would ask of me. A price I still didn't know.

Telling Matt about the secret would ruin the trust he had in me. It could ruin his love for me. And I didn't trust myself not to give anything away once confronted with Lord Coyle's commanding presence. Avoiding him was best.

"On the other hand," Matt said. "We should find out what he wants. He said it was important."

I didn't eat any of my breakfast. I couldn't even swallow my tea. What if Coyle wanted to call in the debt I owed him?

CHAPTER 6

y first reaction upon seeing other members of the collector's club in Lord Coyle's drawing room was relief. He wouldn't call in my debt with them present. Upon further thought, I realized he would have no such qualms asking me to repay him in front of them. Considering his price would be something of a magical nature, it was likely to involve the other members anyway.

Oh God.

I stood just inside the doorway, unable to move until Matt placed his hand on my back and gently urged me forward. Mrs. Delancey embraced me as if we were old friends before sitting and patting the space beside her on the sofa.

"Sit with me, India," she cooed. "You remember Lady Louisa, don't you?"

"Just Louisa," said the woman on my other side. "I don't like titles."

I'd met her at Mrs. Delancey's soiree some weeks ago. She'd been a curious figure, suggesting all manner of things about magic, including hinting that the language of magic had not been entirely lost. She'd considered me powerful. They all did because I didn't need spells to make timepieces work faultlessly. Lord Coyle had also told them that my watch saved my life, but I hadn't confirmed the tale. I suspected it didn't matter. They believed him.

Louisa smiled at me. It was kind and encouraging, yet I couldn't shake the unease I felt around her. At the soiree, she'd been bold with her words, to the point of not caring if she upset her hostess. For a woman so young and in an elevated position, such boldness was unusual. She reminded me of Matt's niece, Hope Glass, the youngest of the three Glass girls. She was fierce and clever, yet manipulative and selfish too. It remained to be seen if Louisa was cut from the same cloth.

Lord Coyle introduced Matt to Louisa. "She has been a member of our little group only briefly, but has quickly inveigled herself into this inner circle. We have Mrs. Delancey to thank for that."

Mrs. Delancey's smile slipped at his caustic tone, but Louisa gave a soft laugh. "They're still getting used to me," she told me in an aside which the entire room would have heard.

"You know everyone else," Coyle added with a flick of his wrist to indicate the other guests.

Aside from both Mr. and Mrs. Delancey and Louisa, there was Sir Charles Whittaker and Professor Nash. Nash wasn't a member of the club, but our first meeting with him had been in Lord Coyle's dining room. He looked rather nervous, his eyes huge behind his spectacles and his finger tapping out a silent rhythm on his teacup. When he gave his head a slight shake at me, I realized why. He didn't want these people to know he was helping Oscar Barratt write a book on magic, and he was afraid we'd say something. I gave him a smile that I hoped was reassuring but may have failed, since I wasn't at all reassured that my own secret was safe. Nash continued to tap his finger against the cup.

"Tea, Miss Steele?" Lord Coyle asked.

"Thank you." The butler peeled away from his unobtrusive position against the wall and poured a cup for me.

"Something stronger, Glass?" Coyle asked.

Matt's gaze wandered to the glass domed clock on the mantel. It had just gone eleven. "Tea will be fine." He waited until the butler let himself out and closed the door, then said, "Is this an ambush?"

Mrs. Delancey laughed musically. "Of course not."

Sir Charles and Mr. Delancey chimed in with reassurances too. Coyle tapped his pipe on the table and opened his tobacco tin.

"Do you mind not smoking in here?" Louisa asked.

A moment of stunned silence enveloped us as we all stared at her. Lord Coyle stared too, his jowls trembling in indignation. "Well, aren't you precocious? This is *my* house, or have you forgotten?"

"I would be most grateful, sir. The smoke makes my eyes water, and the effect is quite unsightly."

He snapped the tin lid closed. "I suppose it is already stuffy enough in here."

Sometimes I wondered if pretty women had a power that other women don't possess, something that went beyond superficial looks. Something that made men do their bidding. Louisa wasn't beautiful but she was certainly pretty with a slim figure I could never achieve. And of course there was her confidence, an alluring quality in both men and women. Coupled with a flutter of her eyelashes, she cast quite a powerful spell.

"I'm surprised to see you here, Professor," Matt said, picking up his teacup. "Have you become a member?"

Nash shook his head. "Lord Coyle was gracious enough to invite me, although I'm not yet sure why." He gave a nervous smile into his teacup before sipping.

"Perhaps his lordship can enlighten us before everyone's imagination runs wild."

"Gladly." Lord Coyle helped himself to cake from the plate then belatedly realized he hadn't offered any to the rest of us. "Cake?" he asked.

Only Mr. Delancey took a slice.

"We are on tenterhooks, my lord," Mrs. Delancey said. "What is this about?"

"It's regarding a little project that Sir Charles and I have been conducting in recent weeks."

Everyone looked to Sir Charles. He pounced on the cake too. "This looks delicious."

Coyle finished his slice then reached for another before going on. "Sir Charles has been watching cast members of Buffalo Bill's Wild West show, trying to determine if any are magicians."

Mrs. Delancey made a scoffing noise, but the others took Coyle more seriously. Only the professor looked as relieved as I felt. It would seem both our secrets were safe, for now.

"Why?" Mr. Delancey asked.

"Chiefly because we suspected the sharpshooters might be some kind of metal magicians," Coyle said. "Their accuracy is astounding. Inhuman, one could say. We suspected they might be manipulating the bullets with a spell."

"That's not what I meant." Mr. Delancey's deep brow furrowed. "Why did you decide to follow them without discussing it with us first?"

Sir Charles waved his hand. "It was a whim of mine. I'm sorry I didn't mention it."

"But you discussed it with Coyle. Why not us?"

"As I said, it was a whim. A passing notion and not one I

wanted to admit to. What if I was wrong? I didn't want to appear a fool in front of everyone."

"You have to admit the idea does sound absurd," Coyle said.

Louisa made a sound of protest. "On the contrary. I think it plausible. Well done, Sir Charles. I like the way your mind works."

Mr. Delancey's frown deepened. He sipped his tea and fell into silence.

"And what did you learn?" Professor Nash asked. "I haven't seen Annie Oakley myself, but I've heard she's a marvelous shot."

"I'm still not sure about her," Sir Charles said. "But while watching the cast members, and following them here and there, I did come to suspect another fellow of being a magician." He nodded at me. "Miss Steele recently confirmed my suspicions. One of the sharpshooters was a paper magician."

"How does that help him shoot accurately?" Mrs. Delancey asked.

"It doesn't. It helped him cheat at cards."

Nash pushed his glasses up his nose. "You said *'was'* a paper magician."

Mrs. Delancey gasped. "It's that fellow who was murdered, isn't it? It was all over the newspapers."

"I rarely read them. That does explain Mr. Glass and Miss Steele's involvement."

"You're helping the police?" Louisa asked. "How noble. Does this mean they know you're a magician, India? If they're aware of magic then that's quite a step forward, wouldn't you say? It's only a short leap from there to official recognition."

Lord Coyle held up his hand. "Don't get ahead of yourself, Louisa. It's not in the police's best interests to publicly acknowledge magic."

"It's not in anyone's," Mr. Delancey said.

Louisa picked up her teacup. "Except for magicians who wish to practice in the open, raise their children without fear, and create beautiful things with their talent."

Mr. Delancey gave his wife a withering look, as if he blamed her for bringing the rebellious Louisa into their midst. Mrs. Delancey did not look up from her teacup.

Only the professor looked intrigued by Louisa's statements. Indeed, not intrigued, but in awe. It wouldn't surprise me if he was half in love with her already.

"I want to apologize to you both," Sir Charles said to Matt and me. "When you called on me yesterday, you caught me off guard. I wasn't sure how much to tell you without checking with Coyle first. He has been the driving force behind this."

"Of course," Matt said with a smile. I couldn't tell if he believed Sir Charles or not. It made sense to me that Sir Charles was reluctant to divulge too much without checking with Lord Coyle. Coyle was, after all, a powerful man. If Sir Charles displeased him, there could be all manner of consequences.

"Can we assume that our presence here means you approve of Sir Charles telling us everything he learned?" I asked Coyle.

"You can," he said. "Proceed, Whittaker."

"You asked me about the victim's lineage," Sir Charles said. "You wanted to know if he was related to Melville Hendry, the paper magician in Smithfield."

"Melville!" Mrs. Delancey cried. "Don't tell me he's involved in this murder too?"

"He wasn't involved in the last one," I said. "Although he was implicated by his...friend."

"*Are* they related?" Matt asked.

Sir Charles nodded. "We keep records of magical families, following each branch as best we can. There are gaps, of course, but in the case of Hendry and Cocker, the link was evident. They share one set of great grandparents."

"Did either of them know?"

"It's likely they did, considering Cocker paid Hendry a visit the day before his death."

Matt sighed and I sat back, deflated. Part of me hoped Hendry hadn't lied. The last thing I wanted was for Hendry to be a suspect in our investigation. He'd been through so much, and he wasn't an emotionally strong character. Our investigation would upset him.

"How intriguing," Mrs. Delancey murmured.

Lord Coyle eyed his pipe with longing then reached for another slice of cake. "We're telling you this on the condition you don't interrogate Hendry. We don't think he has the stomach for murder anyway, nor do we want him to feel intimidated."

"We wouldn't do that," Matt assured him.

"He's skittish, easily frightened, and he has no ties."

"You're afraid he'll leave London?" I asked. "England?"

Sir Charles leveled his gaze with mine. "We're afraid he'll leave this mortal coil, Miss Steele."

"Oh." I felt rather ill at the thought of Mr. Hendry taking his own life because of us. Surely he wouldn't if he were innocent.

Yet the more I thought about our last investigation, the more I realized that didn't matter. Mr. Hendry had no one, and that, more than our questioning, upset him. He was quite alone in the world. It was immeasurably sad.

"We'll conduct our investigation around him," Matt said. "But he is now a suspect, and if we have no other recourse, we will question him."

"Gently," I added.

"He's not guilty," Mrs. Delancey said. "I like him."

Her husband grunted. "The one does not equate to the other, my dear."

"Why does he have no ties?" Louisa asked. "Has he never married?"

Nobody answered her until she prompted Mrs. Delancey.

"Marriage is not on the mind of his kind," Mrs. Delancey said.

"He has, er, relations with men," her husband said, the twist of disgust evident in his voice.

"Ah." Louisa contemplated the teacup and saucer clutched in her lap. "That doesn't mean he will never marry, however. Indeed, he has good reasons to find a wife. It will protect him from gossip and, even more importantly, it might result in children."

"Why more importantly?" Mrs. Delancey asked. "He might not want to be a father."

Louisa looked at her friend as if she were dim-witted. "The lineage must continue."

I blinked at her, unable to form words to express my shock. Were we no different to race horses to her?

"You really do have only one thing on your mind," Mrs. Delancey said with a tart smile.

Nash scooted forward on his chair, his eyes bright. "She's right. We must think of the future."

"I'm not sure we have a say in the matter of Hendry fathering offspring," Lord Coyle said. "Anyway, I prefer to think of the present. And presently, we have the problem of a paper magician's death—a death that Mr. Glass and Miss Steele have been commissioned to investigate. Now that you know what Whittaker was up to, and that Hendry and Cocker were related, you can continue on."

"Carefully," Sir Charles added. "Particularly with our skittish paper magician."

"Who is *not* guilty," Mrs. Delancey said with a pointed glare for her husband. "Despite his proclivities."

We thanked them, although I wasn't quite sure why. We hadn't learned much and I was still convinced that Whittaker hadn't been acting on behalf of the club, despite what he and Coyle said. I told Matt as much on the way home.

He agreed with me. "For one thing, the others weren't aware of it. And for another, I don't trust Coyle."

"Do you think they had a private arrangement?" I asked.

"I do. Whittaker was spying for Coyle, only we caught him. They couldn't risk us telling anyone else, so they decided to beat us to it."

"I wonder if any of them realize it."

"I wonder what they're up to," Matt said heavily.

"Perhaps they're not up to anything. Coyle seems like the sort of man who likes to gather information to use against people in the future. Others trade in goods, he trades in secrets. It's dirty."

He took my hand and kissed my glove. "The less you have to do with him, the better I'll feel."

I stared out of the window but saw nothing of the passing scenery through the tears stinging my eyes.

* * *

WE SAT in the sitting room as Matt told Cyclops and Duke about the meeting. No one had any good suggestions for what to do next so it was fortunate that distraction arrived in the form of Willie. She yawned without covering her mouth and threw herself into a chair.

"Bristow says I missed breakfast," she whined. "Now I'm going to starve."

"He won't let you starve," Matt said. "And it's almost midday."

"Well?" Duke said slyly. "What did you and Annie Oakley get up to last night?"

"Nothing."

Both he and Cyclops snorted.

"It's true! We had a few drinks together and that was it. I came home."

"At five this morning." Duke sounded amused. "Don't deny it. I heard you clomping up the stairs like a sow."

"Five!" I cried. "Willie, what *did* you two get up to? And don't pretend you just had a few drinks. For one thing, The Prince of Wales would have closed well before five. And for another, what is there to do in this city at that time?"

"You'd be surprised," she said. "But I don't expect *you* to know, India."

"True. I am busy polishing my halo at that time of morning."

She pulled a face.

"So what's she like?" Duke asked.

"Fun," Willie said, a secretive smile teasing her lips. "Real fun."

"So what fun things did you two do?"

"I told you, we drank together and that was it. I came home."

Cyclops chuckled. "You don't remember, do you?"

"Course I remember." She sniffed. "I just ain't going to tattle."

"Leave her alone," Matt chided. "Just as long as the police don't come knocking on the door, I don't care what you do."

A knock on the sitting room door had everyone sitting forward, and Willie swore under her breath. Matt glared at her.

Duke hissed, "What *did* you do?"

Willie swallowed and looked to the window, as if

deciding if it was worth the risk to climb out of it. The sitting room was on the second level.

Bristow entered on Matt's command and announced the arrival of Melville Hendry. Willie excused herself and beat a hasty retreat.

"Mr. Hendry," Matt said, rising and offering his hand. "Welcome. We're glad you came. Bristow, bring in tea and some of Mrs. Bristow's finest cakes."

"I won't be long," Mr. Hendry said, wiping the palm of his hand down his trouser leg as he sat. He smelled faintly of coconut, a scent that seemed to emanate from his hair. "I have to get back to my shop. I don't like closing it for long."

"I understand. Is this about the invitations?"

Mr. Hendry tugged on his cuffs. "No. They're with the calligrapher now."

Duke and Cyclops left, closing the door, putting Mr. Hendry a little more at ease, although he still seemed agitated.

"Are you all right?" I asked. "You seem upset."

"Not upset. Just..." He drew in a shaky breath.

"You're not in trouble," Matt assured him. "You're not a suspect in Cocker's murder, if that's your concern."

"I'm not? Oh, thank God." He took a few deep breaths before going on. "I came to tell you that I lied to you yesterday. That man did visit me."

Matt nodded. "Thank you for informing us."

"I was afraid you'd think I killed him to keep our magic connection a secret, that's why I didn't tell Miss Steele." He pressed his fingers into the bridge of his nose and closed his eyes. "I don't know what I was thinking. I'm on edge these days. Ever since Patrick betrayed me, I can't trust anyone."

"You can trust us," Matt said kindly. "India's situation is not that different to yours. She wants to keep her magic a secret too."

I bit my tongue and told myself he was only saying what he thought Hendry wanted to hear, mindful of Hendry's delicate state of mind. "You can trust us," I reassured him. "We want to find out who killed Mr. Cocker, and you might inadvertently know something about his movements in his last few days that could help. So he did visit you. Why?"

"He wanted to learn my spells."

"He asked you? Just like that?"

"He was brazen, that's for certain. He got my name from his grandmother, many years ago. Or, rather, he learned of my grandfather's name—they were cousins. I am my grandfather's only living descendent, and I still run the shop that was once his. Emmett Cocker said I wasn't difficult to find. We had a long talk, but I'm rather ashamed to admit that I didn't particularly like him. He was too...uncouth. Too abrupt, brash. He cheated at cards. Not just once or twice, but all the time. He laughed about it. He offered to teach me how, but I declined, of course."

Bristow brought in tea then discreetly left again.

"Did Emmett infuse his magic into the cards?" I asked, pouring the tea. "Is that how he cheated?"

Mr. Hendry nodded. "He knew a spell that allowed him to *see* the card from a distance with the card facing away from him. Of course, it meant he had to place spells on each card before the game. Apparently the only times he lost was when an opponent insisted on using a different deck, but then Emmett realized he could whisper the spell into the cards he held. Over the course of an evening, he would have placed his magic on most of the cards in the deck, allowing him to cheat."

"Did you tell him what you thought of his scheme?" I asked.

"I did. He laughed," he said, his voice distant. "It was a

horrid laugh, brittle and cruel. He didn't care that he was hurting people, effectively stealing from them."

"Did he know what spells you could do?" Matt asked, accepting the teacup I handed him.

"Not at first. When he told me what he could do, then asked what spells I knew, I told him." He stared into his cup. "I told him everything, stopping short of giving him the words."

Mr. Hendry not only knew how to make strong paper of the best quality, he also knew spells to fold paper into interesting shapes without touching it, and how to turn paper into a weapon. I had a sick feeling that Emmett wanted to know the latter most of all.

"I thought nothing of it, at first," Mr. Hendry went on. "He merely sounded curious, like a family member catching up on news. But then he asked if I could teach him the spells."

"And you refused?" Matt asked.

"I did. He grew very angry. He shouted at me. I thought he'd become violent. I'd seen the gun strapped to his hip and became scared he'd use it, so I told him I'd give it some thought, just to get him out of my home."

"When was this?"

"Early evening on the night he died. I read about his murder in the newspaper the next morning. I was shocked. I think I was still in shock when you came to see me. I wasn't thinking clearly. That's the only explanation I have for not admitting the truth immediately."

I reassured him that he'd done the right thing, but my thoughts wandered in a different direction. According to Hendry, Emmett had his gun with him the night of his death. That meant someone had returned it to Emmett's room later, and that someone had to be the killer.

"Such anger seems out of proportion," Matt said. "And out of character, from what I've heard."

I agreed. Emmett had been charming, on the whole, although he'd displayed evidence of a temper when Willie stopped playing poker. Perhaps that charm slipped when he didn't get what he wanted. I'd found that to be true for most men with false charisma.

"He was likeable at first," Mr. Hendry said. "But when I refused to tell him my spells, he changed." He lifted his gaze to Matt's. "I've seen desperation, Mr. Glass. I've seen it in myself, and I know what it looks like. He was desperate to learn the spell to turn paper into a blade."

Matt stroked a finger over his top lip and I could see he was warring with himself. He suddenly sat forward, his gaze not wavering from Mr. Hendry's. Hendry sat forward too, enthralled by the attention and the understanding that Matt was about to tell him something he should not.

"The police informed us that Cocker is being hunted in America," Matt said. "He cheated a man at cards. Cocker didn't know it at the time, but that man is a dangerous outlaw."

Mr. Hendry swallowed. "Do you think the outlaw came here and...and found him? Killed him?"

"It's possible."

"It's a long way to travel for revenge."

Matt sat back and picked up his teacup. "Some people will go to great lengths for revenge. Their pride drives them. So I believe."

Mr. Hendry nodded slowly. He picked up his cup too but did not sip. "You think Emmett wanted my spell so he could turn his cards into weapons if he found himself in trouble and without his gun."

"We do," I said.

"Sometimes it's not feasible to draw a gun," Matt added.

"The outlaw has a reputation as a quick draw. Cocker couldn't defeat him in a gunfight."

"No one would expect him to kill with cards," Mr. Hendry finished. "Giving him an advantage." He dragged a hand through his hair, yet when he drew his hand away, his hair was still perfectly arranged. "If I'd given him the spell, he could still be alive."

"We don't know that," I rushed to reassure him. "You shouldn't think about it; it'll only upset you."

"He was family, Miss Steele. My only family." His voice cracked. "I should have had more of a care for him instead of dismissing him. Family ought to help one another."

"No cards or papers were found on the body," Matt said. "It's unlikely your spell could have helped him that night."

Mr. Hendry looked reassured by that more than by my attempt to comfort him. Matt was better at reassurance than me, at least where Mr. Hendry was concerned.

After Mr. Hendry left, Matt and I headed to Emmett Cocker's lodgings on Childs Street. Or, rather, we headed to the rear of the property. Matt knocked on the back door while I kept watch at the gate to the alley running behind the row of terraces.

"I'm going in," Matt whispered from the door—the door that was now open. He had a knack for picking locks that he'd learned from his time in his grandfather's gang. It was quite a useful trick.

I joined him at the door but he shook his head.

"Someone has to keep watch," he said.

I glared at him, hand on hip, but he shook his head again and disappeared into the kitchen beyond. I returned to the gate and waited.

And waited.

We'd decided to look around Emmett's lodgings while the Drapers and the other lodger were performing in the afternoon show. It was easier than facing their questions. With only one room to search, I'd not expected Matt to be long, however time dragged. I checked my watch on no less than eight occasions. I paced, sighed, huffed, and glared at the back door, yet no amount of willing him to reappear actually resulted in his appearance.

The arrival of two men at the entrance to the alley set my heart racing. One wore a suit with a tie, the other a neckerchief and no jacket. His sleeves were rolled up and he carried a toolbox. They walked toward me, talking quietly, and hadn't yet seen me.

I had to warn Matt. They might be going to one of the other houses, but I didn't dare rely on that. I banged on the back door then raced to the gate again, where I affected a limp. The men didn't see me until I was mere feet away from them.

"Are you all right, madam?" asked the gentleman in the suit.

"My foot slipped on the cobbles," I said, wincing.

I hobbled past them and both men turned, as I hoped they would. Their backs were to the gate.

"Oh," I whimpered, stopping. "It hurts like the devil."

"Here, take my arm," said the gentleman. "Can I assist you to your destination?"

I glanced past him but Matt did not appear in the alley. Where was he? "Perhaps your man can find a hack and you could help me to it. Slowly." I winced again for good measure.

The second man returned the way he'd come, leaving me with the gentleman.

"Are you alone?" he asked.

"Quite alone." Too late, I realized that was the wrong thing to say to a stranger in an alley with no one else in sight. He might dress like a gentleman but that didn't mean he was. "Although my fiancé should be along soon."

He began to turn to look over his shoulder, just as Matt emerged through the gate. "Ohhhh!" I cried out.

The gentleman gave me his full attention, wrapping his arm around my back to support me. "Your fiancé should not have abandoned you."

"I didn't," Matt said, coming up behind the gentleman. "She wandered off. She does that sometimes. What have you done, darling?"

"I slipped on the cobbles," I said. "My ankle hurts. This kind gentleman is helping me to a waiting hack."

"So I see." Matt gave a pointed glare at the man's arm.

The gentleman withdrew and stepped away. He cleared his throat. "Well then, I'll leave you in the hands of your fiancé. Good day, sir, madam." He touched his hat brim and continued on down the alley. He stopped at the gate to Emmett's lodgings, nodded at us again, and disappeared into the courtyard beyond the fence.

I pressed a hand to my chest. That had been close. Too close. I thumped Matt on the arm. "Why did you take so long?"

"I wanted to have a good look around. Well done, back there. I'll make an actress of you yet."

He took my hand and led me along the alley. I resumed my limp as we passed the second man with the toolbox, and thanked him for his assistance. Back on Childs Street, I dismissed the waiting hack and climbed into our carriage. Matt ordered the coachman to return home.

"It shouldn't have taken you that long to search one room," I said huffily.

A slow, crooked smile lent a wickedness to his handsome features. "You were worried about me."

"I was bored." I crossed my arms and sniffed. "Until those two showed up."

He leaned forward and placed both hands on my knees. That smile didn't waver. "How many times did you check your watch?"

"Five minutes, Matt. That's how long it should take to check one room. Perhaps ten. Honestly, the police have already searched it. What else did you expect to find?"

"I looked through the other rooms too."

I gasped. "You can't do that!"

"Why not? The Drapers are suspects. Why waste a perfectly good opportunity?"

I narrowed my gaze at him. "You're thinking like a criminal."

"And you're adorable when you're cross." He rose off the seat and kissed me on the lips. I leaned into him, eager to deepen it, but he drew back and sat down again.

"You're vibrating with excitement," I said. "Breaking and entering seems to give you joy."

"It's your presence that does that to me."

I rolled my eyes. "I no longer fall for your smooth words."

"The sparkle in your eyes would imply otherwise."

"That's not a sparkle, that's soot. The air is smoky today."

He laughed. "Don't you want to know what I found?"

"Go on then. What did you find in Emmett's room?"

"Nothing. I did, however, find something in the Drapers'. They're in debt. A lot of debt. I found letters of demand from creditors both in the States and here. Some were threatening."

"Danny has gambled away their wages," I said. "Poor May."

"May might not be too innocent. She was probably aware of the scheme Emmett was running and Danny's part in it."

"It seems the scheme wasn't enough to get them out of their debt," I said.

"Not yet, but it might have been enough, given more time."

"Emmett's death ended those hopes. Killing Emmett wasn't in their best interests."

"We can't assume that," Matt said. "Not yet. For one thing, the stairs creak with every step, and their room was close to the staircase. Nobody could have crept up them without the Drapers hearing."

"I don't understand."

"We know someone returned the gun to Emmett's room the night he died. Either the Drapers lied, and they weren't at home, or they returned the gun themselves. I don't believe they didn't hear someone going up the stairs."

"I see your point. But the other resident also heard nothing."

"So he told Brockwell. I want to question him again."

"Brockwell won't like it. He'll think you're overstepping."

"Then we won't inform him until afterward. I'll return to Childs Street tonight, after the show. If the lodger isn't there, I'll wait. He has to return eventually."

* * *

MATT LEFT AGAIN a few hours later, slipping out of the house before dinner, much to his aunt's annoyance.

"He ought to dine with us," she said, toying with the string of black jet beads around her neck. "He's an engaged man now. He must behave as such."

"This isn't a formal dinner," I said. "It's just us."

"His friends are here." She indicated Duke and Cyclops, taking their seats opposite. "As are we. He is no longer free to do as he pleases."

"He ain't in jail," Cyclops drawled. "We don't care if he ain't here. He's investigating, not out drinking."

Miss Glass's lips flattened. "I expected you to agree with me, Cyclops. You always agree."

"Willie ain't here either," Duke chimed in. "Why aren't you cross with her?"

"She's a unique force." She watched as Peter filled her wine glass and picked it up. "One doesn't expect Willie to do the conventional thing."

"Amen," Duke muttered.

We'd hardly begun our soup course when Bristow entered and informed me of a visitor.

"Did you advise him that Matt's not here?" I asked.

"He asked for you," Bristow said.

"Who is it?"

"Mr. Gideon Steele."

Chronos!

CHAPTER 7

$\mathcal{M}$y grandfather had not visited for some weeks. Although I knew where he lived, I had not visited him since announcing my engagement to Matt, so I supposed I couldn't be cross with him. Even so, it was difficult not to be. He irritated me in a way that no one else did. He was selfish, putting his own magical ambitions above all else, including familial ties.

And yet I loved him, in a way. He *was* family.

"Your timing is impeccable, as always," I said, meeting him in the entrance hall. "We've just sat down to dinner. Shall I have Bristow set another place?"

"I'm not staying." Chronos looked past me to Bristow. "You can go. I wish to speak to my granddaughter alone. And don't tell Glass."

"Matt isn't here," I said. "Otherwise he would have come down to see you. Thank you, Bristow, I'll see him out myself."

Chronos watched the shadows until Bristow had retreated completely. Chronos's eyes danced in the lamplight, reminding me of Matt after he'd snuck into the Childs Street house, all youthful mischief and confidence.

"You look different," I said. "Have you cut your hair?"

Chronos touched the white strands floating above his head like weeds in a stream. "I don't have time to visit the barber."

"Why not? What could you possibly be doing these days?"

He took my arm and moved me away from the stairs, even though we were alone. "Come with me, India," he whispered.

"No. I'm in the middle of dinner."

"You can eat later. This is important." He strode across the tiles and removed my hat from the hat stand. "It's warm. You won't need a coat."

"I can't just leave. The others will wonder where I went."

He shoved the hat at me. "Leave them a message. Come on, I haven't got all night. Neither has he."

"Who?"

He grabbed my elbow. "I'll explain on the way."

"No!" I pulled free. "Stop it, this instance. I'm not going anywhere with you until you explain what this is about."

He studied me, hands on hips, and gave an exasperated sigh. "I have the paperwork for the shop. You need to go through it before you sign it."

"Oh. I see."

The shop once again belonged to my family after Eddie Hardacre had been found guilty of fraud and my grandfather found alive. Chronos had said he'd give it to me, but now that the moment had come, I realized I hadn't quite expected it. I didn't need a shop. I couldn't sell timepieces as the Watchmaker's Guild would never grant me a license to do so.

Chronos was hopeless when it came to business matters.

He'd wanted to be a shopkeeper, and left it in the hands of his wife and son, my father. He'd been more interested in finding a magical doctor to help him pursue his experiments. Experiments that had given Matt back his life, twice. For that reason, I couldn't bring myself to resent Chronos. I owed him so much.

I took the hat. "I'll fetch my gloves."

"You don't need gloves." He took my hand and led me outside.

"Bristow, I'll be back soon," I called.

I caught sight of the butler racing down the stairs just as Chronos shut the front door. We headed down the steps to the waiting hansom, its door already open.

"Why didn't you bring the papers with you?" I asked.

"I didn't plan on coming here." Chronos assisted me onto the seat. "I was in the area and just decided to drop in."

"Are we meeting the lawyer at your place? Is he a friend?"

He shooed me over and sat next to me. He gave the driver his address through the hatch above and shut the door. "I have a confession to make, India. The shop papers are not my main reason for getting you to come with me."

I sighed. I should have known he was lying. "Why the ruse?"

"Because I knew you wouldn't come if I told you the truth." He grabbed my arm as if he suspected I'd leap out when the cab slowed. "I didn't wait for Glass to leave the house, I swear. That is pure coincidence, but a fortunate one."

If he didn't want Matt to know, it could only mean one thing. Magic.

"You'd better tell me everything," I said.

He let me go and patted my hand. He also did not wear gloves and his skin felt cool, dry. "There's a man waiting for you at my lodgings. He's French, but that's not his fault."

I pressed my lips together to suppress my smile. "Is he a magician?"

He nodded. "He heard about a powerful magician here in London and wanted to meet her—you."

"How did he hear about me? And who says I'm powerful?"

"Your reputation is advancing beyond this city, this country. The story of your watch saving you is well known among certain circles."

"Who's blabbing?"

"It's gossip. It spreads. And no, it wasn't me." We stopped beneath a street lamp at an intersection. Light and shadows carved out Chronos's cheeks and deepened his eyes, making him seem every bit his age of seventy-one. He patted my hand again. "Just hear what he has to say before you get cross."

"I'm not cross." I sighed. "I *am* cross. You should have been honest with me."

"If I had, would you have come?"

I withdrew my hand. "So he knows about me and about my connection to you. How did he find you?"

"You can ask him that. We're nearly there."

My grandfather lived in a row house not far from Crouch End Station. His neighbors were mostly clerks and bank employees who commuted to their offices in the financial district of London. It didn't seem like the most likely place to find Chronos, except when one considered that he wouldn't want to be near craftsmen or anyone belonging to a guild. Ever since Oscar Barratt and Mr. Force's articles, Chronos was not in favor with the artless who felt threatened by magic.

His landlady greeted us, but Chronos brushed her off

with a quick introduction then led me up to his rooms on the first floor. A man rose from a chair in the small parlor where he'd been reading a newspaper by the light of a lamp. For some reason I couldn't now fathom, I'd expected someone like Chronos; old, a little disheveled with a mad gleam in his eye.

Fabian Charbonneau was nothing like Chronos. He had more in common with the debonair Mr. Hendry. He was dressed in a tailored slate gray suit with shiny black shoes and dark hair, glossy with Makassar oil. His chin and jawline sported a day's worth of stubble. I guessed him to be only a little older than me, although it was difficult to tell. There was something quite serious about him, something earnest, and that was the only similarity to Chronos.

He stepped forward and touched my hand in greeting. Without gloves, the intimate gesture made me blush.

"Sit, sit," Chronos said, waving both hands toward the sofa. "We don't have long to talk, so let's begin."

"Why don't we have long?" I asked.

"If your fiancé arrives home before you do, he'll come straight here. Your butler can't be trusted to keep a secret. Don't pretend Glass is a modern man, India. We both know he wants to keep a tight rein on you."

"He does not! He's quite happy for me to do as I please."

"Unless it involves magic." He indicated Fabian, who'd so far said nothing beyond a polite greeting. "Fabian, tell her why you're here."

"Firstly, tell me how you came to find me," I said. "Chronos wouldn't say."

"Chronos?" Fabian prompted. "You call your grandfather by this name?" He spoke English very well, with a lilting French accent.

Chronos laughed. "She prefers it."

"We were strangers to one another until recently," I told

Fabian. I was determined that Chronos shouldn't get off lightly for the years of abandonment. "I do prefer to call him by his nickname. Grandpapa doesn't ring true."

Chronos grunted in what I suspected was agreement.

Fabian smiled politely. "I heard about you through a friend, India."

"What friend?"

"I am not at liberty to say."

That only made me even more curious.

"What sort of things did your friend say about me?"

"That you fix watches and clocks without a spell. That your watch will act to save you, again without a spell. This is not normal, India. *You* are not normal."

"He means you are extraordinary," Chronos cut in, as if he thought being labeled abnormal would offend me.

"My friend did not know where to find you, alas," Fabian went on. "Except that you are in London and related to the famed Gideon Steele. So I come here today and find him, and then he fetches you."

"Today? You didn't waste time, Chronos." I glared at him, trying to drill in the importance of getting to know this man before he brought me here to meet him. Fabian could have been lying. He could be anyone, working for anyone. Trusting him without question was a mistake.

"Let him finish, India," Chronos said. So he had understood the meaning behind my glare. I was glad I didn't have to spell it out in front of his guest. "Fabian asked Oscar Barratt where to find me and Oscar sent him here."

"Barratt did not know I sought you," Fabian said. "Your grandfather informed me that Barratt could have told me where to find you if I had given your name. But I am glad to meet Chronos first. He says your husband would not like me so it is wise I do not go to you."

"Fiancé," I said with another glare for Chronos. "We're getting married in ten days."

"Ten!" Chronos cried. "Why didn't you tell me?"

"I have."

His spine straightened. "I haven't received an invitation."

I sighed. "You will shortly. Fabian, I still don't understand something. You live in France and yet Oscar's articles were published in a London paper. How did you come to read them?"

"My friend sent them."

"The same friend who told you about me?"

He gave a non-committal shrug.

"Tell me your friend's name," I said.

"I cannot." He smiled apologetically. "I am happy to meet you, India. May I call you India?"

"Please do. I'm happy to meet you too, but you've come a long way, and I'm afraid it's all for nothing. I can't help you."

I rose, but Chronos grasped my hand. "We haven't told you what Fabian wants yet."

"I can guess. He wants me to extend someone's life with their watch and a doctor's magic." I sounded heartless, cruel even, and I immediately regretted my tone. "I'm sorry, Fabian. Truly I am. But what you ask me to do is—"

"It's not that," Chronos said, casting a secretive smile in Fabian's direction.

Fabian studied me with eyes the color of honey. His undisguised interest sent heat spreading across my skin, prickling my scalp, warming my face. It was unnerving yet thrilling at the same time. I wanted to toss his attentions back at him but couldn't think of anything bold enough to say. So I looked away. I had not felt this out of sorts by a man's attentions since meeting Matt for the first time.

"I am not here to ask you to extend my magic," Fabian

said. "Or anyone's magic. I do not wish to take from you, only to give."

"Give what?"

"Knowledge."

I barked a laugh.

"Listen to him, India," Chronos said from the drinks table by the window where he poured a spirit the color of Fabian's eyes into three glasses. "You'll want to hear what he has to say. Trust me."

"That coming from a man who lied to get me here."

"I didn't lie. I really do have the paperwork for the shop to give you." Chronos handed me a glass and another to Fabian. He still smiled. It put me on edge even more.

"We are alike, you and me," Fabian said. "I understand you. I understand you are scared of your power and what others want from you. That is why I want to teach you what I know. Teaching you will protect you."

"Teach me what?" I asked. "More spells? Are you a horology magician too?"

He chuckled softly. "My mother's family are mason magicians. They can make stones of all kinds into any shape. Their masonry is beautiful, perfect in every way. On my father's side, there are iron magicians. They worked as blacksmiths and farriers for many centuries, but most are now engineers."

"They build steamships, bridges, that sort of thing," Chronos added. "The Charbonneaus run an extremely successful business in France. They're wealthy." He saluted Fabian with his glass then drained it.

"What I am trying to say is, I have magic on both sides of my family," Fabian went on. "They are unbroken lineages, sometimes joining with other magic families through marriage. There is even a confectioner magician, like your mother's father."

As much as I didn't want my curiosity to be piqued by this man and this meeting, it was. I couldn't help it. I had wanted to meet someone like him ever since learning of my magic, but it wasn't until now that I realized how much.

"Does iron bend for you without you speaking a spell?" I asked on a rush of breath.

"Sometimes, if I will it very hard."

"And does it save you if you are in danger?"

"No."

"Oh." I sat back again, unaware I'd sat forward.

Fabian smiled. Clearly my frustration and confusion amused him. I couldn't think why, except that he delighted in keeping me frustrated and confused.

"You are special, India," he said. "I have not heard of anyone who can do what you do with your watches without a spell. I cannot, and I am one of the most powerful magicians in France, perhaps Europe."

"Modest too," I muttered into my glass.

He chuckled. "Forgive me. I am not familiar with English humility, but I am learning."

"Speaking of learning, you said you wished to teach me about magic. If I am more powerful than you, what can you teach me?"

"The language of spells."

Professor Nash had told me about the language of magic, as he called it. According to him, the language was fluid, and words evolved over time, much in the same way English had evolved over centuries. According to Nash, only the most powerful magicians could harness the language to create new spells.

"The language has disappeared," I told them. "Except for a few simple spells, of course."

"No," Fabian said. "Much of the language has been passed down from generation to generation among

119

powerful magical families. In secret, of course. Continental Europe is not unlike England with your guilds and fear mongering."

I waited for him to go on, aware of the flutter in my belly, the clamminess of my skin. I drank the contents of my glass to settle my nerves, but the magic of Madeira wine didn't work fast enough.

"You know the language?" I asked.

"Some. There are gaps, alas, so my studies try to fill those gaps."

"Why do you need me if you already know most of the language?"

"Because knowing the words is not enough. They must be put together in a certain way; a way that is part learning, part instinct. Not all magicians have that instinct." He rubbed his fingers together, as if feeling a fine silk. "Only those with strong magic can bring the words to life. They have the instinct."

"He needs help to create *new* spells," Chronos explained.

"A spell caster," I whispered. That was the term Professor Nash used for such a magician. He'd suspected I might have that power. And now Fabian did too. "You've been searching for someone like me."

"For a long time." He smiled. "But not someone *like* you, India. That person *is* you."

CHAPTER 8

*I*t was almost too much to comprehend. Fabian had come so far to find me. *Me*. This powerful magician, with a lineage that matched mine, needed *me* to create new spells. Yet he was the one who knew the language of magic, and I did not. How could I be a spell caster when I knew only two spells?

Chronos must have refilled my glass because he pressed it into my hand and urged me to drink. "You look like you need it."

Fabian's smooth features lifted with his smile. "You are overwhelmed."

I set the glass down. I preferred to have my wits about me for the time being. I didn't want to say something I would regret later. "You claim a spell caster has instinct. But I don't."

"You do or you could not make your watch work without a spell."

"It *saved* you, India," Chronos said, patting my hand. "Fabian says that is a sign of a spell caster, of a magician with the right instincts."

"Yes, but—"

"No buts." He touched my jaw, forcing me to look at him. His eyes were bright and glossy, his smile barely contained, like a youth after his first glass of wine. "This is your destiny, India."

"According to whom?" I jerked away and rose. "It was a pleasure to meet you, Fabian, but I must get home."

"Not yet! There is so much to discuss." Chronos hauled himself to his feet, all youthful appearances gone. He was an elderly man once again, and I felt guilty for not taking better care of him.

"I've heard everything I want to hear for now," I said. "I'll come and see you again soon." I kissed his cheek but he only scowled at me.

"You're being stubborn," he said.

"It is all right," Fabian said. "India has much to think about. Take your time to consider all I have told you."

"Not too long," Chronos grumbled. "I want to see you fulfill your destiny before I die."

I rolled my eyes. "You're not dying, and I don't believe in destiny. Our futures are the sum of our choices. It is not mapped for us at birth."

"You cannot waste your talents. If I'd been given what you have, I would be excited by the possibilities."

"You are not me."

"Clearly," he muttered. "I blame your parents for raising you as artless."

"And why did they do that? Because they saw what magic did to you, how it drove you to abandon your family and responsibilities, and drove you mad."

"I'm not mad." He tapped his temple. "My mind is in perfect working order."

"It is a lot to take in," Fabian said. "Please, India, take your time and think about what I have told you. If you have questions, I will answer them as best I can." He bowed. "I am at your service."

"How long are you in London?" I asked.

"That depends on you."

"Me?"

He smiled. "I have rented a house in Mayfair, not far from where you live."

He knew where I lived? I glared at Chronos, but he was busy looking through the paperwork on the desk tucked into the corner of the room. He found what he wanted and handed the sheets of paper to me.

"These are the deeds to the shop and all its contents," he said. "I had a lawyer draw them up so it's all legal."

Fabian said his goodbyes and Chronos saw him to the door before returning to me.

"It's all yours," he said, pointing to the papers. "Or it will be, once you sign."

"Are you sure?" I asked, still feeling dazed from the conversation with Fabian.

"Very. I never wanted it, and even if I did, I can't use it. The guild won't give me a license."

"They won't let me in, either."

"But you can rent out the premises."

"So can you."

He merely shrugged.

"I don't need the rental income," I told him. "Matt has many investments."

"Just in case," he said.

"In case of what?"

"You know."

"No, I do not."

He sighed. "In case you leave him. These papers transfer the shop to you alone, and specifically state that it won't go to him in the instance of your marriage ending."

"Matt isn't like that and you know it," I said, sounding miffed and not caring. "He wouldn't leave me destitute if something happened between us. Not that it will."

"*You* might decide to leave *him*, India. He is artless, after all."

I wasn't sure if I wanted to laugh or rail at him. "You are quite possibly the least grandfatherly grandfather I have ever met." Considering he'd just bequeathed his shop to me, that wasn't fair, but I didn't retract my statement.

"Speaking of Matt," he said as he watched me sign, "I don't think you should mention this meeting to him."

"I'm going to."

"He won't want you to speak to Fabian again."

"Matt doesn't make decisions for me."

His lips flattened. He was right not to believe me. Matt certainly wouldn't want me to learn from Fabian and become a spell caster, and if I did want it, I would have a difficult time convincing him that it was the right thing to do. But he would never forbid me, of that I was certain.

Chronos handed me a copy of the contract and promised to lodge the other with his lawyer.

"I have to go," I said, rolling up the papers. "May I have a hack fare? I didn't have time to fetch my reticule."

He opened a tin on the desk and plucked out some coins. He placed them on my palm and closed my fingers. "This is everything I've dreamed of," he said, a faraway look in his eyes. "More. My little girl is a spell caster."

"Not yet," I told him. Perhaps not ever, but I did not say that out loud. It would break his heart.

* * *

MATT DIDN'T RETURN HOME until just before dawn. I knew

because I fell asleep on his bed as I waited for him. I awoke with a start as the mattress sank beside me.

"It's just me," he said. I could barely make out his silhouette in the dark. "Is something wrong?"

"No. I just wanted to speak with you when you got home, but I wasn't expecting you to be this late. Or early."

He stretched out alongside me and I curled into his side, realizing too late that he was naked from the waist up. Since I was already pressed against him, there was no point in pulling away now, so I stroked his chest instead, teasing the tiny hairs and relishing the feel of smooth skin pulled taut over muscle.

"I like coming home to you waiting for me in my bed." He put his arm around me and kissed the top of my head. "Are you wearing just your nightgown?"

"With a housecoat. Don't tell your aunt."

"Scandalous." He cupped my breast through the fabric and I groaned, arching into him. "Very, very scandalous."

I tipped my head back and he kissed me. It was a hungry, passionate kiss that devoured me and sent my thoughts scattering. Every piece of me responded to his touch, aching for his mouth, his hands, his love.

My fingers followed the faint line of hair down his stomach to the waistband of his trousers. I wanted to explore, to know what I'd denied myself for so long, and to fulfill a part of me that needed fulfillment.

Matt sucked in air between his teeth. "I was going to tell you what I learned tonight," he murmured against my lips.

"It can wait," I said.

"Yessss. It can."

* * *

WHILE MATT SLEPT through the morning, I headed out with Cyclops to the Masons' home, located next to the family shop. Cyclops didn't protest, but that was because I lied and told him we were visiting Matt's lawyer and I needed to be accompanied. I wasn't sure why he believed such a thin excuse, but he did.

He didn't even question me when we stopped outside the Masons' house. He simply sighed and opened the carriage door. "I should have known," was all he said.

Mrs. Mason greeted me with politeness and Cyclops with a wary nod. "Would you like to come in, India?" she asked, stepping aside. "While your coachman waits with the carriage?"

"Cyclops isn't the coachman, as you can see by the actual coachman sitting on the driver's seat." I waved to our driver. He hesitated then lifted a hand in a half-hearted wave back. "Cyclops is accompanying me this morning," I said to Mrs. Mason. "Is Mr. Mason at home?"

"In the shop. Aren't you here to see Catherine?"

"I have a business matter to discuss with Mr. Mason."

She pressed her hand to her stomach as if my pronouncement made her feel ill. "Shouldn't your fiancé have accompanied you instead of your...friend?"

I smiled. "We'll go next door. Thank you, Mrs. Mason."

"I don't think she likes me," Cyclops said as we headed to the shop.

"She'll adore you once she gets to know you."

"I doubt it," he said heavily. "Catherine says she's very traditional."

I squeezed his arm, secretly pleased that Catherine had discussed her mother in such an honest manner with him. Mere acquaintances wouldn't.

"India! Nate!" Catherine emerged from the other side of the counter and greeted me with a kiss on my cheek and a rather awkward handshake for Cyclops. "What a lovely surprise."

"I hope we're not disturbing you," Cyclops said.

Catherine looked around the shop, which contained only her brother, Ronnie, behind the counter. It didn't feel empty, however. Not with the faint whirring of gears and the ticking of clocks filling the room. "I can spare a few moments."

I greeted Ronnie, a taller version of Catherine with sharper features. Like her, he was blonde and slender but with wide shoulders. He also smiled easily and often.

He came out from behind the counter and repeated the greeting his sister had given us, kissing my cheek and shaking Cyclops's hand, only with less awkwardness. I'd always liked Ronnie best of Catherine's three brothers, perhaps because he was so like her. Orwell, the older one, was earnest and smiled rarely, while Gareth, the youngest, was more interested in flirting with girls than having a serious conversation.

"Is your father in the workshop?" I asked, nodding at the door behind the counter. "I'd like to speak to him. It's about my shop."

Catherine's brows arched. "*Your* shop?"

Ronnie went to fetch his father, returning with Mr. Mason and Orwell. Unlike his three younger Mason siblings, Orwell took after his father, with a sturdier build that would run to fat in middle age. He wasn't as fair as Catherine, Ronnie and Gareth, or as friendly, but he greeted me kindly. Both he and his father ignored Cyclops, as if he were a servant who'd accompanied me and not worth their notice.

I stepped back a little to draw alongside Cyclops. "Matt wasn't available this morning," I told them. "So I wanted to bring someone else who knows about business matters. This is Nate Bailey."

I felt Cyclops's gaze drill into me.

"Mr. Bailey has a head for business," I said.

"And not just the pirate business," Cyclops joked.

Catherine laughed and Ronnie chuckled. Orwell and Mr. Mason stared at him as if they were trying to decide if they should laugh too or hide their valuables.

"It's about India's shop," Catherine told her father. "It seems it has returned to her hands. Is that right, India?"

I nodded. "I want to offer you the contents at a fair price, Mr. Mason. Or I have another idea that you might be amenable to. Orwell might be interested in what I have to say as well."

"You'd better come out back," Mr. Mason said. "Ronnie, Catherine, stay here. Is Gareth not back yet?"

"He's still making deliveries," Ronnie said with a huff.

Mr. Mason led us through to the workshop, the sight of which warmed my heart. Watch and clock parts were scattered on the bench, along with equipment and tools that were as familiar to me as my own belongings. The housing of a mahogany long case clock stood open, a stool pulled up so that its innards could be inspected from a seated position. At one end of a bench, six silver watch chains waited for the six silver watches to be attached, and a beautifully carved Bahnhäusle cuckoo sat silent but proud.

Mr. Mason offered me a stool but I declined. There weren't enough stools for all of us, and I didn't want Cyclops to be left standing. I drew in a deep breath, drawing the scent of metals and polish into my lungs, and smiled.

"I received the deeds to my family's shop yesterday," I told Mr. Mason. "It was returned to my grandfather after... well, you know." The less Eddie's name was spoken, the better. It wasn't his real name, anyway. "My grandfather doesn't want it, so he gave it to me."

Orwell cocked his head to the side. "He just *gave* it to you?"

"He has no intention of making or selling timepieces again. He's an old man and wishes to enjoy his retirement."

I couldn't imagine Chronos doing the things retired men do, like reading in the park or gardening. But Mr. Mason and Orwell didn't need to know that Chronos wasn't retiring from the business of magic.

"I won't be using it either," I said. "I don't want the shop to remain idle, however, and there is quite a bit of stock left in it." I paused, to see if either of them caught on, but they just waited for me to continue. "Enough stock for another watchmaker to walk right in and hit the ground running."

"You're not selling the stock?" Mr. Mason frowned. "Isn't that why you're here? To offer it to me?"

"That was my original intention, but as I thought more about it, I realized it would be a good opportunity for Orwell to lease the shop and buy the stock. I'd sell it to him at cost."

"You could set up a repayment plan," Cyclops said. When they both looked at him blankly, he added, "Like a loan."

Orwell's frown matched his father's. "But...I have this shop."

I'd thought he'd jump at the opportunity. Orwell wasn't the brightest star in the sky, but surely he could see that this was his chance to step outside his father's shadow.

"I thought you might like your own shop," I said.

"He'll inherit one day," Mr. Mason said. "And until then, he should remain here to learn from me."

"Hasn't he been here ten years? Hasn't he learned everything by now?"

"It doesn't come easy to everyone, India. We're not all

magicians." Mr. Mason snatched up a pivot locator and sat on the stool by the long case clock.

"Orwell?" I asked weakly.

"He's not interested," Mr. Mason said, peering into the clock's housing.

I arched a brow at Orwell. He merely shrugged. "This is where I belong. It'll be mine one day, and I can't imagine working anywhere else."

"What about Ronnie?" I asked.

"He's too young," Mr. Mason said.

"And hopeless," Orwell muttered.

I sighed. "Very well. Thank you for listening to me."

"Good day, India," Orwell said.

"If you're still interested in selling the stock at cost, let me know," Mr. Mason said.

"It won't be cost price," I said. "That was only for someone who agrees to lease the shop as well."

He grunted and returned to the clock.

The shop was still empty of customers, and Catherine and Ronnie both stood behind the counter, side by side, very close to the workshop door. Orwell asked his sister to see us out before retreating into the workshop again.

"Well?" Catherine pressed as she walked with us to the front door. "How did it go?"

"You know very well," I teased. "Since you were both listening in."

Ronnie stopped pretending to polish a watch face and threw his cloth on the counter. "I am *not* hopeless."

Catherine escorted us to the carriage, where I made her promise to have tea with us soon. "I feel as though I've hardly seen you of late," I said.

"I've been busy here, and you've been busy with your wedding plans and investigations. But I promise to visit in—"

"Don't tell me when!" I cut in. I didn't want Cyclops to be absent at that very date and time. "Send me a message beforehand."

She gave me a curious look. "Very well. I hope to see you there too, Nate."

"A pleasure," he said in an odd mix of his own accent and an English one. "I mean, it will be a pleasure to see you. Again. Because it's always a pleasure to see you." He hurriedly opened the carriage door and put out his hand to assist me.

Once inside, he leaned his head back against the wall and expelled a long breath.

I patted his arm. "It's all right, Cyclops. We've all made fools of ourselves in front of someone we're infatuated with."

His head jerked up. "I ain't a boy, India, and it ain't infatuation."

"No. Of course not."

He leaned his head back again and closed his eyes. I bit my tongue to stop myself telling him that what he felt for Catherine was love.

* * *

MATT AWOKE SHORTLY after we arrived home. He asked us to join him in the dining room, where Peter was setting out toast, eggs and coffee for a late breakfast.

"May I have some tea, please?" I asked the footman as he went to leave.

"And more toast," Cyclops said. "And an egg if there's any to spare."

"You already ate," Willie said, helping herself to a slice of bacon.

Duke slapped her wrist. "That's Matt's. You already ate too."

Willie shoved the bacon into her mouth and chewed in his face. He rolled his eyes.

Cyclops looked longingly at the bacon. "I'm still hungry."

"That's because you didn't eat enough at breakfast," Duke said. "You know you won't lose weight if you have two breakfasts."

"What will Catherine think?" Willie teased. "You got to watch how much you eat, Cyclops. Maybe you shouldn't have more toast and eggs. I'll eat anything Fossett brings back for you, since I'm such a good friend."

Cyclops crossed his arms and scowled at her.

"I'm looking out for your health and love life," she added.

"I don't have a love life," he growled.

"You will once you lose a few pounds." She patted his belly, which wasn't at all large, and poured herself a cup of coffee.

I headed to the sideboard too, but I got only as far as Matt. He hooked me around the waist and planted a passionate kiss on my mouth. "Good morning, India. You look ravishing today."

I patted his waistcoat at his chest and adjusted his tie so I could stay in his arms. "So do you."

He smiled and kissed me again.

"Cut it out," Willie whined. "Or I'll throw up my first *and* second breakfast."

Peter returned with tea and more food. He left again, passing Miss Glass on her way in.

"What a lovely morning," she said, cheerfully. "What an excellent notion to have breakfast together, although I have already eaten. India, pour me a cup of tea, will you?"

Matt kissed her cheek, earning a smile. "You are looking handsome today, Matthew. Did you have a good night's sleep?"

"No. I was out investigating."

"The pending nuptials must be agreeing with you, then."

"I think you're right." He held out a chair for her while I set a cup of tea and a newspaper in front of her.

"You might want to read that," I said. "We're going to be discussing the investigation and I know how you dislike such talk at the table. The newspaper will distract you."

"It's not altogether too vulgar over breakfast. Dinner is quite another matter." She picked up the newspaper in one hand and the cup in the other. "Is this about India's evening or yours, Matthew?"

Matt looked up from the sideboard, his brows raised. "You went out, India?"

"Chronos was here. He insisted." I picked up my teacup. "Tell us your news first. Did you speak with the other resident of the building?"

"His name is Hadley." Matt sat beside me and sliced the top off his boiled egg. "He was out on the night of Emmett's murder and didn't arrive back until well after the Drapers. Apparently he was with a woman he met three weeks ago. He was at her home all evening but left just before sunrise to avoid notice."

"Why?" I asked.

"Let me guess," Willie said. "She's a respectable woman?"

"A widow," he said, "so Hadley finally admitted after much cajoling and a little threatening."

Miss Glass snapped the newspaper to straighten it.

"He told me he'd marry her if he could," Matt went on, "but he's already married. His wife lives in New Mexico."

"Ah," Duke said. "S'pose that's why he didn't tell Brockwell about being out that night. You believe him, Matt?"

Matt lifted a shoulder. "I can easily check by asking the other members of the show's cast. He claimed a select few of them know about his affair, including the Drapers. He's sorry for not admitting it to the police."

"Not sorry enough to be honest with them."

"Hadley argued there was no reason to be honest since it wouldn't bring back Emmett."

"Good grief," I muttered into my teacup.

Miss Glass snapped the newspaper again but apparently it wasn't straight enough because she did it a third time.

Matt finished the egg before continuing on. "Hadley says May Draper saw him leave The Prince of Wales with his lover the night of the murder and would have known he wasn't at home."

"So?" Willie asked.

"Aside from the Drapers, the house was empty. If she or Danny returned the gun to Emmett's room, there was no one to hear them going up the stairs. Except each other, of course."

"So they're in it together. Makes sense."

"We need evidence, though." He rubbed his temples. "I'm not sure what our next step should be."

"Confront them?" Cyclops asked.

"They'll deny it," Matt said. "We need something more solid, as well as a motive. Let me think about it."

Miss Glass folded up the newspaper. "That's settled. Now, can we talk about our day, India?"

"I seem to be free for the afternoon," I said. "What did you have in mind? A stroll in the park? Call on a friend?"

"Not a friend. I'd like to visit my sister-in-law, if she's back in London."

My body deflated.

"I don't think that's a good idea," Matt said. "Why do you want to see her?"

"Now that Patience is safely married to a highly respected gentleman, and you two are engaged, it's time to bury the hatchet," Miss Glass said. "We'll start with a brief visit, while you ought to think about seeing your uncle at his club, Matthew. A public place is best."

Matt picked up a slice of toast and pointed it at his aunt. "You do remember that they don't like me."

"That's irrelevant. You're family, and family should be on the same side, no matter how much they dislike one another."

"You wouldn't think that if you'd met my American family."

Miss Glass's gaze slid to Willie, who was too busy inspecting the leftover bacon on the sideboard to notice. "All the more reason to get along with your English relatives. Richard is well connected, and you're going to need those connections one day."

"I can get along fine without him."

"This is England, Matthew." She sounded exasperated— and quite serious. "Affairs are conducted differently here. Business is conducted between acquaintances of certain circles, and unless you want to lose what you have, you'll need to get a foot in the door now. Your uncle can offer you that. Believe it or not, he doesn't want the Rycroft title ruined after he's gone."

"It won't be ruined," Matt said, equally exasperated.

"You may not think you need a foot in the door now, but one day you might. Think of your children."

Matt sighed.

I touched his hand. "I'll go with you, Miss Glass."

"But you'll leave if they insult you," Matt added.

"I'm not certain that Beatrice has returned to London yet," Miss Glass said. "But it won't hurt to check."

I didn't think they would have returned so soon after the wedding either, although according to Miss Glass, her sister-in-law preferred the city, even in the summertime. Both the younger Glass girls did too.

"Before you go, India, tell me what Chronos wanted," Matt said.

"He gave me the shop." The other reason for Chronos's visit could wait until we were alone. "Cyclops and I visited the Masons this morning, to offer the lease and contents to Orwell Mason, but he didn't want it. He prefers to stay apprenticed to his father. I'll lease it out to another shop-keeper, I suppose."

"Our lawyer will take care of it."

"I also want the rent directed to Chronos for the remainder of his life."

"Send an instruction to our lawyer."

"*Our* lawyer?"

"He's at your disposal too now, since you are a business-woman in your own right. The deeds are in your name, aren't they? And Chronos did make sure I couldn't take the shop from you, didn't he? I'd expect nothing less from him."

Miss Glass made a miffed sound. "Trust that mad old goat to do the unconventional thing. I know he's your family, India, but there are holes up here." She tapped her head. "He ought not be left alone."

We all stared at her, and Willie snorted with laughter. Duke thumped her shoulder and she pressed her lips together to smother her grin.

Bristow entered and announced the arrival of Catherine and Ronnie Mason to see me. "They're in the drawing room, madam."

"I'll have to put off the visit to Lady Rycroft," I said to Miss Glass. "Perhaps tomorrow. Cyclops, will you accompany me?" I asked before Miss Glass suggested we put off our visit only so far as the afternoon.

"No," Cyclops said flatly. "I'm busy."

Willie grabbed his hand. "No you ain't."

She dragged him to the door while Duke pushed from

behind. Cyclops could have thwarted their attempts, but he put up a lackluster show of resistance.

"Come along, Matt, you too," I said, holding out my hand.

He took it. "I don't intend to miss this."

CHAPTER 9

*I*f Catherine had visited alone, I would have assumed it was to pass the time with me, or an excuse to see Cyclops, but the presence of Ronnie made it more serious.

"I suspect you know why we're here," Catherine said after introductions were made.

"We want to take you up on your offer," Ronnie blurted out.

Catherine sighed. "We had agreed that I would do the talking. What he says is true. We'd like to lease the shop from you, India, and buy the stock, too."

"At cost price," Ronnie added. He looked like a puppy presented with a new toy, all eager bounciness as he sat on the edge of the sofa.

Catherine looked far more composed, except for the frequent glances she cast in Cyclops's direction. Cyclops simply sat in the chair and ignored her. He looked everywhere but at her. Poor Catherine.

"This is wonderful news," I said. "I'd much prefer to rent

it to someone I know. But...are you prepared to be shop-keepers?"

"We're already shopkeepers," Catherine said.

"But do you have enough experience in watchmaking and repairs to operate a business?"

"Ronnie is very good. He might not have as much experience as Father, but he's better than Orwell, although Orwell hates admitting it."

"I'm not as stupid as I look," Ronnie said, laughing.

Catherine sighed. "Do stop talking, Ronnie."

Ronnie's mouth twisted, and he sat back with a huff.

"He's right," Catherine said. "He's very clever and has a knack for watches and clocks. Not the same kind of knack as you, India, obviously, but he's been helping in the shop and workshop ever since he was small. I wasn't allowed in the workshop much, but he was. All that time spent back there must have seeped in, because he can repair almost anything that comes across the counter."

Ronnie's cheeks flushed, and he looked at his sister in surprise, as if he'd never received a compliment from her before.

"You've been learning too," Cyclops said to Catherine. "You've spent a lot of time reading books and tinkering."

It was Catherine's turn to blush, and Ronnie's turn to sit forward again and frown at Cyclops.

"While Ronnie will do all the repairs," Catherine went on, "I feel as though I should know enough about them so that I can talk knowledgeably to the customer and charge the right amount for the task."

"You've certainly thought about it," Matt said. "Did you always plan to have your own shop?"

"I was going to work in Father's," Ronnie said. "But Catherine told me there won't be much to do when Orwell's boys grow. He'll want them to work alongside him, and where will that leave me?"

"Gareth can help out in the shop until Orwell's boys are older," Catherine said. "It'll be good for Gareth. He needs more responsibility than simply doing deliveries. He's grown rather bored of late, and when Gareth is bored...well, let's just say he gets into trouble."

"What about your father?" I asked. "Have you spoken to him about it?"

Catherine and Ronnie exchanged grim glances. "We have. After you left this morning," Catherine said. "He was angry. He says we're too young to set out on our own, and too silly."

"That's Orwell's influence," Ronnie bit off. "He's jealous because I'm younger than him and better. He's been in Father's ear for years, sowing seeds against me."

"It's not quite as dramatic as that," Catherine said, earning a glare from her brother. "But neither Orwell nor Father think Ronnie can service watches on his own, yet he can. I know he can."

"And they don't think Catherine is capable of running the shop alone," Ronnie added. "But she's more than capable. She's a natural shopkeeper. The customers love her. Especially the men."

"Ronnie!" Catherine cried, blushing again. "You make me sound like a loose woman."

Ronnie chuckled. "Have you forgotten that foreman fellow?"

Catherine lowered her head and her shoulders rounded.

"She's friendly and kind," Cyclops said in a booming voice that echoed off the walls of the large drawing room and had everyone sitting up straighter. "She makes people feel comfortable. Because she's pretty, her friendliness gets mistaken for flirting. You should be ashamed of yourself for suggesting otherwise, you being her favorite brother and all."

Ronnie's face grew paler with every thunderous word. By the end, he was the color of Mr. Hendry's fine paper. "Right. Yes. Sorry, Cath." He did not take his eyes off Cyclops, and Cyclops did not take his eye off Ronnie. "You're nice and kind, and clever and...nice."

"Don't be scared of Cyclops," Willie said, smirking. "He won't hurt you. He's just keen to defend Catherine's honor. Real keen, on account of him being—"

"Is that the time?" Duke shot to his feet and grabbed Willie, hauling her to her feet. "We have to go."

Willie chuckled. Cyclops rose too.

"You're going?" Catherine asked. "Already?"

"I can't stay," Cyclops said. "I'm busy."

"No, he ain't," Willie cut in.

Duke scrunched her shirt sleeve in his fist and marched her to the door.

"Bye!" Willie called out over her shoulder. "Nice meeting you, Ronnie. Come visit any time. You and your sister."

"I can't stay," Cyclops said apologetically. "I—I just can't."

Catherine sighed. "I understand." She watched him go, sighing again.

Ronnie studied her from beneath half-closed eyelids. "What was that about?"

"Nothing."

"Is there something going on between you two?"

"No."

He eyed the door through which Cyclops had exited. "Just as well, because our parents wouldn't like it. He's...not the sort of husband they want for you."

"I know that," she spat. "That's precisely why I have no interest in marriage, right now. Perhaps ever. That's why I need to take this opportunity. I need employment outside

Father's shop." She turned to me. I'd never seen her look so distressed, so earnest. "If I don't marry and have no means to support myself, I'll have to depend on my parents forever. I'll have nothing of my own and no money. I'll be reliant on them for the rest of their lives, then reliant on my brothers."

I understood all too well. My father had bequeathed the shop to Eddie, my fiancé at the time of Father's death. When Eddie ended our engagement, I had nothing, not even a roof over my head. If Matt hadn't offered me a house and employment when he did, I could have ended up in the workhouse. The workhouse was a fast way to an early grave.

"I'll put the lease in both your names," I told her. "Might I suggest that all business agreements are made up in both your names, too?"

"I'll be the one getting a license from the Watchmaker's Guild," Ronnie said. "I'm hardly going to cheat my sister."

"I think it's a good idea," Matt said in that open yet authoritative way he had that men often responded to. "Having both names on all agreements will mean you will both want the shop to succeed. You'll work equally hard as each other."

Ronnie nodded slowly. "When you put it like that, it sounds like a good idea."

Matt could convince a Conservative to vote Liberal if he used the right tone.

"I'll visit the Watchmaker's Guild this afternoon to apply for the test," Ronnie said. "Hopefully I can sit it within days."

"In the meantime, I'll have the paperwork for the lease drawn up," I said.

"And the sale of the stock." Ronnie put out his hand to me. "Pleasure doing business with you, India."

Catherine kissed my cheek. "Thank you," she whispered. "You won't regret it. We're going to work very hard."

"The place will need cleaning first," I said. "It's been sitting idle for a while and is quite dusty."

"I don't mind rolling up my sleeves."

"I'll send someone around to help you."

She narrowed her gaze at me.

Ronnie looked toward the door and grunted. "Father's going to be furious."

I wasn't sure if he was referring to the shop or Cyclops, and I didn't dare ask.

* * *

WE WERE ALL ABOUT to sit down to lunch together when Detective Inspector Brockwell arrived. "I am sorry to interrupt," he said, when Bristow brought him into the dining room at Matt's request. "I wanted to update you, but I see you're about to eat. I'll come back later."

"Nonsense," Matt said, pulling out a chair. "Come and join us."

"You're very welcome," I added.

"As long as it's all right with Miss Glass," Brockwell said, bowing in her direction.

"Quite all right," she said. "We're being rather formal today, since we're all here, but don't worry about your attire."

Brockwell looked down at himself and smoothed a hand over his wrinkled jacket. His tie was a little crooked and his sideburns needed a trim, but I couldn't imagine him any other way.

"He looks fine to me," Willie said as she tucked the napkin into her collar.

"I'm sure he does, Willie dear."

Brockwell smiled at Willie. She smiled back. I blinked owlishly at them both.

Peter and Bristow placed plates on the table and stepped

back out of the way. The fish, chicken and salad dishes were more than we were used to for luncheon. Ordinarily, sandwiches sufficed, but Miss Glass had decided that since we were all in the house, something more substantial was necessary, particularly as we didn't know if we'd be home for dinner. Matt was already talking about returning to The Prince of Wales early to conduct inquiries.

Brockwell accepted the dish of Chicken Fricassee from Matt and all but smacked his lips in delight at the feast. "This is most generous of you, Glass," he said. "I'm very grateful to be included in your family repast."

"Think nothing of it," Matt said.

"I only came by to ask India a favor, and to tell you the results of our ballistics tests on the gun."

"No!" Miss Glass's voice cut through the air like a siren. "No, no, no. There will be no talk of the investigation at the table."

Willie muttered something under her breath and dropped the plate of roast potatoes on the table with a thud.

"I thought it was only the dinner table when such discussions couldn't be had," I said.

"Luncheon too," Miss Glass noted. "Breakfast is fine, however."

Brockwell put up his hand, and the knife he held, in surrender. "I'll keep that in mind."

Willie chuckled.

The inspector's cheeks colored as he realized how he sounded. "Not that I'll come by at breakfast time again."

"You might," Willie said cheerfully. "If it's necessary."

"I doubt it would be necessary under any circumstances," Miss Glass said snippily.

Willie grinned into her napkin.

We made polite small talk over lunch before finally retreating to the drawing room. Miss Glass did not join us, for which I was glad. She didn't seem to care much for the inspector. Although I hadn't liked him at first either, I had to admit he was a good man and a thorough policeman. Miss Glass probably didn't like him because he wasn't from the upper classes, but neither was I—nor Matt's friends.

On further thought, it had taken her quite some time to get used to us, so there was hope for the inspector.

Before leaving us, she'd told him smoking was to be confined to the smoking room. Willie waited until she was gone before offering the inspector a cigar.

He politely declined. "I wouldn't want to offend Miss Glass."

"She ain't here," Willie said, taking one from the box.

I took it off her. "She'll smell it. You can smoke alone in the smoking room, if you like."

She looked to Brockwell. "I'd be delighted to join you after this meeting, Willie," he said.

That seemed to appease her and she finally sat, sitting like a man with her legs apart.

Brockwell removed his notepad and a small pencil from his inside jacket pocket. "The bullet almost certainly came from Emmett Cocker's gun," he said, flipping the pages. "Therefore it's likely he knew the killer well enough to allow them to get close enough to his person to retrieve it."

"Which means it wasn't Jack Krane, the outlaw," Matt said. "The only way Emmett would let him close is if he was incapacitated first."

"And there were no signs of a fight or struggle on the body."

"That eliminates one suspect," I said.

"Not necessarily." Brockwell referred to his notes. "What if Krane sent the blonde woman here to lure Cocker into a trap?"

"That's an elaborate scheme," Matt said, "but not out of

the realms of possibility. She's certainly worth finding so we can question her."

"That's the problem," Duke muttered. "Finding her."

"I have some information that may help." Brockwell tapped his pencil on the notepad. "One of the show's cast claims she saw her at a lecture at the New Somerville Club on Oxford Street."

"And?" Matt prompted. "Did you question the staff or other club members?"

"They were most unforthcoming."

"It's a ladies' club," I told Matt. "Gentlemen are not welcome."

"He's a detective inspector," Duke said. "Can't he go in anyway?"

"I could, but would they freely answer my questions?" Brockwell shook his head. "I think not. I would not want to pressure them and have them close off completely."

"That's wise thinking, Jasper," Willie said.

He squared his shoulders and looked thoroughly pleased with her compliment.

"Do you want me to infiltrate the New Somerville Club?" I asked. "Is that the favor you wanted from me?"

"Infiltrate might be too strong a word," Brockwell said. "I'd like you to ask questions."

"That won't get answers." Matt hesitated, as if he were unsure he wanted to continue.

"I have to be more subtle," I offered. Matt nodded. "I have to pretend the blonde is a friend. Perhaps she asked me to meet her there. Indeed, there's a chance she might turn up again anyway, to take advantage of all the club has to offer."

"What does it offer?" Cyclops asked. "Just lectures?"

Brockwell referred to his notes again. "Intellectual and robust debate on political, social and literary questions of interest to the educated woman." He flipped the notebook closed. "Members also have the opportunity to meet with friends for luncheon or afternoon tea for a small cost in the club's social rooms."

"Sounds like a gentleman's club," Matt said. "But for a more intelligent membership." He smirked.

"With less gambling," Brockwell added, also smirking.

"I don't know any members," I said. "They won't allow me in."

"I believe you can join on the night," Brockwell said. "They commonly have newcomers joining just for the lectures. The membership fee is low to attract women of limited means."

"Then I'll go tonight."

"Not tonight. Wait for tomorrow night's lecture. It seems those evenings draw a larger crowd. You'll blend in better."

"Take Willie with you," Matt said.

"You wanted subtle," Duke reminded him.

"I can be subtle." Willie jerked her chin at Brockwell. "Where in Oxford Street?"

"Two-thirty-one, above the ABC tearoom. ABC is the abbreviation for the Aerated Bread Company. The tearoom also provides the meals and refreshments for the club."

"Tomorrow night, then," Willie said. "Do I have to wear a dress?"

"I think you'll be accepted the way you are."

"Don't wear your hat," Duke said. "That way they can see you're a woman. Wouldn't want you to get turned away at the door."

Brockwell pocketed his notepad and pencil. "Have you learned anything useful, Glass?"

"May Draper is lying about that night." He told the detective inspector his theory about the Drapers being home alone on the night of the murder and the likelihood that one or both of them had returned the gun to Emmett's room.

"Unless they weren't there at all, and someone else returned it," Brockwell said.

"I've thought about that, but why lie and say they were home if they weren't? It just makes them seem guilty."

"There is certainly something strange about those two. I don't trust them."

"We're returning to The Prince of Wales tonight to see what we can learn from the other cast members," Matt said. "We established relationships with some on our last visit, and they don't yet know that we're working with you."

"I'm good friends with Annie Oakley," Willie announced.

"You're acquaintances," Duke said. "She ain't your friend."

"She is. We got up to some things the other night that only friends do together, but I can't say what on account of I don't want to put Jasper in a difficult position. And India's too prim to hear it."

I rolled my eyes.

"Since you're going to the pub," Brockwell said, "you might as well ask if anyone saw the blonde woman leave right after the victim on the night of his death. It was late, and most had gone home, but one of the staff claims he saw a blonde woman follow Cocker out."

"Our mystery woman?" I said. "Or May Draper?"

"Could be either. He didn't see her face and couldn't remember her clothes. I questioned Mrs. Draper, but she denied it was her." Brockwell rose and thanked us for lunch. "I'd best be getting back."

"What about that cigar?" Willie asked, picking up the cigar box.

Brockwell hesitated. "You going to join us, Glass?"

"I rarely smoke," Matt said.

"Nor me," Duke added. "Cyclops doesn't smoke. You two go. Your men can manage themselves for a while longer, Inspector."

Willie strode out, expecting Brockwell to follow. After the briefest hesitation, he said his goodbyes to us and trailed after her.

I hooked my arm through Duke's. "I'm proud of you for not thwarting Willie's flirtations."

"I reckon they're past flirting," he said.

* * *

WE WENT EARLY to The Prince of Wales to speak to the staff. The barman confirmed seeing a blonde leave after Emmett the night of his murder. We asked the other staff members about blondes they'd noticed coming and going from the pub in the last few weeks. The only two that everyone remembered were the striking mystery woman and May Draper.

"The Draper woman's not as pretty as the other one," one of the barmaids said as she dried a tankard with a towel. "But she's here most nights. I didn't take much notice of her until I saw her kissing a man in the alley when I took an empty crate out. The same alley where the murder took place."

Matt described Danny Draper but the maid couldn't offer a description as the man had his back to her.

"Thank you," Matt said, slipping her some money.

We didn't have long to wait for May herself to arrive with several other cast members, including her husband. Danny immediately sat at a table with three others, including Matt. May hovered at her husband's shoulder, her glare frosty. I got the distinct feeling they'd just had an argument, and she wanted to continue it but he did not.

With his back to her, he was able to ignore her as he smiled and joked his way through the first round of poker. I wouldn't have guessed he'd been losing terribly, both before Emmett's death and after, but Annie Oakley claimed he had.

"And May don't like it," she said to Willie when Willie asked why May looked so sour. "She tries to stop him from coming here, but he won't listen." She signaled to the barmaid to approach and ordered beers for the three of us.

"Have they always argued?" I asked. "Or is it only a recent thing?"

She frowned as she considered her answer. "Recent. I guess he finally lost too much for her to stomach."

Or she knew Danny couldn't maintain the cheating scheme with Emmett gone, and he was losing for real, now, with no compensation from Emmett.

"Would you say their marriage is a good one?" I asked.

She screwed up her nose. "How would I know? I ain't much of a good judge of marriages. Mine is fine, but that's because Frank understands me. We been together so long now, we're almost the same person."

He must be very understanding to let her go out with Willie all night. Then again, I couldn't imagine this woman asking for permission—or anyone trying to stop her. Just like Willie would never let anyone stop her from doing as she pleased. I was fortunate that I'd found Matt. He wouldn't stifle my ideas or stop me from doing something I wanted to do, either.

Although I was yet to test him fully. Such a test might rise soon.

I dismissed thoughts of Fabian Charbonneau and his spell casting from my mind, as I had done all day. Thinking about it only made me anxious, and I couldn't afford to be anxious. Not with the wedding approaching and the investigation to finish. I had quite enough on my plate to worry about.

Our drinks arrived and Willie immediately drained half of hers. I kicked her under the table in a bid to get her to slow down, but she ignored me. She wiped her mouth with the back of her hand and declared, "I needed that."

Annie didn't even raise an eyebrow at Willie's uncouth behavior.

Willie leaned forward. "I heard May was seen kissing a man who weren't Danny. Just outside here in the alley, too."

I gasped at her brazen statement when it could very well have been Danny. "Don't spread gossip," I scolded her.

She lifted a shoulder in a shrug.

"Where'd you hear that?" Annie asked.

"Barmaid," Willie said.

Annie clicked her tongue. "Typical. Everyone thinks it's fine to gossip about us because we're on show every day. Well, let me tell you, that ain't fair. Our private lives ain't up for public dissection."

"Very true," I said.

Willie wasn't giving up, however. "I only wanted to find out if she was interested in a little...fun," she said, winking.

I almost fell off the stool. What was she doing? "I think you drank that beer too quickly, Willie." I moved her tankard away.

She grabbed it and pressed it to her lips. She peered at Annie over the rim as she sipped.

Annie picked up her tankard too. "Knowing May, she might be." She rubbed her thumb and two fingers together.

I sat, frozen to the stool, unable to quite believe what I was witnessing. "You can't say that."

Annie chuckled. "May's my friend. I look out for her, and I know she's having a rough time, with Danny losing all their money. She'll do whatever's necessary to save him and her marriage. She's done it before. She used to be an actress." She said it as if it explained May's behavior.

"Does Danny know she'll do...that for money?" I asked.

"I don't know." She looked over to where Danny discarded his hand in the middle of the table. Behind him, May winced as if she were in pain.

Could she really have a liaison with Willie? For money? The very notion put me into a bit of spin. My shock must have been written on my face, because Annie chuckled into her beer and Willie slapped me on the shoulder.

"Careful you don't lose that halo, India," she said.

"It's already tarnished after what I've just heard," I whispered in her ear as I rose.

I went to join Matt, Willie at my heels. "I had to ask," she said. "If I didn't, we'd never know if she was kissing Danny in the alley or not."

"We still don't know."

"But we do know she ain't faithful if money exchanges hands. That's something."

We pushed past Duke as he chatted to another man having a conversation about female sharpshooters. I suspected he was planning to steer the conversation to May. Cyclops was with another group of cast members and was probably also attempting to find out more about the Drapers or the victim.

I rested my hand on Matt's shoulder. He smiled up at me. "I'm winning," he said, good naturedly.

"So I see. He has such good luck," I said to May, standing at her husband's back.

"He certainly does," May said cheerfully. If her smile weren't so tight at the corners of her eyes, I would have believed she didn't care that Danny was losing. She was certainly an accomplished actress.

They continued to play for quite some time. I joined

May and we chatted, but I sensed that her attention was on the game, not me. She hardly looked Danny's way, however, as he continued to lose more than he won.

The two other players rarely won. The more Matt won, the more agitated May became. I suspected that was Matt's tactic, but what he planned to do with an annoyed May, I had no idea.

She wasn't the only one getting annoyed. Danny slapped his cards on the table every time he lost and muttered under his breath. After losing a particularly large sum, he kicked over a stool, earning glares from those nearby. Matt tried diffusing the tension with a joke, but Danny was beyond jokes.

May put her hand on her husband's shoulder. "Will you buy me a drink, honey?"

"Get it yourself," he muttered.

Her fingers tightened. "Come and join me for some fresh air. It's getting hot in here, and smoky."

"You go. I'm busy." He nodded at me. "Your new friend can accompany you. Whose turn is it to deal?" he asked the other players.

"Don't be like that, honey. I need you."

"Fresh air is a good idea," Matt said, setting the deck down. "I could do with a break myself. If you'll excuse me." He headed off in the direction of the corridor that led to the outhouse in the courtyard.

May rubbed her husband's shoulder then moved up to his neck. It was a sensual caress and seemed to relax him. He sighed.

Then she pinched him.

I wouldn't have known she'd done it except that he jerked away and glared up at her. She picked up her skirts and moved off in the direction of the door that led to the side alley.

He stood and buttoned up his jacket. "Duty calls," he said to the other players, who laughed. He followed his wife.

I followed him but didn't exit through the same door. It was too obvious. They'd see me. Instead, I left through the door leading to the courtyard. It was quieter outside, and the only light came from the moon and a lamp hanging beside the outhouse door. There was no sign of Matt. The hum of voices from the public bar sounded muffled and distant, whereas the voice of May Draper from the other side of the wall was much clearer.

"You're a fool!" she snapped. "A dang fool, Danny Draper!"

I dearly wanted to see but the brick wall was too high. I could climb onto one of the barrels, but it wouldn't be easy with my skirts. I hitched them up with one hand and sat on one of the barrels then swung my legs up onto another. From there I was able to lever myself to my feet.

I remained in a squatting position and peered over the wall. The moonlight was just strong enough for me to see May pacing back and forth in the alley while Danny sat on a crate, his head in his hands.

"I can't believe you," May said, stopping in front of him. "You're hopeless."

"I can win it back," he whined. "I'm sure I can, darlin'."

"Based on past experience, you won't. And don't call me darling. I'm furious with you."

He stood and went to put his arms around her, only to receive a shove in the chest.

"Don't," she growled. "I can't keep doing this just so you can lose it all. You have to stop *now*."

"Not yet. I know I can win it back."

"How many times are you going to say that?" She shoved him again and he took a step back.

"I mean it this time. I lost my touch because I didn't need

it with Emmett, but I reckon I'm getting it back now. My luck'll change, you'll see."

"Don't mention that name to me again. If you hadn't let him cut you out, we wouldn't be in this situation."

"I didn't *let* him," Danny said.

"That's the whole damned problem!" she cried.

"What does that mean?"

She didn't get a chance to answer. He suddenly ran toward me. Before I could move away, he'd jumped onto something out of my line of sight against the bricks, and clamped his hands over both of mine, holding onto the top of the wall. My heart exploded with fright and my stomach plunged. His face filled my vision, all bared teeth and wild eyes.

"Well, well," he snarled. "If it ain't your friend listening in to a conversation that don't concern her."

CHAPTER 10

I tried to pull my hands away but his grip was too firm. His mouth twisted into a teeth-clenching grin as he ground my palms into the bricks.

"Let me go!" I cried, struggling to free my hands.

Something thudded beside me. "Let her go," Matt growled. How long had he been here?

He reached over the wall and grabbed Danny's collar.

Danny released me and put up his hands in surrender. "She was spying on us!"

Matt shook him so violently, Danny lost his footing and almost fell off the barrel he was standing on. I stood straighter. The top of the wall came to my chest. Behind Danny, May stood with hands on hips. In the pale moonlight, it was difficult to tell if her glare was directed at Danny or me. With a click of her tongue, she stormed off down the alley.

Danny pushed against Matt.

Matt punched him in the jaw, snapping Danny's head back. "That's for frightening my fiancée."

Danny rubbed his face. "She was spying!"

"I heard an argument," I told him. "It sounded heated, and I was worried for May's safety."

He snorted. "And I'm the fucking queen of England."

Matt punched him again. "That's for using bad language in front of my fiancée." He must not have hit him too hard because the punch didn't draw blood. "I'll let you go when you answer some questions."

"What questions?" Danny whined.

"I'm getting to them. Have some patience." He shook Danny.

Danny pressed his teeth together and looked as if he wanted to hit Matt. But he did not. He stood there, hands in the air, and waited.

"First of all, a statement," Matt said. "You were in a cheating scheme with Emmett Cocker."

"No!"

"That's a quick denial, considering you don't know what scheme I'm referring to."

"I can guess," Danny spat. "You think we cheated at cards together. You think I lost on purpose to reel in other players. I didn't. We didn't cheat."

"I don't believe you," I said. "I heard you tell May that you didn't need any luck with Emmett. Why wouldn't you need luck?"

"Because I sometimes won against him. A lot, as it happens. You just didn't see it."

"That's not what everyone else says." Matt jerked his head to the pub's rear entrance.

"You can't trust gossip."

"In the conversation you had with May," I said, "it sounded as if you are having money difficulties."

He shrugged one shoulder.

"May said Emmett cut you out. She was referring to the cheating scheme, wasn't she?"

"I don't know what you're talking about. Why are you asking these questions? None of this has anything to do with you. You're winning tonight, Glass. You ain't being cheated."

"You cheated my cousin," Matt said. "You and Emmett."

"Emmett probably did, it's true. But he's gone now, and if he did, it ain't my fault. I never saw him cheat, and he's never been caught. Not once."

Matt merely smiled, a wicked slash of white teeth in the night. "It was you, wasn't it? You killed Emmett."

"No! I ain't no murderer!"

"You weren't home at the time of his death. You lied to the police."

Danny's jaw slackened. "Who *are* you?"

"We're private agents assisting the police to catch Cocker's killer. I have Detective Inspector Brockwell's permission to do whatever it takes to get to the bottom of the mystery." He smiled as his fingers curled into Danny's collar, pulling it tight around his throat.

I couldn't see the color of Danny's face in the poor light, but I could see his eyes bulge.

"I lied," he choked out. "I admit it. I lied to the inspector about that night."

Matt loosened his grip. "You weren't at home the night Cocker died?"

"No." Danny swallowed heavily. "I went for a walk to clear my head."

Matt barked a laugh. "You expect us to believe that?"

"Believe it or not, it's the truth. I was out walking with May for hours. London's peaceful at night, and it wasn't cold. We were just walking and talking."

"Where did you go?"

"Nowhere in particular. Here and there."

"Did anyone see you?"

"I don't think so. Maybe just a drunk or two. They wouldn't remember us."

"What about the constables on watch duty?" I asked. "Ever since the Ripper murders, the police have had a strong presence at night."

"Didn't that happen in the East End?" Danny asked, all too innocently. "We didn't see anyone who'd remember us. Now, can I go? I've got to find my wife and sweet talk her into forgiving me. She's mad on account of you beating me at poker tonight, Glass."

"Just tonight?" I asked. "Or is it the accumulation of losses?"

"Can I go?"

Matt released him and Danny jumped off the crates. He stuck a finger down his collar and stretched his neck. With a final glare at us, he headed down the alley with an exaggerated swagger.

"I suspect he's lying," I said.

"Your instincts are most likely correct." Matt jumped down then put his hands at my waist and lifted me off the barrel. "Are you all right?" he asked once my feet were settled on the ground. "Did he hurt you?"

"It was more the shock and my annoyance at being caught. I thought I was safe in the low light."

He put his arms around me and drew me close. "What would you have done if I hadn't come?"

"I would have questioned him, just as we did. He would have lied, just as he did. So really, nothing would be different."

"That's quite a convincing argument, but I wish you'd brought Duke, Willie or Cyclops with you."

"I knew you were out here, Matt." I took his hand and led him to the door. "You took a long time in the outhouse."

"I didn't go into the outhouse. I was waiting in the

shadows for a suitable length of time to return when you showed up."

I spun around. "You were there the entire time I was watching them?"

His eyes shone in the darkness, two glittering orbs of reflected moonlight. "I was going to reveal myself to you. I really was. But then I thought about how enthusiastic you would be telling me what you'd learned, and I didn't want to deny you that feeling."

I studied him, but he seemed genuine enough. "That is quite sweet."

"Also, I just like watching you. I'm only a man, after all, and from behind, you're...delightful."

"That's not sweet at all." I squeezed his hand hard, and he chuckled as I led him back inside.

WE WERE at a loose end the following day. Willie and I weren't going to the lecture at the New Somerville Club until later, and we didn't want to question the Drapers any more. Duke and Cyclops had asked after the blonde mystery woman at the pub, but no one knew where she'd gone, although several had seen her before the murder. Three had even seen her in Emmett's company, both in America and England. It seemed they'd been a couple, but no one could explain why she'd been happy to see Duke punch Emmett. It was looking more and more likely she'd left the city— perhaps even the country. Hopefully we'd uncover some useful information at the lecture tonight.

Our day looked quite free, and I worried that Miss Glass would want me to call on her sister-in-law or fuss over the wedding arrangements. I was saved such unpleasantness by something nastier—the arrival of Mr. Abercrombie.

The master of The Watchmaker's Guild would not enter the house. He informed Bristow that he preferred to remain on the doorstep and would speak to me from there. "This is a house of sin, and I don't wish to set a single foot inside. You ought to be ashamed of yourself, working for such *debauched* people. It means you're no better than them."

"Dear me, what will you say once Matt and I are respectably married?" I said as I came down the stairs. "You won't have any excuse to harass the staff and make a scene. I'm sure that will quite frustrate you." I'd heard him rail at poor Bristow from the landing and thought to rescue the butler.

Bristow didn't look in need of rescuing. He seemed quite unruffled. He'd seen and heard much worse in this house. Nevertheless, I wasn't going to let Mr. Abercrombie get away with such ridiculous statements.

Abercrombie's mouth turned down in distaste as he squinted at me through the pince-nez perched on the tip of his equine nose. "You may joke, Miss Steele, but you will get your come-uppance. Good wins over evil every time. God is watching."

It would seem I was to be painted the villain and he the hard-working hero in his version of the story. As much as I didn't want his words to affect me, they took the wind out of my sails. I suspected much of the public would side with him if they were forced to make a choice between the artless and magicians.

"You're making a scene," I hissed at him. "Come inside."

His lips stretched into a thin smile and I regretted letting him see my irritation. "What I need to tell you won't take long. I'm here to tell you that you cannot circumvent the guild's rules. We're onto you. We on the Court of Assistants are far too clever for your ruse to work."

"What rules?" I asked, feeling a little ill.

"Section 6.1 under article four states no magician is allowed in the guild."

"You made a rule just for me? I'm flattered. Perhaps you could name it." I tapped a finger to my chin in mock thought. "I like The Steele Ruling. Or what about The Steele Decree? Law of Steele has a nice ring to it too. There are quite a number of possibilities."

Someone behind me snickered. Since it was such a strange noise for Bristow to make, I turned around and saw that Bristow was no longer there. Instead, Matt, Cyclops and Duke stood at the base of the stairs, each with his arms crossed over his chest. Matt nodded at me but made no motion to join me at the door.

I turned back to Abercrombie. He didn't look quite so cock-sure anymore. I liked to think it was my joking and not Matt's presence that rattled him. "Why would I care to circumvent rules of an organization I do not wish to belong to?" I asked.

"You do wish it. You wish to sell your watches and clocks and make a tidy fortune. Isn't that what you're really planning to do by putting the Mason children in your shop?"

"She doesn't need to earn a fortune," Matt said. "I already have one, and it's entirely at her disposal."

Abercrombie snorted. "Then you're a fool for allowing her free reign. She'll ruin you." He removed his watch from his pocket and checked the time. "I must be going. I simply came here to tell you that your plan won't work. The Mason boy won't be allowed into the guild."

I knew what he'd been building up to, but hearing him say it so cavalierly made my blood boil. "That's not fair."

"He'll never be admitted while he's working from your shop, under your direction."

"He won't be working for me. He and Miss Mason are

leasing my father's old shop, but I won't have anything to do with their business. I'll just be their landlady."

"We can't be certain of that."

"This is ridiculous. You can't stop a young man and his sister from making their way in the world independently of their father. How can you be so cruel to a family that have been members of the guild for generations?"

"Not only that," Matt said, standing at my back, "but unless your constitution specifically mentions non-magicians renting shops from magicians, I'm afraid you can't legally ban them from the guild."

Mr. Abercrombie merely smiled again. "I believe you're selling them the remaining stock. Section 6.2 under article four of our revised constitution states that the sale of goods made by magicians is a banning offence."

"I won't sell them the stock then." I no longer cared about the money. I couldn't let this vindictive man destroy Catherine and Ronnie's dream. "I'll only sell them the tools and furniture."

"I'm willing to give them an interest-free loan until they establish themselves," Matt added.

Abercrombie's smile slipped before stretching again. He lifted his chin and peered down his nose and through his pince-nez at me. "Of course, the rules are irrelevant if the Mason boy doesn't pass the guild's entry test."

"You'll fail him just to get revenge upon me?" I snapped. "Are you truly that cruel?"

"Make no mistake, Miss Steele," Mr. Abercrombie said, voice harsh, "I know why you're installing your friends in the shop. You accuse me of going to great lengths for revenge, but *you* are the one who seeks revenge on *us* because you feel rejected by the guild."

"I do not!"

He scoffed. "Of course you do. Your father told me how

bitter you were when your application wasn't approved. Indeed, he shouted it at a Court of Assistants meeting he burst into."

Rage flashed before my eyes, blood-red and hot. "You are a petty, small man." I wanted to say more, but my mind was too fogged with fury and I couldn't think of the right words.

Mr. Abercrombie smiled, all slick and supercilious.

I shut the door in his face.

Matt circled his arm around my waist from behind. His lips brushed my temple above my ear. "Want me to punch him?"

I leaned back into his chest and released a ragged breath. "I know you're joking, but it is tempting." I drew in another deep breath and let it out slowly, releasing some of my anger with it. "I want you to think of a way to wipe that smile off his face in a non-violent manner."

"The only way to do that is to get Ronnie into the guild."

"Then we've got some thinking to do," Cyclops said.

I'd forgotten he and Duke were there. I pulled away from Matt and took Cyclops's hand. "Catherine will be upset to know the guild is trying so hard to thwart them."

"So you don't want to tell her?" he asked. "That ain't a good idea, India. She should know."

"They both should," Duke added.

I sighed. "You're right. But let's not tell them today. Let them have another day of happiness. It'll give us time to think of what to do."

The door opened and Willie strolled in, wearing the same clothes as the night before. Her hair was unbound, falling in tangles around her shoulders, and her neckerchief was missing. I didn't need to question her to know what she'd been up to.

"Are you just coming home now?" I asked.

"Sure am." She grinned. "That shock you?"

"Not in the least. I've grown quite used to it. But do try to be discreet. The servants don't want to work in a disreputable household."

"Ha!" she barked. "They'll work wherever they're paid the most, and Matt's a good employer." She slapped his shoulder. "Did you leave me any breakfast, Cyclops?"

"There's plenty," he said. "I'll let the kitchen know."

"Where have you been anyway?" Duke asked, walking alongside her to the staircase. "With Annie Oakley?"

"Some of the night."

"And the rest?"

She pressed a finger to her lips and shushed him. "A girl never tells."

He sniffed her. "You still drunk?"

"Drunk on life, old friend."

He groaned. "Sometimes I miss the miserable Willie."

She hugged him and noticed Matt and I following them up the stairs. "You all coming to watch me eat breakfast?"

"You have to help us think," Matt said. "There's been a situation, in your absence."

"Sure." She threw her arms wide, and Duke just managed to dodge being smacked in the head. "I'm a great thinker after drinking a few beers. And liquor."

"This will be interesting," I muttered to Matt. "Where do you think she went after leaving Annie?"

"Scotland Yard, perhaps, to brush up on her investigative skills." He laughed at my gasp. "Or lodgings not far from there."

* * *

THE AFTERNOON PASSED by in a dreamy haze. The day wasn't too hot, so Miss Glass and I went for a stroll through Hyde Park. Even though the weather was pleasant, and our walk slow, she found it taxing. We rested often on the many seats positioned in the shade and watched others enjoying picnics by the Serpentine, or boating on it. It was a nice way to spend the day in the middle of an investigation. Much nicer than visiting Lady Rycroft and her daughters. Thankfully, Miss Glass had received word that her sister-in-law was still at Rycroft Hall. The letter stated they planned to return to London in two weeks and regretted they could not attend our wedding due to pressing estate matters.

They hadn't been invited.

By the time we returned to number sixteen Park Street, Willie had woken and Matt had finished attending to his business matters. Willie and I settled in Matt's office to think of ways to extract information about the mysterious blonde from the New Somerville Club members and staff. By Willie and I, I meant mostly me. She slouched in an armchair and inspected her fingernails, her booted feet resting on a table. I tossed out ideas for conversational topics to use on potential witnesses, and she grunted her approval or rejection. It was a different type of grunt for each. I knew Willie well enough to know the short sharp one meant yes and the long one meant no. I wrote the approved topics on a piece of paper. Once I'd run out of ideas, I counted the number. Only five.

"You need to be less discerning," I told her.

It turned out that I didn't know Willie very well, after all. She came up with a third type of grunt, the meaning of which I couldn't fathom. I was about to ask her when there was a knock on the door.

Peter entered and announced a visitor. "Mr. Barratt is here, madam. Mr. Glass asked for you to join them in the drawing room."

"Thank you, Fossett. Please see that tea is brought in."

I left Willie to her slouching and grunting and headed to

the drawing room. I heard Matt and Oscar before I entered, even through the closed door.

"It was you!" Oscar shouted. "It had to be. No one else knew."

"Calm down," Matt snarled. "It wasn't me."

I opened the door and ordered them to keep their voices down. Matt looked relieved to see me, whereas Oscar merely scowled. "What are you two arguing about?"

"Your fiancé is sabotaging my book," Oscar said.

Matt shook his head and muttered under his breath.

"Sit down," I said. They both sat. "Oscar, how is Matt supposedly sabotaging your book?"

"The printer is ignoring me. He sends every letter back unopened and pretends to be out when I call on him. You two were the only ones aside from Nash who knew about the printer, and I doubt *you* want to stop my book, India."

"Matt doesn't either."

Matt said nothing.

"See!" Oscar cried. "He won't even deny it."

"I can deny it if you want, but you won't believe me," Matt said.

"That is not a denial."

I stood between them, hands on hips. "So you've finished the book? It's ready for printing?"

"I'm still in the planning and research phase," Oscar said more calmly. "I hope to start the actual writing next week."

"Then it could take weeks to finish. Months, even. Is that correct?"

"Correct."

"Then why are you so worried about this printer ignoring you? Commission another printer."

"There are no other printers! Not—" He broke off as Bristow wheeled in the tea trolley.

The short break seemed to dampen Oscar's fire a little,

but as soon as Bristow left, he shot to his feet. He pointed at Matt. "This is your fault, Glass. I know it."

I pressed a cup and saucer into his hands. "Sit down or you'll spill tea on the carpet and I'll be most upset." He sat. "Now, as I recall, the printer was operating illegally because he didn't have a license from The Stationer's Guild. So perhaps he simply had second thoughts about printing your book. Perhaps he's worried it'll draw attention to his operation."

"The voice of reason," Matt said, accepting a cup. "India's offering you a more logical and likely explanation than the one you jumped to. I can assure you, Barratt, I am not in the habit of destroying the livelihood of a man I've never met. Not even to annoy you."

Oscar didn't seem convinced, but he managed to keep his thoughts to himself as he sipped his tea. "He seemed keen to print my book up until a few days ago," he finally said. "Something must have happened, or why else would he suddenly change his mind?"

"How do you know it was sudden?" I asked. "He might have been telling you one thing while secretly considering how dangerous it could be to his business."

"Are you sure you didn't tell anyone else about the book?" Matt asked.

"I'm sure," Oscar said.

"What about Nash? Can you trust him?"

Oscar didn't look quite so certain anymore. "I've just come from seeing him. He assured me it wasn't him, but the truth is, I just don't know him well enough. He's also artless."

"His grandfather was a magician," I said. "And the professor has a keen interest in magic. I doubt he'd do anything to jeopardize the book."

"I doubt it too." He watched Matt over the rim of his cup.

"It wasn't me," Matt said again. "You have my word."

Oscar's entire body heaved with his deep breath. "Then I apologize, Glass. I'm very busy these days—with work, the book, and so many magicians approaching me for advice. And of course, there are ongoing family battles. It's a little overwhelming, and I've become short tempered."

"What sort of advice are the magicians seeking?" I asked.

"Mostly whether to tell the truth about their magic. Some have asked how to find you, India. They want you to extend their magic."

"You'd better not tell them," Matt growled.

"I haven't and I wouldn't. Not unless India wishes it."

So far only one magician had come to number sixteen Park Street to ask me to extend his magic. The leather worker had discovered my address quite by chance from his friend who worked at The Cross Keys tavern, where my grandfather regularly drank. He'd realized Chronos's connection to me after reading Oscar's article in *The Weekly Gazette*. He had not returned, thankfully, but if Oscar started telling magicians how to find me, I might be inundated with requests.

"How many magicians have approached you?" I asked.

"About ten."

That wasn't such a great number, after all. I suspected London housed hundreds of magicians. Perhaps most didn't want to extend their magic or didn't want to bring it to light. It was impossible to gauge the general feeling.

"I met an interesting magician recently, as it happens," Oscar went on.

His mysterious tone should have been a warning, but I barreled headlong into the trap with naivety. "Who?" I asked, offering up the plate of cakes.

"A magical language expert from the continent asked me

where to find your grandfather. I believe you met him, India."

All the breath left my body. I twisted in the chair to see Matt frowning at me. He righted the plate I'd managed to tilt and picked up the cake that had fallen on the floor.

"India hasn't met a magic language expert," Matt said without taking his gaze off me. "Have you, India?"

I swallowed but my throat was too tight and the ball of guilt lodged there was too big. Matt's jaw firmed.

"She has," Oscar said, somewhat delightedly. "His name's Fabian Charbonneau. Her grandfather introduced them. Didn't you know, Glass? Charbonneau wants to teach India the language so she can create new spells. According to him, she's a spell caster."

I felt as though a noose were closing around my throat; each word from Barratt's mouth tightened it. But it wasn't nearly as horrible as watching Matt's eyes grow darker and darker. He didn't speak. He didn't ask me if it were true, or for an explanation; he simply set the plate of cakes on the table.

"It's time for you to go, Barratt," he said with an exaggerated calmness that sent a chill skittering down my spine.

Oscar pushed himself out of the chair. "Of course. India, you know where to reach me if you need to talk about Charbonneau's—" He cleared his throat as Matt turned an icy glare onto him. "Never mind."

He shut the door behind him, leaving me alone with a seething Matt.

CHAPTER 11

I busied myself with the tea things, not daring to look at Matt. I didn't need to see him to know his opinion. I could feel the waves of anger vibrating off him.

"I meant to tell you," I said as I stacked empty cups on the trolley. "There just wasn't a good time."

"Then find a bad time," he snapped. "You should have told me, India, instead of letting me hear it from *him*."

"I know. I'm sorry."

"I'm going to be your husband. You don't think that's reason enough to tell me about something as important as this?"

"I would have told you, Matt."

"When?"

"When I was ready."

"You mean when you'd decided whether to take this Charbonneau fellow up on his offer or not." He squeezed his eyes shut. When he reopened them again, I was reminded of the old Matt, where he was sick and tired all the time. I hated that I'd caused this change in him.

"I haven't been thinking about it," I said heavily. "I didn't want to. It's...overwhelming."

I stared down at the teacup in my hand but hardly saw it through my tear-filled eyes. I hated arguing with Matt. I hated it even more when the argument was my fault.

Matt took the cup from me and grasped my shoulders. "This is why I want you to come to me. Not because I want to tell you what to do, but because I want to share some of the burden." He tugged me closer and settled his arms around me, enveloping me in a warm hug. "I'm marrying you because I want to share your life, and that means the difficult parts of it too."

I bit my wobbling lip and tried not to spill tears into his waistcoat. I didn't deserve to be forgiven so easily, but I wanted to believe that I did deserve such a good man.

Matt didn't rush me to speak, and I waited for the ache in my throat to ease. Then I pulled away and sat on the sofa. He sat beside me.

"Fabian Charbonneau is a Frenchman with a strong magical lineage." I smoothed my skirt over my lap then clasped my hands. "He's one of the few who know the language of magic, although his knowledge is not complete. Despite being an expert, he can't create new spells. That requires a magician with magic instincts, someone the magic responds to."

"And he thinks you are that magician?"

I nodded.

"Why does he want to create new spells?"

"Well..." I began, but did not go on. It was a good question. Indeed, it was the only relevant question. Why indeed. "To see if it's possible, I suppose." Even as I said it, I doubted my answer.

And if I did somehow manage to create a new spell, then what? What would be done with that spell? Who would use it? And would Fabian want me to create another and another? For what purpose?

Matt didn't ask me any of those questions, although I knew he must be thinking them too. He simply placed his hand over mine and stroked my knuckles with his thumb.

I leaned against him, my head on his shoulder. "We can expect Fabian and Chronos to call on me soon."

"Then you'd better think about a response."

I preferred not to think about it at all, but he was right. It was best to be prepared. The problem was, I didn't know what I wanted to do.

* * *

THE NEW SOMERVILLE Club for ladies was a revelation. It was quite small, with a parlor, a reading room and another room set out with chairs and a lectern where the lecture would take place. The reading room was well appointed with recent issues of a variety of magazines, newspapers and periodicals. The armchairs looked comfortable, although the upholstery was frayed at the seams and the curtains faded. I had expected something either overtly feminine with floral wallpaper, or too masculine where smoking was allowed and there wasn't a cushion in sight. I liked this happy middle.

Willie and I arrived early to join up and talk to the staff. There were very few, with only two maids setting out glasses and jugs of water. The only other two staff members were the president of the club and the treasurer. Both appeared too busy to speak to us as they arranged furniture in the lecture room. I wasn't sure how to proceed, but Willie took the lead. Unfortunately she didn't begin with any of the conversation starters we'd noted down earlier. I knew she hadn't been listening.

"A friend asked us to meet her here," she said as she followed Mrs. Broxham the president around the room.

Mrs. Broxham was a short, plump woman with a clipboard in one hand, a pencil behind her ear, and a no-nonsense manner about her. She marched from one side of the room to the other, pointing at chairs that needed to be moved. Miss Ovington, the treasurer, rushed to do Mrs. Broxham's bidding, only Mrs. Broxham was too quick and moved on to the next instruction before Miss Ovington had finished the previous one.

"Maybe you know her," Willie persisted. "She's a member here."

"What's her name?" Mrs. Broxham asked, checking her clipboard.

Willie opened her mouth then shut it again. She hadn't thought this through at all.

"It's a little embarrassing," I said. "We can't recall it."

"Lizzie, that chair needs to move closer. We have to fit another five in," Mrs. Broxham said.

Miss Ovington wove her way between chairs with the precision and grace of a dancer, her arms raised to chest height to avoid bumping anything. She moved the offending chair closer to the one next to it.

"Too close," Mrs. Broxham said, and Miss Ovington moved it back. "What does your friend look like?" she asked us.

She had somehow made it to the opposite side of the room without me noticing. I picked up my skirts and trailed after her.

"She's blonde," I said. "Quite tall with a trim figure, and very pretty. Oh, and American. Perhaps you remember her now. She has a strong accent and isn't easy to forget."

"Not there, Lizzie. *There*." Mrs. Broxham removed the pencil from behind her ear and wrote something on her clipboard. "I do remember her, as it happens. She came to the previous lecture, but I don't remember her name. I wouldn't call her very pretty, though."

"I would," Miss Ovington said, carrying a chair to the other side of the room. "But I don't remember her name either, sorry."

"Can you check the register?" I asked. "We feel awful for not remembering her name and don't want to make fools of ourselves tonight if she comes."

"There wouldn't be any point," Mrs. Broxham said. "There were probably ten ladies at last week's lecture that I've never seen before. Some signed up as new members and others came as guests. I don't remember which your friend was. It could be any of those ten." She pointed at individual chairs with her pencil, her lips moving as she counted.

"What about you, Lizzie?" Willie asked the treasurer.

Miss Ovington looked shocked that Willie had used her first name to address her. "I can't help you, I'm afraid," she mumbled.

Willie followed her out while I contemplated tearing the page from last week's register to get the names of the ten newcomers. The problem was, there'd be far more than ten on there that I didn't know. Going by the chairs in the lecture hall, they were expecting sixty attendees tonight.

Mrs. Broxham suddenly clapped her hands, making my nerves jump. "Lizzie!" she snapped. "Stop gossiping and bring in those chairs."

Willie helped Miss Ovington with the chairs while I contemplated how best to learn the name and whereabouts of the mysterious woman. The president hurried out of the room, and when I went to look for her, she'd disappeared. One of the maids said she'd gone downstairs to speak to the tearoom staff.

Members and their guests soon trickled in. Mrs.

175

Broxham returned with her clipboard and peered over Miss Ovington's shoulder as she wrote names in the ledger, correcting her when she made a mistake, which was often.

I accepted my pamphlet from the woman by the door and joined Willie in the lecture room. We found seats together at the back.

"This is hopeless," Willie whined. "We ain't never going to find her."

"She might show up," I said, watching the first of the members trickle in.

"What if she doesn't?"

"We'll ask around at the interval. Someone may remember her from last week. In the meantime, we get to be enlightened by an intellectual lecture." I checked my pamphlet. "'The effect on the brain of street noises,'" I read.

Willie groaned.

The lecture was quite interesting. A doctor spoke about the brain's structure, followed by another medical professional to tell us about the results of his study into the effects of loud and incessant noises on both the brain and behavior. He concluded that people who live in the city where the noise levels were higher than in the country, needed to leave the city from time to time or risk going mad.

"His voice is driving me mad," Willie muttered.

I was surprised she was still awake. She'd sunk further and further into her chair over the hour and, at one point, I thought I'd heard snoring.

The audience applauded as the first part of the evening came to an end and refreshments were announced. We filed out of the lecture room to the parlor, where sandwiches and fruit cake had been brought up from the tearoom.

Willie and I separated to divide and conquer. I tried to be subtle, and avoided breaking into conversations, but as time wore on and the window allotted to the refreshment break closed, I cut people off mid-sentence to question them. Finally I met a group of women eager to talk about the American friend they'd met at the previous lecture.

"I remember her," said one. "We had a conversation about her homeland."

"So did I," her companion said. "We stood right in this very spot. She was uncommonly pretty."

"She was reasonably pretty, I suppose, but in an understated way."

"Oh, I thought she was extraordinary," the third woman commented.

The second woman looked at her friends like they were blind. "She didn't say much. Indeed, she didn't really seem interested in our conversation. I think she was looking for someone."

"Was she alone?" I asked.

"Yes."

"No, she was with a friend," said the first woman. "Her landlady is a member here, but I don't believe she's here tonight."

"That's right," said the third.

The second woman shook her head. "She was definitely alone. She complained about the membership fee for joining on the night. If she'd been a guest of her landlady, she wouldn't have needed to join and pay the higher fee. She could have paid the lower one. You must be mistaken because she was quite alone. I distinctly remember her complaining about everything. The cost, the food, the lecture. I walked off after five minutes, particularly when she didn't seem to be listening to a word I said. That must have been when she joined you both."

The first and third woman both looked at one another. "I found her delightful," said one, and her friend agreed.

They must have been talking about two different women. "I'm asking about the blonde American," I said.

"Yes," all three chimed.

I blinked. Blinked again. And then the answer hit me like a brick. *May Draper* must have been here that night too! She must have been the one complaining about the cost who'd come alone, and the other was the mystery beauty, the guest of her landlady.

I turned to the two who'd spoken to the mystery woman. "Do either of you recall her name or that of the member she came with?"

One shook her head. The other said, "I think it was Dot or Dotty."

"I'm looking for her, as it happens. It's quite important that I find her. Did she mention where she's lodging?"

Both shook their heads.

I found Willie chatting to a group of women near the table of food. She had a sandwich in one hand and a slice of cake in another. She saw me and grinned.

Mrs. Broxham announced the refreshment break was over and it was time to return to the lecture room. Willie shoved the sandwich into her mouth and tucked the cake into her coat pocket before she joined me.

"You'll never believe it," I said as the room emptied.

Willie mumbled something unintelligible around her mouthful of food.

"She was here, but so was May Draper," I said.

"I know," Willie managed to say.

"Did you find out the mystery woman's name?"

"Dotty."

"Her last name?"

She shook her head.

"Apparently she came with her landlady," I went on. "But she's not here tonight."

Willie wiped her mouth with her sleeve. "Damn."

"Quite. Come on, we'd better return to the lecture."

"Not me. I need a drink and something better to listen to than that boring old coot." She lowered her voice as the last of the women left the room. "This ain't what I thought it would be like."

"What did you think it would be like?"

"A saloon, but with only women."

I linked her arm with mine and together we slipped out of the club while Mrs. Broxham was busy giving orders to clear the refreshment room.

"May hasn't been completely honest with us," I said once outside.

"She's a cheat, like her husband. What'd you expect?"

Oxford Street felt otherworldly in the evenings. During the day, the road and pavements were thick with traffic and pedestrians, but at night, only a few dining premises remained open. The glow from the streetlights held the shadows back and illuminated the shop window displays. The warmth of the day had been trapped in the city by the blanket of cloud, and it would have been a pleasant walk home, but Matt had insisted we take the carriage.

"Think I'll go out for a drink," Willie said. She did not climb into the cabin but remained on the pavement, her gaze focused in the middle distance.

I followed it, peering into the ethereal light cast by the streetlamps. "Willie? Have you seen someone?"

"Don't know. Did you feel like we were being followed on the way here?"

"No. Did you?"

"Maybe. I don't know. I saw a carriage that I thought followed us, but then it drove on after we stopped."

If I were following someone, I'd drive on after they stopped too, to avoid notice. "Do you see that carriage again?" I asked, checking the vicinity. There were two carriages stopped some distance behind us. One appeared to be a hansom, the other a larger vehicle pulled by two horses.

"Don't know," she said, climbing in. "Let's drive off and see if any follow."

She thumped the ceiling and the coachman gave the order to the horse to move on. We watched through the rear window all the way home. No carriages followed all the way; one did take the same route for part of the journey but turned left where we turned right. It had not, however, been one of the carriages parked behind us on Oxford Street.

"What do you think?" I asked as we alighted at Park Street.

"I think you're going inside to report to Matt and I'm off to find someone to have fun with."

"Annie Oakely?"

She gave me a sly smile. "Maybe."

She didn't give the coachman instructions until I was out of earshot on the front stoop. Where she went was her own business, but I was wildly curious. Her secrecy only intrigued me more, although it wouldn't surprise me if she were keeping secrets just to irk me.

THE FOLLOWING MORNING, Matt and I were about to leave the house to speak to May Draper before she left for the day's show, but the arrival of Chronos and Fabian delayed our departure.

"We can tell them to come back later," I said to Matt when Bristow announced them.

"I want to speak to them now," he said. "This is more important."

I didn't agree but kept my mouth shut as he asked Bristow to show them into the drawing room. We met them there two minutes later and had just finished introductions when Bristow announced another visitor.

"Mr. Hendry is here with your wedding invitations, sir," the butler intoned. "Shall I ask him to wait?"

"I don't know how long we'll be, and I know he's busy," Matt said. "Tell him we'll collect the invitations from his shop later and pay for them at the same time."

"Surely he can leave them," Chronos said. "He'll know you're not going to avoid paying him."

"We're trying to build trust between us," I said.

"And it'll give us an excuse to call on him again and ask questions related to our investigation," Matt added.

Bristow bowed out and closed the door behind him.

I smiled at Fabian. "Forgive us for not offering you tea but we have a pressing engagement this morning. I hope you understand."

"Should I return later?" he asked, rising.

"No," both Matt and Chronos said. "We prefer to get this over with," Matt added.

Fabian dipped his chin in a nod. "You are worried, Mr. Glass. Chronos warned me you would be upset by my presence in your home."

"Upset is not quite the scale of it," Matt said. "And I prefer you weren't in the country, let alone my house, but here we are and we must deal with you as best we can."

Fabian's brow creased. "Deal with me?"

"An American phrase."

Fabian seemed unperturbed by Matt's rudeness. Indeed, he seemed prepared for it. I hoped he'd come prepared with answers too, because we had a lot of questions.

"You are the man with the magic watch," Fabian said. "May I see it?"

"No," Matt said.

Fabian merely smiled, unperturbed. "You look very well, very healthy."

"Enough about me. We want you to answer our questions."

Chronos huffed out a breath. "India, may we speak privately?"

"Anything you wish to say can be said in front of Matt," I said. "As my future husband, this concerns him too."

Chronos clasped his hands together, like a preacher urging his congregation to see the light. "I like you, Glass. You're a good man, and India is lucky to be marrying the heir to a barony. But you are not a magician. You don't understand her needs."

Matt arched his brows. "And you do? You've known her for less time than I have."

Chronos didn't seem concerned to be reminded of his abandonment of me when I was a baby. "Let me explain it to you. India needs to use her magic. It's a compulsion, an itch she must scratch. If she doesn't use her magic, a restless sensation builds and builds inside until it bursts forth."

"What rot," I scoffed. "I didn't use magic for twenty-four years, and I felt nothing like what you're describing."

"You were using your magic all the time in the shop, you just didn't know it. Since leaving the shop, you hardly use it at all, because you're not working on watches and clocks. Believe me, the restlessness will soon become noticeable."

"I work on my new watch all the time. I've even used the spell you gave me. I can do that whenever I want, whenever I experience this restlessness you speak of."

"It won't be enough. Soon, your own watch will become a part of you, and too easy to fix. You'll need a challenge."

"Then I'll buy her a clock and she can tinker with that," Matt said.

Chronos turned to me. "So you won't take Fabian up on his offer?"

"I have some questions I'd like him to answer," I said. "We both do. Firstly, I want to know who told you about me."

Fabian hesitated before saying, "Lady Louisa Hollingbroke. I believe you have met her."

I wasn't surprised to hear it had been her. Her interest in magic extended beyond collecting magical objects. She had been the first to tell me about the language of magic.

"How do you know her?" I asked.

"Her father conducted business with my father. We have written to one another for years but met for the first time the day I arrived in London. She warned me you would not be easily convinced about your role."

"My role in what?"

"Not *in* what," Chronos said. "*As* what. Your role as a spell caster."

"Your role as my student," Fabian added. "Now, you have questions. Begin, please. What do you wish to know?"

"Why do you need a spell caster?" I asked.

"To see if it is possible to create new spells at all."

"Yes, but *why* create new spells?"

"How can I put this?" He paused and focused on a framed painting of a snow-capped mountain range hanging on the wall. "Why does a man climb the tallest mountain? Because it is there, and no one yet knows if it is possible until he reaches the summit."

I wasn't sure if it was quite the same thing. "And if I do manage to create a new spell, what will it be used for?"

"That depends on the spell, *naturellement*. It may not be used at all. It may be written down and filed away. Without knowing the spells you will create, it is impossible to say."

"You're being evasive," Matt said.

"I am afraid I cannot be otherwise. I know this troubles

you, Mr. Glass, but let me reassure you. India will decide what happens to every spell she creates." Fabian turned to me. "Is that what you wish, India?"

"It helps," I hedged.

"Of course it does," Chronos said. "You will be in control, India. Never forget that. What woman doesn't wish that, eh? My wife certainly did." He chuckled but it withered beneath my glare.

"What's stopping you from using the new spells for your own gain?" Matt asked Fabian.

"I am a man of honor. I would not promise you one thing then do the other."

"How do we know we can trust you?"

Most men would be offended at having their honor questioned, but Fabian took it in his stride. "That is a good question, and one I cannot answer for you. You must decide. Perhaps investigate me." His eyes crinkled at the corners with his smile. "It is what you are good at, no?" At Matt's lack of response, Fabian's smile faded.

"They are all the questions we have for now," I said. "If you don't mind, we have work to do."

"Of course, of course." Fabian rose and buttoned up his jacket. "Please, Mr. Glass, do not keep India from this."

It irked me that he assumed it was up to Matt to make the decision for me. Clearly Chronos hadn't explained our relationship very well.

"She is a great magician," Fabian went on, his accent thicker. "She is powerful and can be a very great magician. If you love her, you would want that for her, yes?"

Matt's dry chuckle held not a shred of humor. "So if I refuse her, I don't love her? Is that the message you want her to hear?"

"*Non, non, non.*" Fabian placed his hand on his chest, over his heart. "Not at all. You do not understand. My English..."

"I'll let you in on a secret." Matt leaned closer conspiratorially but did not lower his voice. "She doesn't like it when people assume I make the decisions for her, and I can assure you, this decision will be hers."

"With your advice freely given, no doubt," Chronos bit back.

Matt straightened. He was no longer smiling, not even cruelly.

Fabian looked like a gentleman who'd stepped in a horse's deposit with no gracious means of removing it from his shoe. He simply backed away, bowed to me, and left.

Chronos, however, lingered. Knowing him, he probably wanted to stay for lunch, even though it was hours away. I ought to do the right thing and invite him. A good hostess would. Miss Glass would, even though she disliked Chronos. People like her were used to entertaining guests they disliked. It seemed to be a burden her class bore with relative ease. I was not of her class, though.

"That wasn't necessary, Glass," Chronos said with all the authority of a father chastising his son. "He's not bad, for a Frenchman, and you can't blame him for thinking you'll be making up India's mind for her."

"Why can't I blame him for that?" Matt asked. "Perhaps his attitude ought to change."

Chronos threw his hands up and walked off. "There's no reasoning with you when you're in this mood. Good luck dealing with him today, India. You're going to need it."

I suspected he was right.

CHAPTER 12

We managed to catch May and Danny Draper just as they were leaving for the Earls Court Exhibition Ground. The show wasn't scheduled to start for another three hours, but Danny insisted they needed that much time to prepare.

He brushed past us on the pavement, but Matt grabbed his arm, while I blocked May's exit from the Childs Street house.

"We have some questions for you," Matt said.

"We have nothing more to say to you," Danny spat.

"Don't make me use force to extract answers."

Danny swallowed. Matt simply smiled.

"You're not the police," May said, trying to push past me.

I moved to block her again. I was taller, and I liked to think that made me somewhat intimidating. But she only stopped trying to pass me when she glanced at Matt. I suspected his foul mood had more to do with subduing her than my presence.

"If you don't co-operate, we will assume you killed Emmett," I said.

That got the response I wanted. May's eyes widened and her jaw went slack. "B—but...we didn't!"

"Then why are you hindering our investigation?"

"We're not," Danny said.

"Your wife is. She didn't tell us she met with the blonde woman, Dotty. She knew we were searching for her—"

"I did not!" May cried.

"You knew," Matt growled. "We've wasted our time looking for her, and I do *not* like wasting time."

May stepped back from the threshold. I followed, crowding her so that she took another step back. Matt thrust Danny through the door and followed him. He slammed the door shut.

"Tell us about Dotty," I said. "If you don't, we'll leave you to Scotland Yard's men. They'll have no qualms detaining you until you give them answers."

May hesitated.

"Tell them!" Danny urged her. "Or they'll think we killed Emmett."

"All right." May put up her hands, warding us off. "Dotty was Emmett's girl, back home. She followed him to England and their relationship continued for a short while. It was all very secretive."

"Why?"

"Because he has a wife."

"Why did you go to the New Somerville Club to speak to Dotty?" Matt asked.

"I heard she was going to a lecture there. I didn't know where else to find her so I went too. She avoided me all night, but I caught up to her outside afterward. I wanted to ask her why she and Emmett ended their relationship. I knew she had, because whenever I saw her outside our lodgings, she would glare up at his window. She looked mad. I wanted to find out why."

187

"I don't understand why you would care," I said.

May lifted one shoulder.

"So she could blackmail Emmett," Matt filled in. "She hoped to learn something that she could use to force Emmett to include Danny in his cheating scheme again."

"What scheme?" May asked, too innocently.

Neither Matt nor I bothered to answer her. "So did Dotty tell you why their relationship ended?" I asked.

One side of May's mouth curled up. "She's with child. His child. When she told him, he refused to believe it was his. He told her to get rid of it as he wouldn't give her money and he couldn't marry her."

That explained why she glared angrily at Emmett at the pub and liked it when Duke punched him.

"Bill Cody doesn't want that kind of scandal getting out," she went on. "He would fire Emmett if the newspapers reported it."

"So you threatened to tell Bill Cody if Emmett didn't include Danny in his scheme again," I said. "Did he try to silence you and you shot him?"

"No, no, that's not what happened," Danny said, standing with May. He took her hand, but she snatched it away. His shoulders sagged. He looked every bit the pouting youth denied a treat.

"You're partly right." May crossed her arms. "Yes, I spoke to Dotty so I could find something to blackmail Emmett with. But I didn't approach Emmett. I was worried he'd get angry and began having doubts. He has a temper. A violent one. I didn't tell you before for this very reason—you would assume I'd killed him."

"Thank you for telling us," I said. "It's best to be honest so we can concentrate on finding the real killer. So you both knew Emmett was cheating at poker, is that correct?"

Danny sighed and nodded. May nodded too. "We don't

know how he did it," she said. "He wouldn't reveal his secrets. Do you want to know where to find Dotty? I can tell you, if you like. She gave me her address in the hope that I would spy on Emmett for her and feed her information about him. She was jealous and wanted him to herself."

I wrote down the address on the notepad I carried in my reticle. It wasn't too far away. We could visit next.

"I know you think Dotty killed Emmett," May said with a troubled frown. "But treat her gently. She's with child"

"You think I'd manhandle a woman?" Matt asked.

May gave a small shrug. "You've been rough with Danny."

"As far as I'm aware, he's not a woman."

Danny laughed nervously. "Some say she does wear the trousers in our relationship."

May glared at him and his smile vanished.

"One more thing," Matt said. "Where were you really on the night of Emmett's death?"

"Walking with Danny," she said without missing a beat. "I believe he told you that, Mr. Glass."

Matt's lips thinned. "I'll make a guess and say you didn't see anyone on your walk except a drunk or two who wouldn't remember you, even if we managed to find them."

"That would be a good guess."

I didn't believe her, and nor did Matt. "She didn't accompany him on his walk," I said as we returned to the carriage.

"He didn't go for a walk," he said.

I gave Dotty's address to the driver and we climbed in. Matt removed his hat and raked his hand through his hair, leaving it delightfully tousled.

"May could be setting Dotty up to take the blame for Emmett's murder," he said, staring out of the window. "She gave us the address too readily."

"And mentioned her jealousy. Why wait until now to place the blame on her?"

"Because she just realized she's the prime suspect in the murder. That's why she admitted everything—the cheating, the blackmail—and wants to shift blame to someone else. Dotty's the most obvious alternative."

"Do you think May is innocent?"

"Not in the least, but I'm not sure she's guilty of murder, either." He hadn't turned from the window during our conversation. Either he was particularly interested in the scenery or he was avoiding looking at me.

"Are you all right?" I asked, taking his arm.

"Fine."

"You're still thinking about Fabian Charbonneau."

"I am."

"We should talk about the possibility of me being a spell caster and what it means." I hugged his arm.

"Not here."

I sighed. He was right; it wasn't the best place, and we were almost at Dotty's, but it did feel as though he was avoiding the conversation. I could hardly blame him when I had avoided the conversation for so long too.

"Later, then."

He put his arm around my shoulders. "Later."

* * *

DOTTY'S LANDLADY hadn't seen her since she left the house on the previous Thursday evening—the night Emmett was murdered. "I'm quite worried about her," she said as she stood in the doorway of her modest terrace house. "It's been almost a week."

"Did she take her things?" Matt asked.

The landlady's gaze narrowed. "Why do you ask?"

"We're trying to find her."

"Why? Who are you?"

"My name is Matthew Glass, and this is India Steele. We're private inquiry agents helping Scotland Yard in the murder of Emmett Cocker."

"Murder!" She clutched her throat. "That's nothing to do with Dotty. She's a good girl."

"We only want to ask her some questions about him," I said.

"I don't believe you do work for Scotland Yard. When I reported her missing they said nothing about her involvement in a murder." She tried to close the door but Matt put his hand against it. The landlady slipped further behind the door and peered around it at us.

"Can we take a look at her room?" Matt asked.

"Certainly not. If the police want to look through it then they may do so. Not you."

We left her and drove to the Victoria Embankment, but Brockwell wasn't in his office. One of the constables said he was making inquiries all day and wasn't expected back at New Scotland Yard until late afternoon. He suggested we return tomorrow.

"Doesn't he want to solve this damn murder?" Matt muttered as we returned to the carriage.

I quickened my pace to keep up with his long strides. "I'm sure his inquiries are important too. Be fair, Matt. He can't be everywhere at once."

His only response was to lengthen his strides more.

Our journey home was conducted in silence. I was acutely aware of him sitting beside me, staring out the window, his temper simmering away just beneath the surface. I suspected one little word would set it off, so I didn't speak. I'd wait for his temper to cool and his reason to return.

When we arrived home, and I finally looked at him, I was surprised to see that he hadn't been brooding at all. He'd been sleeping. That worried me more.

"Matt, wake up," I said, shaking him gently.

He frowned sleepily and looked through the window. Then without a word, he opened the door and offered me his hand.

"Are you unwell?" I asked, stepping out.

"No."

"But—"

"I'm fine, India. I just need to use my watch."

My stomach dropped and an immense weight pressed down on me. "But...my spell, and Gabe's...they're no longer working?"

He clasped my hand. "It has been several weeks since I needed to use the watch. This is normal. It's how it was last time after Chronos and Dr. Parsons performed their magic."

"Oh."

"I expected to use it every few weeks. At least it's not every few hours." He managed a smile.

He was right; I shouldn't be worried. Yet part of me had hoped that my spell would be strong enough that he wouldn't need to use the watch again for some time— perhaps ever. I was a fool to think my magic was *that* powerful.

Clearly Fabian and the others were wrong about me.

We were surprised to find Catherine and Ronnie Mason waiting for us in the drawing room, though not as surprised as Cyclops, who arrived home five minutes later. Once the shock wore off, however, he glowered at me as if I had invited her and deliberately not told him.

"Catherine and Ronnie were here when Matt and I got home," I said huffily. "Come in and sit down, Cyclops. They were just about to tell us their news."

"I don't think that's wise," Cyclops said. "I should go."

"Do stop avoiding me," Catherine said snippily.

"I'm..." He swallowed beneath her stern glare and plopped down on the nearest chair.

"That's better. I don't like that you're avoiding me, Nate. Not now, when I need your wisdom and broad shoulders to lean on."

Cyclops's face lifted. He seemed quite pleased to hear her refer to his shoulders as broad. Her brother simply stared at her, unblinking.

"Is this about the guild?" Cyclops asked.

She sighed. "It is. We've just come from the hall where we had a meeting with Mr. Abercrombie. He informed us we couldn't use any of your stock, India, if we are to obtain a license."

"He was here yesterday," I said. "They added new rules to the guild's constitution forbidding members to sell stock made by magicians. I am sorry. We should have immediately informed you."

"You've been busy, I understand. But what are we to do?"

"Nothing," Ronnie grumbled. "We can't afford to buy stock at full price. Not the amount we're going to need."

"You can still use the tools and other equipment," I said, looking to Matt.

"And I'm going to give you an interest-free loan," he added.

Catherine gasped.

Ronnie began to shake his head then stopped. He got up and offered his hand to Matt. "Thank you, sir. I was about to refuse but that would be foolish. We'll take you up on your offer."

"That's not wise," Matt said, shaking his hand. "Not without asking questions first. There could have been conditions attached."

Ronnie's face fell. "Are there?"

"No, but you should still have asked."

"I will, next time I'm offered a business deal that seems too good to be true."

Catherine threw her arms around me. "I'm hugging you because it would be inappropriate to hug Matt," she said.

I laughed. "I like to think I had something to do with it, but it was all his idea." I pulled away and felt awful for what I was about to say. I didn't want to dampen her spirits. "Abercrombie won't make it easy for you to get your license, Ronnie. He made it very clear the test will be so difficult that you'll fail."

"Don't worry about me," he said smugly. "I'll be prepared."

"His knowledge is very good," Catherine said. "He'll do well at the written part of the test, and the practical part shouldn't be a problem, either. He's been fixing timepieces for years."

I hoped she was right, but I wasn't so confident. There were older styles of clocks that the Masons would never have seen before in their shop, ones with complicated, outdated mechanisms.

I walked Catherine and Ronnie out, but Catherine excused herself. "I left my reticule behind."

A moment later, Matt emerged from the drawing room, leaving Cyclops and Catherine alone. When Ronnie realized, he looked somewhat caught between fetching his sister and leaving them to their privacy. To help make up his mind, I took his arm and led him down the stairs.

"You must practice between now and when you sit the test," I told him.

"I will."

"Every day, several hours a day."

"I haven't got several hours. I have to help in Father's shop."

"Then you must sacrifice your spare time."

"I will, India."

"Even if it means losing sleep."

He screwed up his nose. "If I'm tired, I won't be able to think properly."

"It'll only be temporary, but this is very important, Ronnie. Mr. Abercrombie and the other Court of Assistants members will want you to fail, and they'll give you very difficult questions to answer and near impossible tasks to complete. You must be prepared."

He patted my hand. "I'll be fine."

"I don't think you understand the depth of Mr. Abercrombie's hatred of me. He'll delight in seeing you fail. Failing you is the closest he can get to failing me."

"Don't worry. *He* might want me to fail, but not everyone there does. Some are friends of my father's. They won't let Abercrombie get away with dubious tactics."

"India is just nervous," Matt said. "She thinks she's sitting the test herself."

Ronnie laughed.

"I wish I could sit it for you," I said.

Catherine came down the stairs without Cyclops. She wasn't smiling, but there was a light to her eyes, a rosy glow on her cheeks. *Well, well.*

Her brother didn't seem to notice, however, as he and Matt had a brief discussion about paperwork for the loan. I studied Catherine as her gaze wandered back up the staircase. She sighed deeply when it became obvious Cyclops wasn't going to join us.

"I wonder what they spoke about," I said after we shut the door on the Mason siblings.

"You are *not* going to ask him," Matt said. "It's none of our business."

I chewed the inside of my lip.

"India," he warned.

"Don't you need to use your watch? You look tired. I'm going to find Miss Glass to see if there's anything she needs."

I left him and went in search of his aunt. I found her in her room, writing letters. She didn't need me. After a quick check of the rest of the house, I headed outside to the mews and found Cyclops in the stables, mucking out a stall.

"Did you give the stable boy the afternoon off again?" I asked.

He and Duke had a habit of coming out here to work when they needed to exorcise their demons. The physical exertion seemed to soothe them. Willie could often be found out here with them, sitting on the trough edge, giving orders. Cyclops was alone today, however.

"I know why you're here," he said, before I could speak. "And there ain't nothing to say that you haven't already heard. Nothing's changed."

"Did Catherine want it to change? Is that why she spoke to you?"

He scrubbed a patch of the floor with the broom, the rhythmic *swish* of bristles on stone a not unpleasant background noise. "She apologized for snapping at me."

"And?"

His strokes became more vigorous, the rhythm erratic. "She said she was annoyed with me for abandoning her when she needed me the most."

"That's actually rather sweet. I can see why it upset her that you'd run off at the first sight of her. She does need you now, Cyclops, even if it's just as a friend. Abercrombie and the guild are a formidable foe, and she's a young woman. Going up against them is intimidating."

"She's capable," he said.

"That doesn't mean she wants her friends to leave her to it."

"I told her I'd be at her side, no matter what. That she can count on me."

"Then what's the problem? Why are you scrubbing the top layer off that area of the floor?"

He stopped and leaned on the broom handle. "She kissed me."

"Oh. I see." I smiled. "That is good news."

His gaze lifted to mine. "Why?"

"Because I see that you liked it or it wouldn't be bothering you so much."

"You don't understand, India."

"I do understand. You've given me two reasons why you can't be together." I held up a finger. "Someone in America wants you dead. But that's in America, not here." I held up another finger. "And her family don't want her to be with a man who isn't like them."

"They're worried about her. Worried about people treating her differently. And so am I."

"That's something you can conquer together. I won't pretend it'll be easy, but if you have one another, you'll get through anything."

He shook his head and began sweeping the same spot on the floor again. "It's too hard."

"The harder it is, the sweeter it will be when you finally give in to love." I patted his arm. "I know Catherine, and I suspect she won't give up on you easily."

"That's why I've got to be cool to her. I can't let her see what I really think of her." He bent his back and put his shoulder into one hard sweep of the broom. "I can't let her know I liked that kiss."

Going by Catherine's smile as she left, I'd say he failed.

* * *

THE STRANGE MOOD that had come over Matt since the meeting with Fabian and Chronos lingered through dinner and into the evening. He did look less tired after using his watch, though, thank goodness. While Willie, Duke and Cyclops decided to go out, he sat silently by the unlit fireplace, staring at the grate.

Once we were alone, I perched on the arm of his chair and stroked his hair. "You're still mad at me for not telling you about Fabian, aren't you?"

He peered up at me through thick black lashes and my heart tumbled over with a thud. I could stare into those warm eyes all night. "I admit I was upset, but I know how you feel," he said. "Overwhelmed describes it aptly." He pulled me onto his lap. "I think we both need a distraction tonight."

My smile started slowly then spread, matching the blush that crept up my throat and warmed my cheeks. "I like being distracted by you."

He kissed me softly, his lips pillowing mine. His hands splayed at my lower back, pinning me against him. I sighed when he broke the kiss. It had been too brief.

"But I wasn't referring to that kind of distraction," he added, his eyes smoky.

"Oh."

His grin was lopsided. "But I'm seriously rethinking my evening plans now."

"What did you have in mind?"

"We'll search Dotty's room."

I drew back. "I think my idea is better. Yours is madness."

"You don't have to come. I'll go alone."

"And what if you get into trouble? If you go, I'll go. You need someone to watch out for you. How do you plan on getting in with the landlady there? I'm going to assume we're not scaling the wall and climbing in through the window if you invited me along."

"Nothing so adventurous. The local police station is going to send her a message about an update on the missing Dotty and her presence is required to assist with their inquiries."

"I'm not sure that's a good idea. When she learns there's been a mistake, she'll suspect something. It will also be upsetting."

"We're trying to find Dotty. Since the landlady won't let us into the room, we have to resort to unconventional methods."

"Or we could wait for Brockwell."

"And waste valuable time? What if we can't speak with him tomorrow, either?"

There would be no convincing him. He'd made up his mind. I rather thought he was being honest about needing the distraction tonight.

* * *

THE LANDLADY LOCKED the front door and deposited the key in her reticule. She looked up and down the street before heading off in the direction away from us. The evening was still early and the streets safe enough for her to walk to the nearest police station where we assumed she'd reported her tenant missing. We calculated we had twenty minutes at a minimum to search Dotty's room. First, we had to get in and locate it.

Getting in wasn't a problem with Matt's toolkit. He had the front door open in seconds. Finding Dotty's room took a little longer, but we found it on the second floor and immediately began searching through her things with the lamp turned down low.

"Her travel documents," Matt said, holding up papers he'd found in the top drawer of an escritoire. "There's a steamship ticket to the United States, and identification. Her full name is Dorothy Campion."

"So she hasn't left the country."

I didn't like rifling through Dotty's dresser drawers but it was better for me to do it than Matt. There was nothing unusual hidden among her unmentionables, but the fact that the drawers and trunk were full of underthings and clothes meant she hadn't found alternative accommodation. It was beginning to look like something terrible had happened to Dotty. Nobody willingly left all their belongings behind.

Matt checked under the bed then began skimming his fingers over the wallpaper, feeling for hidden compartments. I searched her dressing table for more clues. Among the hair combs, pins, perfume and powder were a few items of jewelry, all of which were paste or inexpensive beads. I moved aside a small pile of handkerchiefs to discover the pile didn't just contain handkerchiefs. Something hard was wrapped in one of them.

I unwrapped it and stared at the watch in my hand. It looked familiar. At first I assumed I must have seen Dotty checking it, that night at The Prince of Wales, but that didn't seem right. For one thing, it was a man's watch. For another, it was a fine piece and would have cost a considerable sum. It seemed out of place among the cheap jewelry.

And then it struck me. It wasn't Dotty I'd seen checking this watch, it was Emmett.

"Matt," I said, brandishing the watch. "She did it! She killed Emmett! That's the only way she could have his watch in her possession. She stole it from him, along with his other belongings, after she killed him to make it look like a robbery."

"You're sure it's his?"

"It's distinctive." I turned the watch over. "And it has his initials engraved in the back."

"Well done, India. I think we're done here. Let's go."

The words were hardly out of his mouth when the click of the front door opening set my heart racing. I gasped and covered my mouth. We'd stayed too long.

If I were the landlady, the first thing I'd do after returning from a fool's errand would be to check Dotty's room. Matt must have thought the same thing. His gaze flew to the window then darted around.

"Hide under the bed," he whispered as he extinguished the lamp.

I looked out of the window and down. It was too far to jump. "There's a drainpipe. I might be able to manage it." My skirts would be a hindrance, and I'd never climbed down a drainpipe before, or out of a window for that matter, but there was no other option.

"My fiancée is not climbing down a drainpipe. Hide under the bed. I'll go out through the window and draw her attention away from the house."

"How?"

"I'll think of something. Slip outside once she leaves."

I remained by the window and closed it after him, as he needed both hands to hold onto the drainpipe. I was torn between watching him descend and not daring to, in case he fell.

My mind was made up for me when a floorboard creaked, perilously close. I shut the window as softly as possible and eyed the gap beneath the bed. It wasn't high and my skirts were full.

The door handle rattled as it turned.

Defying the stiff boning of my corset, I flattened myself to the floor and slid under the bed. Panic and my corset laces made my breathing shallow, ragged, and loud in my ears. Dust drifted up my nose, and a sneeze threatened.

The door swung open and a rectangle of light fell across the floor, reaching the bed. Footsteps approached and the hem of a skirt came into view.

"Is someone in here?" asked the landlady.

My nose tickled. I pinched it in an effort to hold back the brewing sneeze and held my breath to ensure silence. I couldn't last long without air. Matt had better hurry. Why hadn't he knocked on the front door yet?

He must have fallen.

CHAPTER 13

I closed my eyes, as if that could shut out the landlady and my perilous predicament. If she were observant, she'd notice the things on Dotty's dresser had been moved. If she looked under the bed, she'd see me. Perhaps she didn't suspect...

"Who's there?" she asked.

She suspected.

Where was Matt? He must have fallen and injured himself or he would have come, by now. It didn't bear thinking about, yet it was all I could think about. That and the landlady discovering me. All sorts of scenarios played out in my head, and all of them were awful. They tumbled around in my mind, making it difficult to concentrate. Being unable to breathe properly certainly didn't help. I felt foggy, and my vision blurred, but at least I no longer wanted to sneeze.

Any moment now and I would need to draw a breath or pass out. Either way, it would reveal me.

I heard footsteps again, but this time they receded. The

landlady had departed. That's when my head began to pound.

No, not my head. Someone was knocking on the front door, very loudly.

Matt! *Thank God.*

I slid out from beneath the bed and sucked in several deep breaths. Then I tiptoed to the door and listened to Matt, below. I couldn't hear his words but his voice was a beautifully sonorous sound to my ears.

I crept closer to the stairs to listen. He was telling the landlady that I had gone missing and that he thought my disappearance was linked to that of Dotty. He sounded beside himself with worry. The landlady was doing her best to direct him to tell the police, but he was having none of it.

I tiptoed down the stairs, pausing on the first floor landing when they came into view. Matt kept his gaze on the landlady, but even so, I knew he knew I was there.

"You have to help me find her," he begged. "I need to know everything about Dotty."

"I sympathize," she said haughtily, "but it's nothing to do with me. You should go to the police."

"They're hopeless! Have they found Miss Campion? No. Are they even looking?" He threw his hands in the air. "I doubt it. They're fools." He squeezed the bridge of his nose. "Please, madam, help me find her. She's the most precious thing in the world to me. If I lose her..."

The landlady sighed. "Are you sure something terrible befell her?"

"It must have. Why would any woman leave me voluntarily? I'm rich and handsome and excellent company."

"Perhaps she left you because you're proud and conceited."

"No, that can't be it." He sounded thoughtful, but I didn't look at his face. I was too busy walking as swiftly and quietly as possible toward the back of the house. "Everyone says I'm charming," Matt went on.

"I'm sorry but I can't help you. Please leave, sir."

"You can't give me any clues about the whereabouts of Miss Campion? I'm convinced it will help me find India."

"No."

"I suspect they knew each other in the past." His voice had a desperate eagerness to it, as if he were trying to convince her before she slammed the door in his face.

I couldn't hear what she said, however, as I found the kitchen, scullery, and finally the door that led to a courtyard. I lifted the latch and slipped through the door before closing it softly behind me. I raced down the lane and met Matt at the corner. He grinned but all I felt was immense relief. The experience was over and neither of us had been caught or hurt.

"There you are," he said, drawing me into his arms. "Perhaps I should return and tell the landlady you showed up because you missed me too much."

"I missed your pride and conceit." I pressed my forehead against his shoulder and steadied my breathing. "The next time I break into a house, remind me not to wear a corset."

"Next time I break into a house, remind me not to bring you." His arms tightened.

"I would have come anyway." I took his hand and we headed in the direction of the carriage, which waited two streets away. "At least we were successful. We know Dotty killed Emmett. It's the only way the watch could be in her possession."

"We'll inform Brockwell in the morning. He can search her room, find the watch, and take the credit."

"I wonder what happened to her. I hope it's nothing awful. She may be a murderess but I can't help worrying about her. She is a woman all alone in a foreign country, after all."

"I don't think you need to worry," Matt said. "I suspect she's fine, wherever she is, safely away from London's police."

"Why do you think that?"

"We didn't find any money in her room. Not a single farthing. Did you find a reticule?"

"Only one," I said. "Most women have more."

"So we can assume she had a reticule and money on her when she went missing."

It did make me feel better, although now I thought of her as more of a cold-blooded killer than before. "She murdered Emmett, came back to her room briefly, left the watch behind, gathered all her money but took nothing else with her. She suspected the police would come for her and it was best to make it look like something terrible had befallen her by leaving her belongings. That way she could make her escape."

"And start afresh."

Matt helped me into the carriage and he gave the coachman the order to return home.

"I'm filthy," I said, looking down at the dust covering my dress. "The landlady isn't all that thorough in her house-keeping."

I brushed my gown but Matt stayed my hand. "Allow me." His fingers skimmed over my breasts in a poor attempt at flicking the dust off.

We spent the remainder of the journey kissing and...dusting.

* * *

"I'VE HAD another thought about that watch," Matt said the

following morning at breakfast.

I'd just finished telling the others about our escapades. Willie was impressed with my nerve, but Cyclops eyed Matt as if he'd lost his mind for taking me along. Duke was too busy tucking into a sausage to reveal his thoughts.

"What is it?" I asked Matt.

"What if May Draper put it in the drawer to implicate Dotty?"

I sat back, feeling somewhat breathless again. Why hadn't we thought about that possibility last night? Probably because we were both too energized at our success and somewhat distracted in the carriage.

"Whoa, slow down," Cyclops said. "You think May killed Emmett and is blaming it on Dotty?"

"She lied to us about where she was that night," Matt said, buttering his toast. "Both the Drapers lied. And she gave us Dotty's address too easily when she was cornered."

"So," Willie said, pointing her knife at Matt. "Did May kill Dotty too?"

"It's a possibility. Or she has taken the opportunity that Dotty's disappearance presents to blame her. Dotty's not here to defend herself."

"But what about the lack of money?" I asked. "We found nothing in Dotty's room," I told the others.

Matt bit into his toast as he considered that.

Duke finished his sausage and stole a piece of bacon off Cyclops's plate. "You don't need this if you want to look good for a certain pretty blonde."

Cyclops watched forlornly as the bacon disappeared into Duke's mouth.

"Perhaps Dotty didn't have much money to begin with," I said. When Eddie threw me out, I'd had only a few coins to my name, all of which fit into my reticule. "If she carried a reticule filled with all the money she possessed, and was then accosted, then it's no wonder we didn't find any in her room. Her attacker kept it all."

"She should have sold the watch if she was poor," Willie said as she chewed. "I would have."

I pushed my plate away. This talk made me feel ill. Poor Dotty.

Matt took my empty teacup and filled it from the pot at the sideboard. "If Dotty hasn't run off voluntarily, because she committed the murder, then she has probably met with an unfortunate end at the hands of the killer—"

"May or Danny Draper," Willie cut in. "Or both."

"—because she knew too much," Matt finished.

That silenced us all. Even Duke pushed his plate of food away, although he pulled it closer again after a mere five seconds.

All talk of the investigation ceased upon Miss Glass's arrival at the breakfast table. She'd eaten in her rooms, as she often did in the morning, but joined us for a cup of tea and gossip.

"I had a letter from Beatrice this morning," she announced, accepting a cup from Matt.

"Another one?" I said. "She has become quite the correspondent in her absence."

"She misses London keenly, as do Hope and Charity. Patience is happily settled at Lord Cox's estate, although I suspect that is a lie to rub my nose in it."

"Rub your nose in what?" Willie asked.

"The excellent match Patience made. Lord Cox's estate is grand, and I believe he's on fifty thousand a year."

"Fifty! Well fu—"

"Willie!" both Matt and Duke snapped.

"Sorry. Forgot myself on account of my shock. How much do you make, Matt?"

"None of your business."

"Fifty," she said to the slice of bacon on her fork. "I'd say she fell on her feet. Lucky he changed his mind and married her."

I swallowed half my tea with one gulp. It burned as it went down.

"Why would Aunt Beatrice need to lie about Patience's happiness?" Matt asked Miss Glass. "I'm sure she is happy. They're a good match."

"He has *four* children, Matthew. Four! That's twice as many as anyone needs. I believe three of them are boys, and all are under the age of twelve. Patience will be regretting her choice soon enough, if she doesn't already. Imagine the noise. I have a headache just thinking about it."

"We can assume you won't visit her, then," Matt said, warring with a smile.

"I'm old. She can come here and visit me—leaving the children behind, of course."

"This is a terrible dilemma you've put us in, Aunt," Matt said, suddenly serious. "India and I wanted to outdo Patience and have five children."

"Don't be ridiculous. You can't fit five into this house."

"You could share a room with the girls, if we're blessed with any."

"Or with Willie," I said.

Miss Glass looked as though she believed us, but only until Willie barked a laugh. "You two are darned funny. Don't worry, Letty, they're just pulling your leg."

"Thank goodness for that!" Miss Glass said. "I felt faint for a moment."

Bristow entered and handed Matt a note. "It's from Hendry," Matt said, reading. "He's reminding us about the invitations and asked if we'd like to collect them in person or do we want him to deliver them."

"We'll be busy all day," I said.

"I'll go," Miss Glass said. "I could do with an excursion."

"Take Polly with you." I didn't want her to be alone if she had one of her episodes again.

"What about you three?" Matt asked his friends.

"I'm going to watch Dotty's lodgings," Duke said. "If she returns when we ain't looking, it could be a disaster."

"And I'm going to make sure Ronnie is studying," Cyclops said. At our silent stares, he added, "Not a word from any of you. I ain't going to see Catherine. It's nothing to do with her. I want Ronnie to succeed, that's all." He got up and stormed out of the dining room.

"And what about you, Willie?" Matt asked.

"Ain't none of your business," she said, rising. "But I'm going to have some fun."

"Why am I the only one working?" Duke asked.

"Standing on the street half asleep ain't working."

"I won't fall asleep."

Willie snorted.

* * *

As much as we wanted to question May again, Matt and I went directly to New Scotland Yard to report to Brockwell. Fortunately he was in and prepared to see us. I didn't consider the detective inspector to be a man of action, and certainly not someone who moved at a rapid pace, however once we told him what we'd discovered in Dotty's room, he took on a new persona. He strode into the common area and barked orders at his men to search the room, taking particular note of any watches.

"You coming, sir?" one of them asked as he headed out the door.

Brockwell shook his head. "I have to question a suspect. You're in charge of the search, Sergeant."

The sergeant puffed out his chest and saluted Brockwell before leaving.

Brockwell returned to his office with us in tow and retrieved his hat from the hat stand. "Thank you for the information, but I have to ask, how did you get into Miss Campion's room?"

"You don't want to know," Matt said.

The inspector pressed his lips together. "The landlady didn't let you in, did she?"

"I think you should assume whatever eases your conscience."

"Very little about this eases my conscience, Glass. If my superiors ask for details, I will be forced to tell them."

"And I'll give Munro the answers he wants."

That didn't smooth the frown on Brockwell's brow in the least. "If you don't mind, I have work to do now." He walked off along the corridor.

We followed him all the way outside. Matt dogged his steps, as did I. I wasn't yet sure what Matt had in mind, although I had an inkling. He wouldn't want to end our involvement now.

"That will be all, Glass," Brockwell said, stopping on the curb.

"You're going to question May Draper now, aren't you?"

"It's the wisest course of action at this juncture."

"Not really. May I suggest another?"

Brockwell sighed. "You will whether I want it or not."

Matt smiled. "You know me so well."

"Just get on with it, Glass." Poor Brockwell sounded like he had a thousand burdens on his shoulders and Matt was the biggest.

"May Draper is a consummate liar. With her husband giving her an alibi, you won't get anywhere by questioning her. I suggest you speak to someone who knows them well to give you a more accurate picture first. Someone who can possibly give you ammunition to use in your interrogation."

"Annie Oakley?" I asked.

"William Cody."

"Buffalo Bill?" Brockwell scratched his sideburns. "He must be a busy man. It'll be hard to get hold of him."

"You're the best detective inspector in London. He'll respect that."

"Kind of you to say, Glass, but he won't know I'm the best."

Matt slapped Brockwell's shoulder. "That's why I'm coming along, to tell him."

"And me," I said.

"Of course. We're a team."

Brockwell merely sighed.

* * *

WE FINALLY LOCATED both Annie Oakley and Bill Cody at the exhibition grounds. Annie sat on a stool in the shade of the grandstand with a rifle across her lap, polishing the barrel to a sheen. Cody squatted in the middle of the arena, inspecting a horse's leg, while riders put other animals through their paces. The Drapers were nowhere to be seen.

I waved at Annie when she looked up.

"What're you doing here?" she asked.

"We want to speak to Mr. Cody."

I hurried after Matt and Brockwell, striding across the arena. Clouds of dust kicked up by the hooves hung in the breathless air and cloyed at my throat. I paused to cough and almost got in the way of one of the riders.

"You there!" Cody shouted. "Do you want to get trampled?"

My apology earned me a scowl from the star himself.

"I've answered all your questions, Inspector," Mr. Cody said, flicking a hand at the rider to lead the horse away.

"I have more," Brockwell said.

Mr. Cody stood with hands on hips, feet apart, looking like the impressive cowboy from the posters. He gave Matt and I a thorough inspection. "I've seen you two before."

"At The Prince of Wales," Matt said, holding out his hand. "I'm Matthew Glass, and this is my fiancée, India Steele. We're assisting Detective Inspector Brockwell with his investigation."

"Where you from, Glass?"

"California, mostly. My mother was a Johnson."

Mr. Cody's gaze slid to Brockwell.

"He knows who the Johnsons are," Matt said, smiling.

"Interesting friendship you two got."

"We're not friends," both Matt and Brockwell said.

I managed to hold my smile in check—just.

Mr. Cody's gaze wandered around the arena, taking in Annie and the cluster of cast members with her, the riders, and the collection of Indians setting up their camp display. "So what's this about now? Be quick, Inspector, I've got a show to prepare."

"What can you tell us about May and Danny Draper?" the inspector asked.

Mr. Cody's gaze snapped to Brockwell. "You think they killed Emmett?"

"I'm trying to piece together a picture of a number of people, including the Drapers."

"So they're suspects."

The inspector waited for him to go on.

"Now look here, Inspector, I'm not a gossip. Not everyone in this cast is as clean as a preacher's daughter, but whatever they've done in the past is all forgiven here, as long as their misdemeanors stay in the past. I ain't going to rat on the Drapers—or anyone else."

"You wouldn't want to be harboring criminals, Mr. Cody. Would you?"

Buffalo Bill watched his riders again. "Good day, gentlemen, ma'am. Mind your step on the way out. You wouldn't want to get those nice boots dirty."

Brockwell huffed out a breath.

"You wouldn't be gossiping," I said quickly. "You'd be giving us helpful information to catch Emmett's murderer. You see, we think May has lied to us. We need to learn more about her before we confront her. We need to know what sort of people the Drapers are."

"You put forward a good case, Miss Steele, but the answer's still no. I'm not a snitch."

"Answer the question, Mr. Cody," Matt said, a steely edge to his tone. "If you don't, Brockwell will be forced to stop today's show and turn away your customers."

Mr. Cody rounded on him. Then he turned a hard glare onto Brockwell. "You wouldn't dare," he snarled.

"I can shut it down now," Brockwell said. "It would be better to do it well before it's scheduled to begin, to give you time to organize refunds."

Mr. Cody's lips worked and his moustache twitched, but no sound came out. He resumed watching the horses. After a moment, he said, "May Draper is a woman of many talents. Before she married, she worked for Madame Le Clare in Bellevue, Texas."

"Am I correct to assume that Madame Le Clare is not really French?" Brockwell asked.

Mr. Cody nodded. "She was a brothel madam. May met Danny there, so he knows what she was. They joined my troupe about a year after their marriage, when I spotted them working at a small time show. She shot a tin cup at thirty paces and Danny was a good trick rider. They're not the best at what they do, but I've found married couples work better than singles. Having his wife around makes the husband behave. Usually."

"Danny Draper doesn't behave?" Matt asked.

"He's a gambler. You know that."

"And he has a lot of debt," I added.

"True, Miss Steele. So much debt that I know May returned to her old profession sometimes to pay creditors who talked tough. I reckon Danny don't know the half of it, but he sure knows some. She's always getting him out of a bind. If it weren't for her, his creditors would have caught up with him by now."

"She told you all this?" I asked. It seemed unlikely that a woman would confess such intimate secrets about herself and her marriage to the man who employed her.

"She came to me for a loan once. I wouldn't give her anything but she told me what she'd need to do to get a particularly dangerous creditor off their backs. I felt sorry for her, so I gave her a hundred dollars. It must have helped, because she hasn't come asking for more, and they seemed happier for a time."

"For a time?" Brockwell prompted. "Did that change?"

"About two weeks ago, Danny seemed worried again, real intense when he played cards. He and May argued a lot about money too."

Their change of moods coincided with Emmett ending the partnership with Danny.

"Seems their creditors either followed them here to England or Danny accumulated new ones," Mr. Cody went on. "Knowing him, it could be both."

"Speaking of being followed here," Matt said, "what do you know about Emmett Cocker's troubles back in the States? I heard someone was out for revenge."

"Jack Krane? He caused Emmett some problems before we left, and it wouldn't surprise me if he came here to get his revenge. But I haven't seen him around."

"He might have sent someone to exact revenge on his behalf."

"That he could, Glass. In fact, that's probably why Emmett was murdered. It seems more likely than the Drapers doing it. Their pasts ain't the cleanest, but they're not murderers."

"Do you think May has returned to her old ways again to pay off Danny's debts?" Matt asked.

"I wouldn't want to suggest that about a woman," Mr. Cody said, still watching the horses.

"You're a gentleman," I told him. "Thank you for telling us this much. It's very helpful."

Mr. Cody merely grunted.

"What do you now about Emmett's girl, the blonde named Dotty?" Brockwell asked.

"I've seen her around, both here and back home," Mr. Cody said. "But I don't know her name. Now is that all? I'm a busy man."

"Of course, sir." Brockwell removed his hat and took a giant stride to stand in front of Mr. Cody. He cleared his throat. "Could you spare two tickets to your show, sir? I'd like to bring someone. She says she's already seen it but I think she'd like to go again. She told me how grand the performance was, how ingenious and—"

"Fine, fine." Mr. Cody whistled and a man with a clipboard talking to the Indians looked up. Mr. Cody pointed at Brockwell and held up two fingers. The man nodded.

We thanked Mr. Cody and collected Brockwell's tickets.

"You're bringing a friend to the show?" I asked him as we headed toward the Warwick Road exit. "That's wonderful."

"I have friends," he said, defensively.

"But this is a female friend. You've not mentioned her before."

Matt clapped Brockwell on the shoulder. "Good luck."

Brockwell scowled. "My private life is not a topic I wish to discuss with either of you."

"I'm relieved to hear it." Matt's smirk faded. "Look who finally showed up to work."

I followed his gaze to where May and Danny Draper made their way toward us. Danny carried a pack slung over his shoulder and May clutched a gun case.

"Good morning," May said through her smile. "This is a surprise."

"Something the matter, Inspector?" Danny asked.

"Not at all." Brockwell smiled back. "We had more questions for Mr. Cody and were just on our way."

"Oh. Good." Danny focused on the arena behind us. "What type of questions?"

"The kind I can't inform you of."

May took her husband's arm. "We should go. We're late."

"Wait one moment, if you please. I have some questions you're required to answer."

"Not now," she said. "Mr. Cody has no truck with tardiness. You understand."

"I do."

She smiled and began to walk off, taking Danny with her. Matt moved to block the way. "The detective inspector isn't asking, Mrs. Draper. If you don't want to speak to us here, you can come to Scotland Yard. It's your choice."

Danny swore under his breath. May huffed and released her husband. "Go on then," she snapped.

"Where were you the night of Emmett's murder?" Brockwell asked.

Danny clicked his tongue impatiently. "As we already told Mr. Glass—"

"I know what you told Mr. Glass and Miss Steele. I'd like the truth this time."

Danny swallowed. Husband and wife exchanged glances.

"Come on," Matt urged. "It's not hard. Did you see Emmett that night?"

"No!" May said. "I assure you, neither of us saw him after we left The Prince of Wales."

"So where did you go?"

The Drapers exchanged another glance. Danny gave a slight, barely perceptible shake of his head.

"We know you didn't go for a walk," Brockwell said. "Nor were you at your Childs Street lodgings. So where were you?"

"That ain't your business!" Danny spat. "Now move out of the way." He shoved Matt but Matt hardly moved. He continued to block the way.

Brockwell joined him. "Calm down, Mr. Draper."

"I am calm!"

"Danny," May warned.

"Stay out of this!" The veins in Danny's throat throbbed above his tight collar and his face flushed. He shifted his weight from foot to foot and glared at both men. I was reminded of a boxer sizing up his opponent.

Neither Matt nor Brockwell moved, despite Danny's growing agitation. I took a surreptitious step back, just in case his temper exploded.

"Tell us, Mr. Draper," Brockwell pressed. "Where were you that night? What were you and May doing? Something to get you out of debt? Something you hardly dare speak of?"

"Stop!" Danny screamed in the inspector's face. "Stop your damn questions!"

Matt put a hand on Brockwell's shoulder. "That's enough, Inspector."

Brockwell ignored him. There was a brightness to his eyes, a mad gleam as he focused on his prey. It was as if Matt and I weren't even there. "Either you tell us where you were that night or I will have to assume you killed Emmett Cocker."

"No!" May blurted out on a sob. Her fingers tightened around the gun case handle. "We didn't kill him. We were nowhere near The Prince of Wales at that time."

"Enough, May," Danny said, breathing heavily through his mouth. "Don't say anything."

"Why do you want her to stop, Mr. Draper?" Brockwell asked oh-so-innocently. "Is it because you're afraid she'll implicate herself in the murder?"

"She's not a murderer."

"Are *you*? Is she lying to protect *you*?"

Danny's hands curled into fists at his sides. "We're not murderers."

"You both lied to us about your whereabouts that night," Brockwell went on like a boulder hurtling down a hill. "You hated Emmett Cocker for ending the cheating arrangement you had with him, and May lied about knowing Dotty Campion. Did you kill her too, May?"

May gasped. She dropped the case and covered her mouth with both hands. The movement distracted me and meant I didn't see Danny swing his fist until it was too late.

CHAPTER 14

*D*anny struck Brockwell in the mouth, sending the inspector reeling. Matt caught and steadied him, but his hat fell into the dirt.

"Danny!" May snapped. "You dang fool!"

Danny shook out his hand, all blustery anger gone. He blinked innocently at his wife.

"Oh, Danny," she said on a sigh, grasping his hand in both of hers. "You've gone and hurt yourself, you silly boy."

He bowed his head and she kissed his forehead. It was rather touching, and for the first time, I hoped they weren't guilty of the murder. These two loved each other, in their own way, and it would break their hearts to be separated.

It also explained why one would cover up the other's murdering misdeeds with a bundle of lies.

Brockwell dabbed at his cut lip with his handkerchief. "Mr. Draper, you're under arrest for striking an officer of the law."

"Wait!" May cried. "Don't arrest him. Danny was only defending my honor. If we confess, will you let us go?"

"Depends what you confess to."

220

"Not murder," she said quickly. "We didn't kill Emmett."

"You don't have to do this, May," Danny said gently.

Two cast members dressed in cowhide chaps and big hats walked past, their spurs tinkling with each step. They continued to stare at us long after they'd passed by.

"I do have to," May said, lowering her voice. "But you've got to promise you won't tell anyone. Not even Cody."

"Agreed," Matt said. "Go on."

"The night Emmett died, I was...spending some time with one of the men Danny played cards with."

"You mean soliciting?" Brockwell asked.

Danny looked like he'd throw another punch.

"No," May said, taking hold of her husband's right arm. "It was just a little fun. No harm done. Danny knows all about it and he...looks the other way."

Danny wasn't looking the other way now. He looked like he wanted to strangle Brockwell for bringing the matter up.

"So you don't do it for money?" Brockwell asked.

"Of course not, Inspector. That would be illegal."

"May I ask the name of the man?"

"James Lester. He has rooms in a house on Glebe Place, Chelsea."

Brockwell wrote down the name and address in his notebook. "And where were you while your wife was...entertaining, Mr. Draper?"

"In the vicinity," Danny growled.

May clutched his arm. "Now do you understand why we didn't want to talk about it?" she asked. "It's not something a husband and wife like to admit."

Danny's jaw clenched, and I swore I heard his teeth grind.

"Is that all?" May asked.

"Not quite," Matt said. "Emmett Cocker's watch was

found in Dorothy Campion's belongings. Did you put it there?"

She squared her shoulders. "No, I did not. Why would you suggest such a thing?"

"Because it was convenient that you suddenly remembered where Dotty lived after we interrogated you, and even more convenient that incriminating evidence was found in her room."

"Perhaps it was convenient because *she* killed Emmett. I'm not even sure I know what his watch looks like."

"It's a gold chronograph LeCoultre," I said.

"We didn't steal it," Danny spat. "Not on the night he died, not before, and not after. We didn't give it to that woman, and we didn't put it in her room. Got it?"

May lifted her chin. "Come on, Danny. We've answered everything we have to."

He picked up her gun case and together they marched off toward the arena.

"Are you all right, Inspector?" I asked. "That cut looks nasty."

"Don't mind me, Miss Steele. It's a hazard of the job."

Matt picked up Brockwell's hat and dusted it off. "Your interrogation technique leaves something to be desired, but it got results. I'm impressed."

"Spoken like a man," I said. "But yes, it did get results. Well done, Inspector. So what do we do now?"

"Now, I check up on James Lester of Chelsea." Brockwell patted his jacket pocket where he'd slipped the notepad. "You two should go home. I'll let you know the outcome."

I went to walk off, but Matt didn't follow. He stared at the looming arena behind us, a magnificent structure that in less than an hour would be home to the spectacular Wild West show presented by Buffalo Bill.

"Matt?" I asked.

He joined us and we walked out of the exhibition grounds through the Warwick Street gate. "They're still holding something back," he said.

"They'd be foolish to," Brockwell said.

"I know, but I can't shake the feeling."

"You Americans and your feelings." Brockwell chuckled only to wince as his lip pained him. "You wear your emotions on your sleeves."

"May certainly is emotional," I said. "But not nearly as emotional as Danny. Do take care of that lip, Inspector. Don't let it fester."

We parted ways, with Brockwell taking a hack to Chelsea, and Matt and I taking our carriage home. He was distracted on the drive, however, often peering through the rear window, and I couldn't engage him in discussion, no matter how many times I tried.

"What is it?" I finally asked.

"I think someone's following us."

I peered through the window too. Hansoms, growlers and omnibuses all vied for position on the road behind, but I couldn't discern a particular one that appeared to be following. When we turned into Park Street, none turned with us.

"There's no one there," I said, facing the front again.

"There was. I think."

"Willie thought someone followed us from the New Somerville Club the other night, too."

He opened the door as the carriage rolled to a stop outside number sixteen. "If I were still a gambling man, I'd wager all my money on Whittaker."

I accepted his assistance down the step to the pavement. "He does seem a likely candidate. Is he spying for the club or Lord Coyle?"

"And does he know more about the murder of Emmett Cocker than he lets on?"

A message from Duke waited for us on the hall table along with the rest of the mail. It simply stated that Dotty Campion had not returned to her lodgings and that no one connected to the case had called there. He would continue to watch the building for the rest of the day.

Cyclops and Willie hadn't returned home, but Miss Glass waited for us in the sitting room. She handed me a small pile of invitations, tied with a dark blue ribbon.

"Thank you for collecting them," I said, untying the ribbon. My fingers warmed from the magic heat in the cards, but I was soon distracted by the luxurious silkiness of the cards themselves. "The quality is superb." I stroked the topmost card then offered it to Miss Glass to feel.

"It's no wonder he has such a good reputation," she said.

"You do recall that he's a paper magician, don't you?"

"Is he? No, India, you hadn't mentioned it. I'm the last to know these things around here."

"Feel it, Matt," I said, offering him an invitation.

He touched the card and nodded dutifully, but his mind was elsewhere. He excused himself and left the room.

Miss Glass and I sat on the sofa together and checked each invitation. I gave her hers, and set aside Duke, Cyclops, and Willie's. It was quite unnecessary for them to have invitations, but Mr. Hendry had insisted, and Miss Glass enjoyed receiving one.

"He's quite an unusual fellow," she said, reading over her invitation again. "Rather...how should I describe him?"

"Emotional?"

"Insistent."

"That doesn't sound like Mr. Hendry. What did he say to you?"

"He asked why you and Matthew hadn't come in person.

He seemed quite put out that you'd sent me to collect these."
She placed her invitation on the table beside the others and
removed her spectacles. "He was almost rude about it."

"Perhaps he thought we didn't appreciate the magnifi-
cence of his work enough by sending someone else in our
stead. He doesn't know how important you are to us." I
patted her hand and she seemed to perk up a little at my
compliment.

"That must be it."

* * *

AFTER ENDURING a luncheon with Matt where he still
seemed distracted, I confronted him when we were alone
afterward. "Are you worried that we haven't heard from
Brockwell yet? Or that we don't have a task of our own to
accomplish?"

"It's Whittaker," he said. "I want to confront him about
following us."

"We don't know for certain it was him."

"It can't hurt to ask."

I wasn't so sure we should confront him. Sir Charles and
Lord Coyle were slippery fish. Suspecting them of spying
was one thing, but getting them to admit it was quite
another.

Matt gathered my hands in both of his and raised them
to his lips. "Whittaker admitted that he's spying on magicians. It's no great leap to assume he's spying on you, despite
his denial."

"I suppose."

"He needs to know we're aware of him following us. It's
the only way to get him to stop."

"Or he might be more careful not to get caught next
time."

Matt would not be swayed from the idea of confronting him so we set out again that afternoon. "There," he said, peering through the back window. "I'm sure that black Clarence, three behind, has been with us ever since we turned out of Park Street."

The Clarence didn't follow us all the way to Sir Charles's Hammersmith house but veered off one street before. I tended to agree with Matt that we were certainly being followed, but wasn't convinced it was Sir Charles.

"We'll know for certain if he's not at home now, but will arrive shortly after we knock, walking from that direction." He nodded toward the end of the street.

My breath caught. "My God," I whispered. "Every time we've come here, he hasn't been home, but has arrived on foot soon afterward."

Matt looked rather smug.

"He *is* following us," I went on. "When he sees that we're on our way to visit him, he alights from his carriage around the corner and walks here just in time to catch us before we leave. And you knew."

"I've only just guessed. This will confirm it." He knocked on the front door of the row house.

True to form, the housekeeper announced that Sir Charles wasn't at home, but as we turned to go, he hailed us from the pavement.

"Good afternoon," he said cheerfully. "To what do I owe the pleasure of this visit?"

"We'd like a word." Matt sounded cheerful too. It set me on edge.

"Do come in."

"This won't take long." Matt waited for the housekeeper to return inside then his features set into hard planes with severe edges. "Stop following India."

Sir Charles pressed a hand to his chest over his heart. "I can assure you I'm not."

"Don't lie to us. You've been caught. If I catch you again, you will get another visit from me. It won't be as polite as this one."

Sir Charles laughed nervously. "Come now, Glass, what is this? Let's be friends again."

"We were never friends. And do not feign innocence."

"I *am* innocent!"

Matt grasped Sir Charles by the front of his jacket and pulled him closer. He towered over him and was certainly the more powerful of the two. It was no wonder Whittaker swallowed audibly.

"Do not follow India again." Matt shook Sir Charles, causing Sir Charles's bowler hat to tilt. "Do you understand?"

"Matt," I said carefully. "The housekeeper is watching through the window."

Matt let Sir Charles go, shoving him for good measure. "This is your final warning."

Sir Charles took another step back, out of Matt's reach, and smoothed down his scrunched jacket. "I—I'm simply following her to gain some information about your investigation into Cocker's murder."

"Why? Because you killed him?"

"No! The outcome interests us."

"Us?" I prompted. "Do you mean the collectors?"

He nodded without taking his eyes off Matt. "I didn't kill him. Nor did anyone else in our little group. What possible reason could we have for killing a magician?"

His point was valid, but I didn't trust him. There could be another motive we hadn't thought about.

"May I go inside now?" Sir Charles asked, regaining some of his composure.

"Be sure to tell Coyle that you've been warned not to follow India," Matt said. "The warning applies to him as well."

"I told you last time, all my research is for the whole of the club, not just Coyle." He removed his hat and smoothed a hand over his sleek hair. "May I enter now?"

Matt stepped aside and Sir Charles strode past, head high.

"I don't believe him when he says he's spying on behalf of all of the club members," I said as we returned to the carriage. Mrs. Delancey had told me about the time she'd overheard Sir Charles and Coyle discussing Mr. Hendry. The information was news to her, and wasn't shared with the other members. It wouldn't surprise me if Sir Charles and Lord Coyle were still keeping secrets from them.

Matt eyed the door through which Sir Charles had gone. "I don't trust him, either."

CYCLOPS WAS at home when we returned, and he was not alone. Both Ronnie and Catherine were with him. Ronnie paced the drawing room floor, chewing on his thumbnail, while Catherine spoke quietly with Cyclops on the sofa. They sat very close, their knees almost touching.

Cyclops shifted away when we entered. "Here she is," he announced. "India, we need your help."

Ronnie stopped pacing and released a deep breath.

Catherine rose and took my hand in hers. "I hope you don't mind us dropping in like this."

"Not at all," I said. "Is the tea still warm?" I went to pour cups for Matt and me, but he refused.

"I have a letter to write," he said.

His thoughts must still be on Sir Charles, Lord Coyle

and their club. He'd promised me he wouldn't confront anyone else today, but I wasn't sure writing a letter to Coyle was a good idea.

"It's not to him," he said, reading my mind. "Just my lawyer." He kissed my forehead, excused himself, and left.

"Tell me what's wrong," I said to Cyclops as I sat with my tea. "You all look worried."

"I'm tied up in knots," Ronnie said, resuming his pacing. "I'm going to fail the guild's entry test, India. I know I am."

"You have to calm down," I told him. "You're going to find studying difficult if you're tightly wound like this."

"It's not that. They're going to cheat. It won't matter how much I study, they're going to make it so difficult that I'll never pass."

"Catherine assured me your theoretical knowledge is very good, and your practical skill is excellent."

"It is," she said. "He should pass."

"If the test was fair," he added, stopping before me. "But we all know it won't be."

I wanted to reassure him, but he'd see right through the lie. He was right, and we all knew the test would be exceptionally difficult. There might be others on the guild's Court of Assistants who still called the Masons friends, but Abercrombie would have final say on the test's contents. I wouldn't put it past him to change the test altogether without notifying other guild members.

Ronnie suddenly dropped into a squat and grasped my arm. A little tea spilled over the rim of my cup and pooled in the saucer. "You have to do the test for me, India."

I blinked at him.

"Ronnie!" Catherine cried. "That's not what we discussed."

"You were going to ask her to help you study," Cyclops added.

"Studying won't be enough. You know that." Ronnie rubbed his palms on his trouser legs. "You know it too, India."

I certainly did. More than anyone. "It's impossible," I told him. "You'll be in a room inside the guild hall. They check you before you enter to make sure you're not carrying spare parts or notes."

"They'll check to make sure you're not India," Cyclops added with a wry twist of his lips.

"What if you snuck in after me?" Ronnie asked. "Orwell says the examiner doesn't stay in the room. Once he leaves, you can enter and assist me."

"Don't be ridiculous," Catherine bit off. "You're being a coward."

"I'm being practical. You know they'll make it hard."

"Hard, but not impossible. You can do it, Ronnie. I know you can. Now come on, let's go home. India has too much on her plate already; she doesn't need you adding more."

Ronnie stood. "The test is scheduled for early evening on Monday, India."

Catherine grabbed her brother's hand and dragged him to the door. "Good afternoon, and thank you for helping my brother study, Nate. I'm sorry for the trouble you've gone to for him to turn around and ask this."

"No trouble," Cyclops said with an awkward smile. His eye positively sparkled.

The Mason siblings saw themselves out. I felt sorry for Ronnie. I truly did. But I couldn't do what he asked. If Mr. Abercrombie caught me, he might have me arrested for trespassing.

With more than one senior policeman on my side, it would probably come to naught. The worst Mr. Abercrombie could do would be to shout at me and fail Ronnie. It was possible Ronnie would be banned from applying for guild membership for the rest of his life. But Ronnie would likely fail anyway because of his association with me. Mr. Abercrombie would see to it.

Cyclops narrowed his gaze at me. "Stop it, India."

"Stop what?"

"Feeling guilty. It's not your fault."

I smiled weakly and sipped my tea.

* * *

DETECTIVE INSPECTOR BROCKWELL finally paid us a visit later that afternoon. I'd been on tenterhooks since seeing him off after interrogating the Drapers at Earls Court. It should not have taken him this long to report on his visit to May's alibi, James Lester of Chelsea.

"It's about time," I told Matt as we waited for Bristow to show the inspector into the drawing room. We'd heard his arrival but decided not to greet him at the door, instead saving the discussion for somewhere more private.

"Of course he's coming now," Matt said. "It's almost dinner time."

I didn't know how he could treat the visit so lightly after a nerve-wracking wait. "Well?" I asked Brockwell the moment Bristow announced him. "What did Mr. Lester have to say?"

Brockwell eased himself into a chair and shifted his weight until he found a comfortable position. He stroked his sideburns and eyed the door. "Is your cousin at home, Glass?"

"She's been out all day," Matt said.

"Is that so?"

"If you're looking for someone to smoke with," I said, impatience making my voice harsh, "Matt will join you in the smoking room later."

"No, no, that's quite all right. It's too close to dinner time for a cigar."

"Would you like to stay for dinner, Inspector? If I tell Mrs. Potter now, she can put on more."

"Thank you for the kind offer, but I have plans."

"Oh?"

"With my colleagues. I'll be working this evening, searching for the Drapers."

Matt sat forward. "They've disappeared?" At Brockwell's nod, he said, "Have you alerted the railway stations? The ports?"

"And all major coach terminals. Thank you, Glass, I know how to do my job."

Matt sat back, looking skeptical, but thankfully he kept his mouth shut.

"You'd better start at the beginning," I said. "What happened with Mr. Lester?"

Brockwell removed his notebook from his inside jacket pocket and licked the tip of his finger. He flipped through the pages far too slowly for my liking until he finally found the one he needed. "Lester confirmed that he and Mrs. Draper had a liaison on the night of Cocker's murder. It was *not* a financial arrangement, however, the following morning, Mr. Lester found his pockets were empty and his watch gone. He confronted her that afternoon after the show, discreetly of course, but was run off by Danny. Upon seeing Danny, Mr. Lester realized he'd noticed him the night before loitering near his home. It's his belief that Mrs. Draper placed his trousers near the window then unlatched the window to allow Danny access. Danny stole the watch and money while Mrs. Draper and Mr. Lester were otherwise engaged."

Matt shook his head. "Their marital arrangement astounds me."

"Why weren't they arrested for theft at the time?" I asked.

"Mr. Lester never reported it," Brockwell said. "He was too embarrassed to admit he fell for Mrs. Draper's charms, and he says the value of the stolen items wasn't very high. It would also have been difficult to prove unless the identifiable item—namely, the watch—was found in their possession."

"The Drapers knew you would learn of the robbery after we forced May to give up her alibi," Matt said. "They've gone into hiding or left the city altogether."

"They are experts at disappearing, according to information I received via telegraph not long ago." Brockwell returned the notebook to his pocket. "They committed minor thefts in various states in America using a similar method as that used against Mr. Lester. They both went to jail but were released after serving brief sentences."

"William Cody knew it too," I said.

"Or guessed," Matt added.

Brockwell checked the time on the mantelpiece clock. "I must return to Scotland Yard to coordinate the search." He pushed himself out of the chair with a deep sigh. "It's going to be a long night."

Bristow entered with a piece of paper that he handed to Brockwell. "A constable delivered this, Inspector. He says it's urgent."

Brockwell read the paper then tucked it into his pocket. "Excellent news. She's been found."

"May?" I asked.

"Miss Dorothy Campion."

CHAPTER 15

"We're coming with you to speak to her," Matt said, rising.

"That might not be possible," Brockwell said.

"Don't exclude us now, after all the assistance we've given you."

"I mean it might not be possible because she's having difficulty speaking. She's in hospital. Her throat was cut and she has lost a lot of blood."

The constable gave us more details as we drove to London Hospital. Dotty had been brought to the hospital unconscious. She had no identifying documents on her, and the baker who'd found her and transported her on his cart didn't know her. She'd regained consciousness several days ago but had been very weak and unable to talk. Today she indicated she wanted to ask something, so the staff gave her a piece of paper to write on. She'd written her name and asked after Emmett Cocker. Aware of the murder from the newspapers, the staff notified police immediately. It wasn't known whether they'd informed Dotty of his death.

I wasn't looking forward to breaking the news to her. She

was carrying Emmett's child, and now it looked like she wasn't responsible for his death but had been a victim too. With Danny and May Draper fleeing, it seemed more apparent than ever that they were the killers.

The familiar stark and imposing surroundings of London Hospital looked even more stark and imposing cloaked in dusk's ethereal light. I almost expected to see Willie sneaking out after a liaison with her nurse friend, but I recognized none of the staff going about their tasks with silent efficiency.

A young nurse escorted us to the women's ward, stopping at the fourth bed on the right. I hardly recognized Dotty. Her face was as white as the bandages around her throat. Her blonde hair, arranged neatly over her shoulders, was almost the same shade. The only color came from the web of blue veins on her eyelids and the dark shadows underneath. She was still beautiful, only now her beauty was fragile, ghostly.

"She's asleep," the nurse whispered.

Dotty's eyes cracked open and she managed to rasp, "No."

"Don't try to sit up," the nurse said, laying a hand on Dotty's shoulder. "This is a policeman and two of his..."

"Assistants," Brockwell filled in. He introduced himself to Dotty using his full title, but her gaze fell on me. She recognized me.

"My name is India Steele and this is Matthew Glass," I said. "I saw you at The Prince of Wales once." I sat on the bed and smiled gently at her. "We've been looking for you."

"Emmett's murder?" Dotty asked, the words barely audible.

We all moved closer to the bed to hear her. "You know," I said.

"I told her," the nurse said. "She asked so..." She

235

shrugged. "Apparently she has something to tell you about it. I'll leave you now, but please don't tax her. Dotty, if talking hurts too much, use that notepad and pencil."

I took the notepad and pencil from the nightstand and offered them to Dotty.

She gave a small shake of her head. "I can manage."

"Did you witness Cocker's murder?" Brockwell asked, drawing out his own notepad and pencil.

"No," Dotty whispered. "I heard the gunshot after I left him. I returned to see if he was all right, but he wasn't. He lay on the ground, bleeding." She swallowed and winced in pain.

"Take your time," Matt said.

"Did you see who did this to you?" Brockwell pressed.

She shook her head.

"I'm going to ask you some simple questions," Matt said. "You can nod or shake your head in answer. You knew Emmett in America, didn't you?"

She nodded.

"And followed him here."

Another nod.

Matt looked to me, and I suspected he wanted me to take over and ask the more personal questions.

"We spoke with May Draper," I said. "She informed us that you're carrying Emmett's child."

Her hand fluttered at her waist. "Not anymore."

"Oh. I am so sorry."

"The murderer caused two deaths that night." With her rasping voice, it was difficult to tell if she was upset or not. Her eyes didn't water but they were distant, though that could have been a result of weakness from the blood loss.

"You came to England to tell Emmett," Matt went on. "And ask for his financial support?"

Dotty nodded.

"But he refused to help?"

She nodded again.

Matt paused so I took over. "You were angry with him yet you still loved him, didn't you?"

"It's difficult to explain," she whispered. "He wouldn't help. I needed money. The night before he died, I asked him again to support the baby."

"Again?"

"I asked him the previous night, too. He claimed he had none after paying back a large debt." She swallowed with effort. "I had to beg." Another swallow and her eyelids fluttered before focusing on me. "He finally gave me his watch to sell."

That explained Emmett's LeCoultre watch being in her room. "You took the watch back to your lodgings?" I asked.

She nodded.

"If he gave you the watch, why did you return to the lane the following night?" Brockwell asked. "The night he died?"

I didn't like his accusatory tone. Dotty was a victim, not the murderer, and she was battling through her pain to help us.

"A watch, no matter how fine, wouldn't sell for enough money to keep me and a baby for long," she said.

The money from the sale of a LeCoultre should keep her for a year if she lived frugally. But she would need Emmett's ongoing support, not just a year's worth of funds. Finding work while taking care of a young child would be very hard.

"We argued," she went on. "I said some cruel things. Things I regret now." She closed her eyes and took a moment to gather her composure before opening them again. "He wasn't a bad man. If it wasn't for his occasional outburst, he would be wonderful."

"But people were after him," I said. "People who thought he cheated them and wanted their money back."

She nodded.

"So you met Cocker in the lane on the night he died," Brockwell said, his pencil hovering over the notepad. "You argued about money and the baby. And then what?"

"I left. It was late. The saloon closed and there was no one about. I walked down the street and was some distance away when I heard a gunshot." She swallowed and her face twisted with pain.

I offered her water from the jug but she shook her head.

"I raced back to the lane," she went on. "It was dark. Too dark to see properly, but I saw the body lying on the ground and suspected it was Emmett. I couldn't see if he was alive. I was about to go further into the lane when something in the shadows moved. The same time I realized someone was there, I also heard a click. I've been around guns my whole life and I knew that sound was a revolver's hammer striking the primer."

"The barrel was empty," Matt said, enthralled by her tale. "There were no more bullets."

She nodded. "You don't know what relief is until you're shot at but no bullets are fired."

"The killer must have assumed you saw his or her face," Brockwell said. "He or she didn't want you identifying them to the police." He indicated her bandaged throat. "Hence the attack."

"What did you do?" I asked.

"I knew I had to escape," Dotty said. "I thought I could outrun him. I just had to get to a busy street first. So many thoughts jumbled through my mind in mere seconds, but I didn't even get the chance to turn." She frowned. "It happened so fast."

"Was there someone else in the shadows closer to the entrance of the lane near you?" Brockwell asked. "An accomplice who wielded the knife?"

She shook her head.

"Did the killer throw a knife then?"

She touched the bandages at her throat and swallowed. "It wasn't a knife that did this. It was..." She shook her head. "It sounds ridiculous. You won't believe me."

"We'll believe you," I said on a rush of breath.

"It was a deck of cards."

A deep and profound silence settled over us. We knew of only one person who could turn cards into weapons— Melville Hendry, the paper magician.

"A breeze must have whipped them up." Dotty shook her head at me. "But I don't remember feeling one. And cards can't do this, no matter how strong the wind."

"Perhaps you were mistaken," I said weakly. What else could I say? I couldn't tell her the truth. "Did the killer think you were dead? Is that why he left you there?"

"I suppose. He didn't stop to check but ran right past me as I lay there. I managed to crawl out of the lane before I fell unconscious."

"That explains why the baker saw you but not the body of Emmett Cocker," Brockwell said. "Even so, he should have reported picking you up that night after reading about Cocker's murder."

"Not everyone reads the papers," Matt said.

Dotty touched the bandage at her throat. "If the baker hadn't found me and brought me here..."

I patted her hand. "Don't think about what might have happened. The good news is you're going to be fine. Once you've recovered, you can return home to America."

Her lower lip wobbled, and I suspected she was thinking about her lost child. I didn't know what to say to comfort her, so I just patted her hand again.

"Thank you for your time, Miss Campion," Brockwell said, pocketing his notebook. "That will be all for today."

"You think I'm mad, don't you?" Dotty whispered.

I touched the hair at her temple, gently pushing it off her forehead. "Not at all. There are many inexplicable things in this world, and your tale is just one of them."

"India," Matt said quietly. "We have to go."

"You should rest now," I said to Dotty. "I'll come back soon."

Brockwell was already at the ward door when Matt and I caught up to him.

"Hendry must have assumed Dotty saw him," Matt said as we strode outside. "He didn't realize the streetlight at the lane entrance meant he could see her face clearly but she couldn't see his."

"I can't believe it's him," I murmured. "He never struck me as a killer."

"He always struck me as mad," Brockwell said. "Ever since he lied to protect his friend, even though he suspected Sweeney was implicating him. No man in his right mind does that."

I could have said a man in love did, but I wasn't sure Brockwell understood love. He was far too logical to believe in something he couldn't explain.

"May I borrow your carriage?" the inspector asked, climbing into the cabin of our waiting growler. "You two can catch a hack back to Park Street."

"I'm going with you," Matt said, also climbing in. "India, do you have money for a hack?"

"I do but—"

"Driver!" Brockwell shouted. "Smithfield! Now!"

The carriage was away before Matt had closed the door and I could warn them to be careful. I was a little put out that they'd not even considered taking me with them. I was, after all, the only magician of our trio and therefore the only one to really understand Mr. Hendry. At a time like this, and with a man like him, understanding might be needed. At least Matt and Brockwell were smart enough not to confront him inside the shop where weapons in the form of paper covered the shelves and countertop. They would draw him outside first.

I hoped.

Darkness had truly settled into every corner of the city by the time I arrived home. Miss Glass and Willie had already dined together informally while Duke and Cyclops were nowhere to be seen. Bristow informed me that Miss Glass had retired early to her room while Willie was in the smoking room.

I found her sprawled in the wingback chair, one leg dangling over the chair arm, blowing smoke rings. I coughed and opened a window.

"There you are," she said, waving the smoke away from her face. "Where've you been?"

"It's a long story, and I don't want to repeat myself. Where are Cyclops and Duke?"

"Don't know where Cyclops is. Probably drowning his sorrows over not being with Catherine. I s'pose Duke's still watching Dotty's place."

I swore, earning a snicker from Willie. "My apologies, that was uncalled for," I said. "In our haste to get to the hospital, we forgot he was still there."

"Hospital! Is it Matt?"

"No, it's Dotty. We found her." I told her Dotty's story from beginning to end. "Matt and Brockwell have gone to arrest Mr. Hendry now," I finished.

Willie simultaneously dropped the cigar onto the ashtray and sprang out of the chair. "I got to go to Hendry's."

"Stay here. They can manage on their own."

"How can you be so calm? Hendry's magic makes him

more dangerous than he looks. I'll fetch my Colt. Go tell the coachman to bring the carriage back round."

"He's with Matt. I caught a hack home from the hospital."

Willie's swear word was far worse than mine. "Then send Fossett to fetch a cab."

"Willie—"

"Do it, India!"

I intercepted her as she strode toward the door. "We're not going anywhere," I said, grasping her shoulders. "I know you're worried. I'm worried too. But Matt and Brockwell are both capable men. We'll only get in the way."

"Spoken like a silly female who ain't good for anything but sitting home and sewing all day." She shoved my hands off. "I ain't that kind of woman, India, and I didn't think you were, either."

Her words were like a slap to the face, a stark reminder of the differences between us. She was impulsive; I was more rational. She was attracted to danger while I fled from it.

Yet the sting of her words lingered. I'd never been a genteel female who conformed to type. I'd worked in my father's shop from a young age, and I never took to the domestic arts, although I did them out of necessity after my mother died. I preferred to converse on a broad range of topics, not limiting myself to neighborhood gossip, fashion and marriage. I did not appreciate being called a silly female.

I picked up my skirts and raced after her. If she was going then I would go too. Someone had to keep her in check and save her from bursting into Mr. Hendry's shop in the midst of a tense standoff.

The knocker pounded on the front door as we passed through the entrance hall. "That's probably Matt," I said to Willie. "I'll get it, Bristow!" I called out.

I opened the door and my stomach plunged.

Mr. Hendry stood on the stoop.

"Good evening, Miss Steele. I apologize for coming at this late hour, but I need to have a word."

I froze, unable to think of what to say to this man; this murderer. With each passing second, Mr. Hendry's smile slipped. I ought to say something innocent, but I could think of nothing. I felt as foolish as Willie claimed me to be.

She nudged me aside and opened the door wider. "Come in, Mr. Hendry."

"Willie—"

She pinched the back of my hand and turned on a bright smile for Mr. Hendry. He stepped past her and she closed the door. She stood in front of it, blocking his exit.

She'd gone quite mad. We had no weapons, yet Mr. Hendry had several. The mail and invitations were still on the hall table beside my reticule.

Bristow emerged from the shadows at the back of the hall and I beckoned him closer. "Please take the mail and invitations up to Mr. Glass's office then...polish the silver." That would solve two problems—removing the paper products and keeping him out of harm's way. "Oh, and pass me my reticule."

A small crease formed on Bristow's brow, the likes of which I'd never seen before. His face was usually arranged so agreeably. "I polished the silver this morning, madam. Shall I do it again?"

"Er, yes. Please do."

"Very good, madam." He gathered up the mail and invitations, handed me the reticule, and headed up the stairs.

I pulled my watch from the reticule and pretended to check the time then clasped it in my hand. This new watch had never saved my life like my old one. It hadn't even chimed when Mr. Sweeney threatened our lives. I'd worked on it many time since, yet nowhere near as often as my old one. Whether it was enough to chime in the face of danger or save my life now, I was yet to discover.

I had a sickening feeling I was going to discover the answer tonight.

Mr. Hendry's gaze remained on the staircase. "Is Mr. Glass here?"

"He'll be back soon," I said. "What did you want to talk to him about?" It seemed absurd to have a casual conversation with him, but I wasn't yet sure how to proceed. Confront him and we risked him overpowering us and getting away. It only made sense to confront him if we had a weapon. My fingers tightened around my watch.

"Empty your pockets," Willie barked.

I groaned. Clearly she didn't think the same way.

"Pardon?" Mr. Hendry looked from me to Willie and back again. In that moment, I realized he knew that we knew. There was no point pretending anymore.

"Empty your pockets," I said. "Remove anything made of paper. Do it slowly and do not utter a word."

He unbuttoned his jacket and plucked a deck of cards from his inside pocket. He placed them on my outstretched palm. "If you let me go," he said, "I won't hurt you."

I gave the cards to Willie. "Throw these outside."

She opened the door wide enough to slip the cards through then shut it again. "I'm deputizing myself and India," she said. "Mr. Hendry, you're under arrest for the murder of Mr. Emmett Cocker and the attempted murder of Dorothy Campion."

"So she is alive," he said flatly. "I knew I should have made sure." He was so cool and calm, not at all like the emotional man I'd come to know. He'd always seemed so tightly wound, his nerves frayed. Had committing murder changed him? Or had this calculating, cold man lurked beneath the surface all along?

"You also murdered Miss Campion's unborn child," I added.

"She was with child?" Mr. Hendry's body caved in, as if all the breath suddenly left his body. "I—I didn't know."

"We're going to wait here until the police arrive," Willie told him. "India, fetch Bristow back. Send him or Fossett to the nearest police station. We ain't waiting for Brockwell and Matt to return."

"It's not wise," I cautioned her. "I don't know what his magic is capable of, and I don't want the servants getting injured."

"All the paper and cards have been removed."

I would not be swayed. The only way to be entirely sure that Hendry's magic would be rendered impotent would be to render him unconscious. If he couldn't speak a spell, he couldn't fling the papers at us.

I searched the vicinity but few potential weapons presented themselves. The lamps were all attached to the walls, there were no candelabras, and the clock and vase were too heavy to wield effectively. There were only three potential weapons—the silver salver on the hall stand, the umbrella in the umbrella stand, and Willie's fists.

She didn't look at me, however, so I couldn't convey the message to her. I inched back to the umbrella stand.

"I didn't know about the baby," Mr. Hendry said again, hands in the air. "You can't blame that on me."

"You're a low down son of a bitch," Willie spat. "And to think, we defended you last time. Matt and India convinced the police you were innocent of Baggley's murder."

"I was innocent!" He wiped his hand across his forehead, which glistened with sweat.

"Did you come here tonight to ask about the investigation?" I asked. "Is that why you offered to do our invitations? Because you wanted an excuse to come here and check on our progress? You became cross with Miss Glass when she picked up the invitations because you wanted it to be one of us so you could ask questions."

His fingers twitched and he nibbled on in his bottom lip. He could no longer stand still, shifting his weight from foot to foot. "I should have made sure she was dead," he said, tapping his fingers nervously against his thigh. "I scoured the papers for any news of her but there was none. I *knew* she didn't die that night, or it would have been reported along with Cocker's death. Damnation!"

"Please keep your voice down, Mr. Hendry," I said as calmly as I could. "You don't want to alarm the rest of the household, and nor do we. Let's keep this between ourselves."

He scrubbed a hand over his mouth and glanced at the staircase.

"You used Emmett's gun, didn't you?" Willie asked.

"I don't carry one, but he did. The fool. He let me get close enough that I could retrieve it from him. He wasn't too smart. He didn't realize my intention until it was too late."

"Why did you kill him?"

"He was pestering me. He wanted my spells. Every day, he showed up at my shop and offered me something for them. I told him I didn't want his money or anything else he had to offer. That's when he threatened me."

"With what?" I asked.

"With exposure. He was going to tell the police he caught me with a boy. You must believe me, I wouldn't do *that*!"

"You killed him over a threat?" Willie cried.

"I couldn't go to jail. I couldn't then, and I won't now. They'll execute me for murder. Do you understand? Have mercy, Miss Steele." He looked like he'd burst into tears or throw himself on the floor and beg.

"Don't appeal to me," I said. "I have no sympathy for you."

He moved toward me, stopping when Willie ordered him not to move. He put his hands in the air again. "Let me walk away," he said. "I promise not to harm anyone again. I'll live quietly in hiding. Please, Miss Steele. You understand the pressure I've been put under, how my magic alienates me from the rest of the world."

"You alienate yourself." I closed my hand around my watch and willed it to be ready if needed. An encouraging flare of warmth responded. I inched back. Just a little further and I would be in reach of the umbrella stand.

Mr. Hendry's eyes watered and he swiped his nose with the back of his hand. "You can't do this to me, Miss Steele." His voice became high-pitched, panicked. "How could you condemn me to death? We are two of a rare kind. We ought to be protected."

"Do not compare us. We are not the same."

He sniffed. "You've been with the artless too long. They've persuaded you into thinking you're something perverted, something that should be suppressed."

"They've done nothing of the sort."

But he wasn't listening; his wild eyes looked right through me. There was no point trying to reason with him. "Listen only to those who would applaud and revere us, like Lord Coyle and his friends." He moved toward me again.

"Get back!" Willie ordered. "Stay away from her!"

But he kept coming, his hands out—in appeal or to capture me, I couldn't tell.

I didn't wait to find out. I lunged to the side, throwing myself at the umbrella stand. It toppled over, clattering onto the tiles, and the umbrella slid out, too far away for me to grab.

I lay sprawled on the floor, Mr. Hendry towering over me. His lips moved with his whisper.

"Willie!" I cried. "Stop him before he completes the spell."

"There ain't no paper here no more." Even so, she dived toward him.

He dodged her and careened into the hall table. The silver salver and clock fell off, smashing on the floor. The noise would have been heard throughout the house.

There was no time for me to worry about Miss Glass walking down the stairs into danger, however, because the windows suddenly blew inward. Glass shattered, spraying sharp, jagged shards over the entrance hall.

I flung my arms up to protect my face and head. I didn't see what happened to Willie but I heard her gasp of pain.

And then came the *swish swish* of something flying through the air.

The cards.

They were no longer outside, and Mr. Hendry was going to use them to cut us to shreds.

CHAPTER 16

$\mathcal{I}$ cowered beneath my arms, not daring to peek out. I could feel something tugging at my skirt, dragging at my sleeve. Fabric tore. Something sharp as a blade nicked the skin on the back of my hand, drawing blood.

I opened my mouth to scream at Mr. Hendry.

It was drowned out by the boom of a gunshot.

It reverberated around the hall and echoed in my head. The *swish swish* of the flying paper suddenly stopped. I peeked through the cover of my arms and saw Mr. Hendry squatting amid a shower of papers floating to the floor. He'd stopped chanting his spell and now peered into the shadows.

Time seemed to slow. I registered the strangeness of my surroundings. The settling papers made it look as though a snowstorm had struck. Pages of a newspaper were among them, and then I spotted a book I'd been reading. I'd left it in the sitting room. The library wouldn't have been a good place to hide after all.

Willie lay flat on the floor, her hands over her head, sheets of paper partially covering her.

Something in the shadows at the back moved. The shooter?

Mr. Hendry's whispers began again. He'd been distracted only, not shot, by the hidden shooter. He could not be allowed to start his spell again. There was an abundance of potential weapons for him already surrounding us.

I hauled myself to my feet and threw myself at him, slamming into his crouching form.

He toppled backward, smacking his head on the floor. I fell on top of him and clamped my hand over his mouth. His gaze shifted to a point past my shoulder as someone emerged from the shadows.

"You can get off him, India. If he speaks again, I'll shoot."

I couldn't believe my ears. "Miss Glass!"

She stood a few paces away, Bristow at her side. She clutched Willie's gun in both hands. They shook but the determined gleam in her eyes left me with no doubt she would follow through on her threat.

Bristow cupped her hands, raising them slightly. "You want to kill him, not castrate him," he said.

I took a moment to steady my jangling nerves and to take stock. I crouched at Willie's side. The back of her arm was covered in blood and the back of her waistcoat sported several tears, but she was alive. She sat up with my assistance and frowned at Miss Glass.

"That's my gun!"

Sometimes, her priorities were a little skewed.

"I didn't think you'd mind if I borrowed it," Miss Glass said.

"Bristow?" I prompted.

"We heard the noise and investigated from the landing," he said, nodding at the staircase. "Miss Glass suggested we locate Miss Johnson's weapon. We didn't load it, however. We only intended to threaten him."

"I always keep it loaded," Willie said.

"We came down via the service stairs," Bristow went on.

"Just in time, too," Miss Glass said, her hands lowering again. "This becomes heavy after a while."

Bristow took over and we all breathed a sigh of relief. I still wasn't sure where the first bullet had ended up. Thankfully, not in either Willie or me.

The front door suddenly burst open and Matt rushed in, Brockwell and two constables on his heels. All paused and took in the sea of paper, Bristow with the gun, and Mr. Hendry lying on the floor.

"Blimey," one of the constables muttered.

"India." Matt waded through the papers, kicking them aside. He clasped my arms and dipped his head to peer into my face. "Are you all right?"

I nodded.

"Willie?" he said. "Aunt?"

"You're bleeding," Brockwell said, inspecting Willie's arm. He pressed his handkerchief over the shirt sleeve at the cut.

She thanked him and took over, her fingers touching his before he withdrew. "It ain't too bad. Could have been worse."

Matt spotted the paper cut on my hand and kissed my knuckles. "Any other injuries?" he asked.

"Only to my dress and my nerves." I inspected a tear on my skirt. The card had cut cleanly through it. If that card and the others had been directed at my throat then I would need hospitalization with life-threatening injuries like Dotty. Or I may not have been as lucky. I didn't for a moment think Mr. Hendry missed on purpose, but rather he had trouble controlling his magic with so much paper around. The result was chaos that proved too much for him.

Brockwell sent his constables outside before asking us what happened.

"Mr. Hendry came here to learn how our investigation was proceeding," I said. "He hoped to glean some information about Dotty's whereabouts."

Willie kicked Mr. Hendry's foot. He drew his legs up. "He realized she wasn't dead when the papers didn't mention her body was found near Cocker's, so he wanted to finish the job," she said.

"When he learned we'd found her, and that we knew he murdered Emmett, he spoke his spell and this happened. Paper came from everywhere."

Matt picked up a sheet near his left foot. "This is from my office. It'll take all day to put it to rights again."

"The broken windows?" Brockwell prompted.

"He had a deck of cards in his possession which we threw outside for safekeeping," I said. "I think they belonged to Emmett."

"They did," Mr. Hendry said, sitting up. He rubbed the back of his head and winced. "You hit hard, Miss Steele."

"You punched him?" Matt asked me.

"I sort of threw myself at him and he hit his head on the floor." I spotted my watch half hidden beneath a piece of paper and picked it up. "It didn't even chime."

"The broken windows?" Brockwell asked again. "Are you saying the cards broke them?"

"Aye," Willie said. "We threw the cards outside thinking he couldn't use them out there. Seems we were wrong. They smashed the windows and flew in here. Underneath all this paper are shards of glass."

"I'll have the servants set it to rights immediately," Bristow said.

Willie took the gun from him and aimed it at Mr. Hendry. I got the distinct impression she was keen to use it.

"Yes, do clean this up," Miss Glass said, reaching out a hand toward Matt. "Take me to my room, Harry. I need to lie down. All this excitement is overwhelming."

"Harry?" Brockwell asked as he watched Matt escort Miss Glass up the stairs.

"She suffers from memory loss, particularly in times of high excitement," I said. "She thinks she's a young woman again and that Matt is his father, her brother, Harry. She'll be all right by the morning."

I went in search of Polly and sent her up to Miss Glass's room with a pot of chocolate. By the time I returned to the entrance hall, Brockwell had left, taking Mr. Hendry with him, and the clean up operation had begun, led by Mr. and Mrs. Bristow.

Willie tucked the gun into her waistband and patted the handle as if it were a good pet for obeying orders. "There was only one bullet in it."

Bristow paused, papers in hand. "So he could have kept speaking his spell and there was nothing we could have done about it?"

"We could have punched him in the mouth," she said.

"Should have done it anyway," Mrs. Bristow chimed in. "On account of him making all this mess for us to tidy up."

Matt returned just as the front door opened. Cyclops and Duke stopped on the threshold, twin expressions of shock on their faces.

"What happened?" Cyclops asked.

"Mr. Hendry came here and spoke a spell," I said. "He's the murderer. Emmett wanted his spells, Hendry refused, so Emmett threatened to make up terrible stories about his...proclivities."

Duke gathered some papers near the door. "He just came here and confessed?"

"We confronted him," I said. "Dotty was found in hospital and she told us—"

"She's been found?" He straightened. "And no one thought to tell me?"

"Sorry," Matt said with a sheepish shrug. "We were busy."

Duke shoved the papers into Matt's chest. "Then you can clean this mess up yourselves. I'm starving."

"Dinner's in the warming pot in the kitchen," Mrs. Bristow called after him as he marched past her. "Help yourself."

"I better go too," Cyclops said. "Before he eats it all."

"Where've you been?" Willie asked him.

"I met Duke at Dotty's house."

"You've been there the whole time?"

"For the last hour."

"And before that?"

"Waltzing with the queen in Buckingham Palace," he said over his shoulder.

The tidying up operation took almost an hour, and that didn't include sorting through the papers. We stacked them on Matt's desk in his office but he put the task of re-organizing them off until the morning.

"I can't believe his spell did all this," I said, slapping the top of one of the piles. "Although I don't think he intended to. He just wanted to use the cards as weapons and this was an unintentional consequence." I sighed. "He'll hang for murdering Emmett."

"Try not to think about it."

It was impossible not to. No matter how different I was to Mr. Hendry, we were connected by our magic. I understood some of his struggles, although not all. Not nearly all.

"I wonder if paper magic will die out with him," I said. "Neither he nor Emmett had children, after all."

"It depends if they had siblings or other cousins."

"Coyle and his friends would know." That was a troubling thought, although I couldn't quite explain why. Another troubling thought was the failure of my watch. "It didn't chime, despite the danger," I told Matt. "I've tinkered with it dozens of times since Mr. Sweeney's arrest, yet it still doesn't work."

"I'll take it back to Mason's and inform him, shall I?"

"Don't joke, Matt."

"Perhaps you need to tinker with it hundreds of times. You'd had your old watch for years and this one mere weeks. Give it time, India."

"I'm beginning to think it's something my father did to my original watch. Perhaps there's nothing I can do. Perhaps the magic was already in the old one when I received it." I blew out a frustrated breath. "I wish I knew."

Matt took my hand and led me to the chair behind the desk. "Sit down and try to relax."

"I can't."

It turned out that I could relax quite easily when he massaged the tension from my shoulders. Even time seemed to slip away without me noticing.

"That was wonderful," I murmured when he stopped. "Come here and let me thank you."

He leaned over me from behind and gave me an upside down kiss. I smiled against his mouth until he deepened the kiss. It was just what I needed after the evening I'd had.

"No wonder you two are still up here," came Willie's voice from the doorway. "Come down to the drawing room and have a drink with us. We've opened the good brandy."

"I should have closed the door," Matt muttered.

"We'll join you as long as no one plays poker," I said to Willie. "I can't face a deck of cards for some time."

* * *

I SPENT the following morning mending my dress while Matt put his paperwork to rights. A glazier had come first thing to measure up for replacement windows and the household was getting back in order, including Miss Glass, who was her usual self once again.

"You must visit the dressmaker for a final inspection, India," she said. "Now that the investigation is over, we can go today."

"If you wish."

"And check with Mrs. Potter about the menu."

"She has it all in hand," I said.

"What about the flowers?"

"They'll be delivered fresh on the morning of the wedding."

She did not mention the invitations, for which I was grateful. Willie, however, wasn't quite as tactful.

"I think you should invite Jasper," she said.

It took me a moment to remember that Jasper was Detective Inspector Brockwell. "Any particular reason?" I asked slyly.

"He's become a friend," she said, returning to her sewing. Like me, she'd been fixing the tears in her clothing, only she was all thumbs and much slower.

"So I've noticed."

Willie pricked her thumb, drawing blood. "The devil take it," she muttered. "I hate sewing."

"Give it to me," Miss Glass said. "You are quite hopeless at all the feminine arts, Willemina."

"You're an angel, Letty." Willie passed the waistcoat,

needle and thread to Miss Glass. "I can deliver an invitation to Jasper tonight if you like, India. I've got to return his handkerchief anyway."

"Tonight?" Miss Glass asked.

"He'll be busy all day with work."

"Leave the poor man alone when he's off duty. He won't want to be bothered with you after a long day."

Willie opened her mouth but I vigorously shook my head at her. It was best for Miss Glass not to know everything Willie got up to.

Cyclops entered and requested to speak with me privately. I followed him across the hall to the library. He checked the vicinity before closing the door.

"Is something the matter?" I asked.

He leaned back against the door. "Have you given any more thought to helping Ronnie with his test?"

"Are you referring to helping him study for it?"

"No."

"I didn't think so." I sat down near the fireplace and asked him to sit too. "Cyclops, I know you're worried, but it's not possible to sit the test for him without getting caught. Anyway, I thought you and Catherine were against the idea."

"She is. Don't tell her I've talked to you about it."

"Dishonesty is not a good foundation on which to build a relationship."

"We don't have a relationship."

I cocked my head to the side and raised my brows.

"I've been thinking about it and decided Ronnie's right," he said, forging ahead. "Abercrombie'll make the test too hard for him to pass. Ronnie's clever but he ain't you, India."

"Flattery won't work, Cyclops. What you're asking me to do is absurd."

"What does it matter if you get caught? You won't be doing anything against the law, just against guild rules—

and you ain't a member anyway." At my hesitation, he plunged in. "I want the best for Catherine. She desperately wants to open this shop with Ronnie. She needs her independence, India, and she's too vibrant to stay in her parents' shadows. I want her to be happy."

"It sounds to me like you ought to court her."

"That's a different issue."

"Is it?"

He glared at me, so I let the matter drop and returned to the one at hand.

"You're asking me to cheat, Cyclops. I don't feel right about it."

"Abercrombie is the one who's cheating. He's going to make the test too hard for anyone except you to pass. That ain't fair."

"No, but I don't like being a party to anything nefarious." I could hear an invisible Willie whispering in my ear about how safe I was being, how dull and sensible.

"We don't have to tell Matt," Cyclops added.

"Of course I do. We have no secrets from one another."

The words tasted like ash in my mouth. With the turmoil of the last few days, I'd pushed thoughts of my agreement with Lord Coyle to the back of my mind. But they would not go away completely. They never would while his favor hung like a guillotine above my neck.

Bristow knocked on the door and entered. "Lord Coyle is here, madam. He'd like to speak to you and Mr. Glass."

My conscience was a powerful thing, to conjure him up at the very moment I thought about him. "What does he want?"

"He did not specify."

Of course he wouldn't confide in the butler. Bristow waited for my response and I waited for... I didn't really know. A miracle, I supposed.

Cyclops rose and made his excuses but I caught his hand.

"Stay," I said. "Please."

He frowned. "Why? Matt's on his way down, ain't he, Bristow?"

"Fossett is fetching him, sir. Is everything all right, Miss Steele? Shall I ask his lordship to return another day?"

Bristow and Cyclops waited for my decision, but I never got the chance to make it. Matt strolled into the library, leading Lord Coyle.

Bristow bowed out and Cyclops followed, closing the door behind him. I considered leaving too, but that wouldn't solve anything if Lord Coyle had come for his repayment.

His lordship eased himself into one of the deep armchairs with a groan. The leather creaked beneath his weight as he settled. He pulled out a handkerchief from his jacket pocket and dabbed at his flushed, sweating forehead. He looked as if he'd walked here, yet I could see his carriage through the library window, waiting at the curb.

"You seem troubled, Coyle," Matt said.

His lordship continued to dab at his face with his folded handkerchief. "I am greatly troubled, Glass. Indeed, I'm angry."

My own face suddenly felt very hot yet the rest of me went cold. "What about?" I asked, my voice small.

"The police arrested Hendry."

Oh. That was all. Thank goodness I had avoided the confrontation. For now.

"He's going to be executed," Coyle went on. "And you two had a hand in the investigation and his arrest, I believe."

"Did Whittaker tell you that?" Matt asked.

Coyle's gaze locked with Matt's. "I asked you to be gentle with Hendry. You assured me you would treat him carefully."

"That was before we learned he was a murderer."

Coyle thumped the chair arm. "Bloody hell, Glass! Do you know what you've done?"

"Helped get a dangerous man off the street?"

"He was the last of his kind. He and his cousin, Emmett Cocker, were the only paper magicians left in the world."

"That you know of."

"The line dies with Hendry. Paper magic will become extinct. Doesn't that sadden you?"

Matt merely glared at him.

Lord Coyle appealed to me. "You understand, don't you, Miss Steele? We're about to lose a precious resource."

"It is hardly our fault," I shot back. "Blame Mr. Hendry for killing his cousin. As to the line dying with him, I can say with some confidence that it would have done so anyway. You know his proclivities. He wouldn't have fathered children."

He lifted a hand in a dismissive wave. "Something could have been arranged to insure the continuation of his magic."

I barked out a laugh. He didn't know Mr. Hendry very well at all if he thought it would be that easy.

"Hendry knew a spell to turn paper into weapons," Matt said. "That made his magic far more dangerous than any other. I, for one, don't think its disappearance should be mourned."

Lord Coyle removed a cigar from his pocket and plugged it into his mouth.

"No smoking in here, please," I said. "I don't want the books to smell."

He removed the cigar but didn't return it to his pocket. He wedged it between his fingers and pointed at Matt. "You should never have meddled in this affair."

"Brockwell would have found the killer without our help," Matt said.

"I'm not so certain." Coyle regarded me from beneath pendulous, fleshy eyelids. On the surface, he looked indolent, but I knew him to be a man of action. If his desires were thwarted, he had the means and power to follow through on his threats. "I would appreciate it if you didn't meddle again in affairs that don't concern you," he added.

"This concerned us," I said quickly. "Duke was a suspect. We initially offered our assistance to the inspector because Duke was implicated."

Coyle's lips puckered before he shoved the cigar between them. He rocked himself out of the chair and lumbered to his feet. "You've created a headache for me and work for my lawyers."

"You're a fool, Coyle," Matt said. "Let justice take its natural course."

I gasped. "You want to clear Hendry? But you can't! He's guilty."

"Is he, Miss Steele? It's my understanding that Miss Campion didn't see the murder being committed nor did she see the person who cut her throat. Her story of cards flying about will be laughed out of court. I doubt Commissioner Munro will want magic mentioned at all, so what does that leave? Nothing. The prosecution do not have a case, let alone a solid one. My lawyer will tear it to shreds."

"You would risk having that man roam the streets?" Matt growled. "All because you want the paper magic line to continue?"

Lord Coyle walked off, his heavy, rolling gait slow but determined. "Don't worry. Hendry won't have any need to retaliate against either of you if the case is dismissed. I will, however, get an assurance from him that he'll leave you alone, if you like."

"If we *like*!" Matt snapped.

I shook my head at Matt in warning. He marched past

Coyle, opened the library door then the front door, wide. Wisely, Coyle left without another word, and Matt slammed the door behind him.

Willie and Miss Glass emerged from the sitting room. "What's all the commotion?" Miss Glass asked.

"An unwelcome visitor," Matt said. "Don't trouble yourself, Aunt."

She returned to the sitting room but Willie wasn't as easily dismissed. Matt told her that Lord Coyle would see that Mr. Hendry got off the murder charge.

"It weren't ever going to be easy to convict him," she said. "Not if magic were kept out of it. Dotty ain't a good witness, since she didn't actually witness anything."

"Coyle didn't have to make it easier," Matt said. Some of the steel had left his tone, however, and he no longer looked like he wanted to throttle Lord Coyle. "He's setting a dangerous precedent by interfering. Where will it end? How far will he go to protect magicians?"

That was a sobering thought. The more I got to know Lord Coyle and his friends, the more it looked like they would do anything to keep their collections safe, and that meant keeping magicians safe. While it was admirable in theory, in situations like Hendry's, it undermined everything I believed in. Justice shouldn't be influenced by those seeking to bend it to suit themselves.

The worst of it was that I felt quite helpless, and Matt must too.

And he would not like feeling helpless. Not one bit.

* * *

Detective Inspector Brockwell invited me to accompany him to see Dotty. He showed up on our doorstep, two days after Hendry's arrest, with the request when he could have sent a message.

"Is she still in hospital?" I asked as I accepted my gloves from Bristow.

Brockwell didn't seem to have heard me. He was too busy glancing up the staircase, his head cocked to the side as if he were listening.

"Jasper!" I said to get his attention. "She isn't here."

He removed his hat and scratched his sideburns. "I don't know who you're referring to, India."

I smirked. "Acting coy doesn't suit you, Inspector."

"What happened to Jasper?"

"Nice attempt at a deflection." I accepted my hat from Bristow but did not put it on. "Are you sure you want me to go with you, or was it simply a ruse to come here and see Willie? I don't want to intrude."

"No, no, please come. I'm not very good with women. If I'm not interrogating them, I get tongue tied and I blush a lot."

"How did you manage with me?"

"I pretended I was interrogating you. It helped." His face reddened, proving his point.

"You're fine with Willie. Indeed, you seem to have won her over."

"She's not a woman. I mean, she *is* a woman, just... different to most."

"Very true," I said, following him out.

"She's easy to talk to."

I contemplated warning him that Willie might not be looking for a relationship with him, but I realized I wasn't sure what she wanted from Brockwell—or from anyone, for that matter. It was also none of my business. They could muddle through their affair without my opinion.

We found Dotty where we'd last seen her, in the fourth

hospital bed in the women's ward. Her color had improved considerably, and she no longer looked like a ghostly apparition. She smiled upon seeing us and I smiled back, even though my heart was heavy. What we were about to say would make her smile disappear.

"How do you feel?" I asked.

"Better," she said, her voice much stronger than the last time I'd seen her. "Still a little tired, but the doctor said that happens after substantial blood loss. They say I'm fortunate to be alive at all."

"When will you be discharged?" Brockwell asked.

"In a few days. Is the trial going to be soon?"

Brockwell and I exchanged glances.

"Only I'd like to go home to America as soon as the doctors say I'm able." She looked from Brockwell to me and back again. "What is it? What's wrong?"

"It's not official," the inspector said, "but I wanted to keep you informed. There is unlikely to be a trial."

"Why?"

"Insufficient evidence."

"I thought that fellow confessed when confronted."

"He retracted it. He claims he was tricked into making it."

Dotty touched the bandages at her throat. "So there'll be no justice for Emmett."

"You'll be safe," Brockwell told her. "Hendry knows now that you can't identify him."

I sat on the edge of the bed and touched her hand. "It's not fair." It sounded pathetic, but there was nothing more to say. Dotty was right; Emmett would receive no justice. Lord Coyle and his lawyers ought to feel ashamed of themselves.

"There is also the matter of the Drapers," Brockwell went on. "It seems they have disappeared."

"You can't find them?" I asked. "Good lord, this is turning into a debacle."

Brockwell looked offended. "My men tried their best, India. They cannot be everywhere, on every road and at every port."

I sighed. "I'm sorry. I'm frustrated."

"I am not happy about it either."

"They're experts at disappearing," Dotty told me. "They've done it before, so Emmett said. He never quite trusted them, which perhaps explains why he decided to cut Danny Draper out of his cheating scheme."

"One must trust one's partner in crime," Brockwell said. At my arched look, he added, "So I've learned from years of catching criminals."

We thanked Dotty and I promised to visit her again before she left England. Brockwell and I parted ways at the forecourt, only I didn't return home. I wanted to make another call, one that I didn't think would be particularly welcome. Not when they heard what I had to say.

CHAPTER 17

I was in luck. Not only was Mrs. Delancey at home, but she had another visitor whom I very much wanted to see too. Lady Louisa greeted me with slightly less effusiveness than her hostess, although she did look pleased to see me. Her smile waned, however, when I did not return it.

"India, dear, what a lovely surprise." Mrs. Delancey beckoned me to sit beside her. When I refused, she looked devastated. "I insist. You must come and have tea and cake with us. Aren't we fortunate, Louisa? India, you are most welcome. We do enjoy your company. India?" She patted the cushion next to her again. "Sit. You're making my neck ache."

I remained standing after the butler bowed out and shut the double doors. "This isn't a social call. I've come to tell you that you ought to be ashamed of yourselves for what you did."

Mrs. Delancey clutched the black ribbon choker circling her throat. "My dear, I am not aware that we have done anything. Are you, Louisa?"

Louisa set down her teacup on the table calmly and

deliberately. I suspected she knew precisely what I was talking about. Mrs. Delancey, however, was either in the dark or was playing the silly female.

"This is about Mr. Hendry, is it not?" Louisa asked.

I nodded. "Lord Coyle's lawyer is working on his case, and he will likely succeed. Mr. Hendry won't even go to trial. He will walk free in a matter of days, perhaps hours."

"But that's excellent news," Mrs. Delancey said. "So why are you upset, India?"

"Because he's a murderer!"

"Yes, but he's not *dangerous*. I believe his cousin threatened him. It's natural to strike out when backed into a corner."

I hadn't expected understanding from her. It wasn't why I'd come. I had only wanted to make it known how I felt about the situation and about their involvement in it. "You are selfish and greedy," I said. "All of you."

"Greedy?" Mrs. Delancey echoed.

"Greedy for magic. You wish to possess it and control it."

"No, India," Louisa said. "You are quite wrong on that score. We don't want to control magic. We want to protect it."

Mrs. Delancey looked at her like she was mad. I suspected she and Mr. Delancey did want to possess magic, or the objects infused with magic. They were the sort of people who wanted a house full of unique, beautiful things, the rarer the better. *They* were greedy. Louisa was different. Professor Nash too, although he wasn't a member of the club. As to what Sir Charles Whittaker and Lord Coyle wanted, I no longer knew.

"If Mr. Hendry harms anyone else, it will be your fault," I said. "All of you will be to blame for setting him free."

Mrs. Delancey dismissed my concerns with a flick of her wrist. Her numerous rings flashed in the sunlight. "Don't worry about that. Mr. Hendry will be made to understand that he can't go about killing people. Lord Coyle will press it upon him and you know what his lordship is like. He can be quite persuasive in making one see his point of view."

"Mr. Hendry should pay for his crime," I tried again.

"Believe me, he will pay," Louisa said with a wry twist of her mouth. "He will be indebted to Lord Coyle, for one thing, and I do not advise that."

Indeed.

"He'll resist at first," Mrs. Delancey added, reaching for her teacup. "But he'll come to see it's the best course of action."

"I don't understand," I said. "What course of action?"

"He's going to marry and have children."

I laughed. I couldn't help it. Like a sneeze, it erupted from the depths of me and just burst out. "You make it sound so simple, but I know he won't agree to that."

"He will if he wishes to keep his magical gift quiet," Louisa said. "And avoid re-arrest."

"Don't worry," Mrs. Delancey quipped. "It's all in hand. A suitable bride will be sought from among the best families."

I cocked my head. "Best?"

Mrs. Delancey and Louisa shared a look but neither clarified. I was quite certain that "best" in this context had to do with magic and not social standing.

I couldn't quite believe it. While Lord Coyle had said the same thing, when he had called on us, I'd not really taken him seriously. One couldn't force a man to marry against his will, after all. Yet these two spoke of it as if it was inevitable, and Mr. Hendry's love for men not a consideration.

"Now that you've got that off your chest, India, come and sit with us," Mrs. Delancey said, once again turning on a smile. "Let's get to know one another better."

"I can't," I said. "There is one thing I wished to ask you, though, Louisa."

Mrs. Delancey pouted at my snub.

"Is this about Fabian?" Louisa asked.

"Who?" Mrs. Delancey said.

If Mrs. Delancey knew nothing about Fabian Charbonneau then perhaps others in the collector's club didn't know about him either. Why had Louisa not informed them?

"Why did you tell him about me?" I asked.

"He's been looking for someone like you, someone with extraordinary power," Louisa said.

"My power isn't proven."

Louisa gave a languid, elegant shrug. "So I told him about you. His visit here is nothing to do with me. I didn't know he'd come until he showed up at my house."

"Who is this fellow?" Mrs. Delancey pressed.

"An old family friend with an interest in magic. He came from France to meet India. He wants to study the language of magic with her."

I waited for Louisa to tell Mrs. Delancey about spell casting, and Fabian's belief that I could create new spells, but she did not. Mrs. Delancey seemed satisfied with the answer that Louisa offered.

"Does Lord Coyle know about Fabian and his visit?" I asked.

Louisa picked up her teacup and watched me over the rim. "I suspect so. He does tend to discover everything eventually."

I couldn't argue with that.

* * *

I MANAGED to avoid Fabian Charbonneau by either pretending not to be at home or claiming to have a headache. I even heard Matt tell the Frenchman that I was suffering from delicate nerves before our upcoming wedding. I almost gave myself away when I giggled on the landing.

"The funny thing is," I told Matt later, when we sat together in the drawing room, "I'm not in the least nervous about getting married."

"I am," he said, stretching out his long legs.

"Sad to see your bachelor days end? Worried we'll grow bored with one another? Or that we'll grow apart? Afraid your unique edges will be smoothed?"

He frowned at me. "I'm not, but now I'm worried about how *you* feel."

"I don't think we'll grow bored. We'll be fine, particularly if the children stay with us." I nodded at the door through which Cyclops and Duke entered.

"You are," Duke baited his friend.

"Am not," Cyclops growled back.

"You are."

"Say it again and I'll thump you."

"You—" Duke swallowed the rest of his words when Cyclops rounded on him. He ducked away and came to stand beside me, as if I could protect him.

"Dare I ask what you two are arguing about?" I said.

"Nothing," Cyclops mumbled, striding to the window. He paused, glanced outside, and returned to the door but didn't exit.

Sensing the danger had passed, Duke sprawled on the sofa and crossed his arms. "He won't admit he's moping."

Cyclops crossed the floor to the window again. This time he didn't even look out but turned and strode back. "That's because I ain't."

"Then why are you wearing my rug thin?" Matt asked idly.

Cyclops looked at the rug beneath his feet and sat on the sofa, rubbing his palms down his thighs. "Catherine sent a message earlier. She says Ronnie is anxious about the guild test tomorrow. She thinks he's not going to even try because he doesn't think he can pass."

"See?" Duke said smugly. "You do care for Catherine. If you didn't, you wouldn't worry about this."

Cyclops lowered his head, and I shot Duke a glare. He wisely clamped his mouth shut.

"This means a lot to you," Matt said quietly.

"It means a lot to her," Cyclops said. "She wants to be a woman of independent means, and this is the only way. If she opens the shop with her brother, they can move out of their parents' home, and she can keep house for him and assist in the shop. It's what she wants."

"Catherine has always had a strong character," I told them. "When she sets her mind to something, she doesn't stop until she achieves it."

I didn't tell them that I was mostly referring to her flirtations. She used to flit from one fellow to the next, leaving broken hearts in her wake. Until Cyclops. She was no longer distracted by compliments and charm at every turn. Setting her heart on something as grown up as a shop was a welcome change. A year ago, I would have thought it a passing whim, like her flirtations, but not anymore. Now it was different. *She* was different.

"I hope Ronnie attends the guild at the scheduled time," Cyclops went on. "Catherine is worried he won't."

"It's only three days away now," Miss Glass said as she entered the drawing room, Willie at her heels.

"No, it's tomorrow," Cyclops told her.

"The wedding is tomorrow?"

"Never mind. You're right, the wedding is three days away."

Miss Glass patted her heart. "For a moment there, I

thought I'd had one of my turns again and lost two whole days. Thank goodness there's still time."

"Time for what?" Matt asked with a worried glance at me. I didn't know what she was talking about either, either. Hopefully it wasn't about her family coming to the wedding after all.

"For Willemina to find a dress to wear," she said.

Silence.

Duke and Cyclops erupted in laughter. Matt appeared to be biting the inside of his cheek to contain his smile.

Willie's face darkened. "I ain't wearing a dress. India says I don't have to, so I ain't."

"India is being polite," Miss Glass said, picking up her spectacles from the table. "She really does want you to wear a dress." She put the spectacles on and gave Willie a thorough inspection. "Something in pink, perhaps."

"Pink!"

"You're right, pink is too feminine, and no one believes you to be feminine."

Duke hooted and slapped his knee. "Go on, Willie, get a pink dress for the wedding. Do it for Cyclops. He needs a good laugh."

Cyclops wiped the tear off his cheek but couldn't stop his grin. "I'll pay you to wear a pink dress with lace and ribbons, Willie."

Duke slapped Cyclops's shoulder and they fell over one another, laughing. There was nothing like teasing the third member of the trio to bring the other two closer together.

Miss Glass pinched Willie's shirtsleeves at the shoulders. Willie jerked away. "I ain't wearing a dress, Letty, so don't go sizing me up. If a dressmaker delivers anything with a skirt for me, on the morning of the wedding, I'll send her away again."

Miss Glass peered over the rim of her spectacles. "At least put on a new waistcoat and jacket."

Willie looked down at her waistcoat and brushed at a stain to no avail. "All right, but it won't be pink."

Miss Glass clapped her hands. "Marvelous! I know a dressmaker who specializes in waistcoats and jackets. She takes her cues from gentlemen's outfits, but they're suited to a woman's shape. You'll look very becoming, Willemina, as long as you wear trousers and not buckskins." She fixed her gaze on Willie's buckskins. "I don't suppose you'll consider riding breeches?"

"No!"

"Lady Kitty Hargrave wears a blue riding habit with white trousers from a Saville Row tailor, and she's quite the fashion setter."

"She sounds like someone I'll like." Willie gave her a hard smile. "Introduce us and I'll go to her tailor."

I wasn't sure Miss Glass fully understood Willie's meaning at first, but then a slow blush crept up her cheeks.

"Your usual trousers will be fine," she said, removing her spectacles.

She sat as Bristow entered the drawing room. "Mr. Gideon Steele," he announced.

Chronos stepped around Bristow and greeted Miss Glass with a small bow. "Good afternoon, madam. Isn't this a pleasant family gathering?"

She looked taken aback by his deference and pleasantness. Usually Chronos paid her very little mind, but now he gave her his full attention and a smile. "How are you, Mr. Steele?" she asked.

"I'm fit as a fiddle, thank you." He turned to Willie. "And you, Willie? How are you?"

"Fine," Willie said, as confused by Chronos's attention as the rest of us.

"India driving you mad with her bridal demands?" He chuckled.

"No."

"She's very fortunate to be marrying into such a diverse and interesting family," he went on. "There'll never be a dull moment, eh, Cyclops?"

Cyclops's eye narrowed. "Are you feeling all right, sir?"

"Very well indeed." Chronos eyed a spare chair and arched his brow. "May I?"

"Of course," Matt said. "You know you don't need an invitation to join us. You're always welcome here."

"Thank you. Most kind." Chronos sat. "You're very lucky to be marrying such a fine gentleman, India." He was up to something, but I couldn't decide if I ought to be worried or not.

"Dinner is still two hours away," I told them.

He put up his hands. "No, no, no, that's not why I'm here."

"Then why are you here?"

"To see my granddaughter before she weds."

"The wedding is three days away, and you're invited. That's three days on which you can see me, including the day itself. Or are you going somewhere? Will you miss it?"

"I wouldn't miss it for the world. You're my one and only grandchild, and a wedding is a special day. Of course I'll be there."

If only he'd made an effort to be with me on other important days of my life, I might have believed him. "Come now, Chronos. Out with it. What do you want?"

"India," he purred. "I don't have an ulterior motive for seeing you."

I arched my brows and waited.

The silence weighed heavily until he finally sighed.

"Very well. I want to know if you've invited Gabriel Seaford to the wedding."

"Of course. It's the least we can do after he saved Matt's life. Besides, we like him. He's a good man."

"And you wish to remain friends. Good, good. Very wise. Keep him close. It'll make it easier, next time. You ought to consider asking him to join you on your honeymoon, too."

Matt barked a laugh, but I simply stared at Chronos. He was utterly serious, and the more I thought about it, the more I realized his point was a valid one. What if Matt's watch stopped working while we were away? It would take days to return from France. Days that he might not have to spare.

Miss Glass collected her spectacles and book and stood. "If you're going to have such a morbid discussion, I'm leaving."

Chronos waited until she was gone before addressing me again. "I've just come from the hospital where Gabe works; he told me you haven't even brought up the topic of the watch with him since that day."

"Why were you visiting Gabe?" When he avoided my gaze, I added, "This is about Fabian, isn't it? Did you introduce him to Gabe?"

"No." I glared at Chronos, and he eventually slumped into the chair. He wasn't a good liar, just a frequent one. "Yes," he muttered.

"Fabian wanted to find out more about Gabe's doctoring magic, didn't he?"

"Can you blame him? Gabe's magic is incredibly rare." He pointed at Matt. "He did something so fantastic that it's hard to believe. Fabian simply wanted to talk to him about the experience, magician to magician."

"And question him about the words he used?" Matt

275

prompted. "To help fill the gaps in Charbonneau's knowledge?"

I clicked my tongue. "Honestly, Chronos, you've got quite a nerve. Poor Gabe is new to his magic and is probably still coming to terms with his power."

"Not to mention he was at work," Matt said. "A place where he can't freely discuss magic."

"They get busy in hospitals," Willie chimed in with authority.

"As it turns out, he didn't have much time to talk to Fabian," Chronos said with a defiant lift of his chin.

"So you came here," Matt said. "You hoped to learn if Gabe is coming to the wedding so you could talk to him there, perhaps encourage him to seek Fabian out."

I gasped. "Chronos! That's low, even for you. There will be no talk of magic at the wedding. Is that clear?"

"But—"

"Is that clear?"

He crossed his arms and pouted, looking every inch the defiant child after a scolding.

"Did Fabian send you here?" I asked.

"He mentioned that you've been avoiding him." He straightened. "So I thought I'd try to persuade you to talk to him."

I stood and peered through the window. I spotted Fabian loitering several doors away. He saw me and lifted a hand in a wave. I beckoned him to come and informed Bristow to let him in.

"Does your invitation mean you'll help him?" Chronos asked, eyes brightening.

"It means I refuse to let an acquaintance stand outside on a warm day when I could offer him refreshments inside."

Chronos's mood lifted upon Fabian's entry, although he restrained himself and did not bring up the topic of magic again. Peter brought in tea and I poured. I'd expected Duke, Willie and Cyclops to make their excuses and leave, but they seemed curious about Fabian. He seemed just as interested in them.

"You are from the Wild West show, no?" he asked, indicating Willie's clothing.

"Lord, no," Willie blurted out. "Our outfits are gen-u-ine, not like what them two-bit actors wear."

"Actors? Are they not real cowboys and natives?"

"They can ride and shoot, but they're actors, mark my words. They shoot at tin cans and cigarette boxes." She tapped her chest. "*We* shoot at real outlaws, on account of we work for the law back home. Here, too. Did you read about the murder of that American sharpshooter?"

"Ah, yes, India and Mr. Glass captured the killer, no?"

"And me," Willie said. "I helped."

"Then you will perhaps know he is being released soon," Fabian said to me.

"How do you know?" I asked.

"I just know."

"I bet you do," Matt muttered.

"Fabian has contacts, both on the continent and here," Chronos said. "He knows everything that happens in the world of magic and magicians. It's likely he knew about Lord Coyle freeing Hendry before you did, India."

"Are you a friend to Lord Coyle and his group of collectors?" I asked Fabian.

"Not a friend, no," Fabian said. "They are artless."

"You can still be friends to them. The artless are not our enemy."

Fabian's gaze flicked to the faces of my friends. He gave me a tight smile. "Of course."

"Hendry will owe Coyle for the rest of his life," Chronos bit off. "It's deplorable."

"Why?" Duke asked.

"Because Hendry is a magician. He shouldn't owe an artless anything. He should be lauded, revered by the likes of Coyle."

Fabian nodded slowly. "I agree, *naturellement*. And yet I also agree with Coyle's terms. How can you not, *mon ami*?"

"What terms?" Cyclops asked.

"Marriage and children," I said. "Lord Coyle and his friends want to see the paper magic bloodline continue. Since Mr. Hendry is the only living paper magician, the future of the lineage is in his hands."

"He won't like it," Willie said with a shake of her head.

Fabian contemplated his teacup. "Then he should not have killed the only other paper magician who could father children."

"That's all that matters to you lot, ain't it?" Willie spat. "The continuation of the line, the future of magic. You don't care what Hendry wants."

"I said I was against it!" Chronos cried.

"You're just like Oscar Barratt, railroading everyone, forcing them into your way of thinking. What about fairness? Justice? Maybe India would rather live a quiet life than be an object of curiosity. Maybe some magicians don't want to practice their magic because they know the trouble it'll cause. Maybe some don't want to change who they are to secure the future of their lineage."

I suspected that last statement was the main point of Willie's tirade. I wished I were sitting closer, to take her hand and reassure her that no one would ask her to change. We liked her just the way she was.

She shot to her feet and stormed out before I could say anything, however. I watched her go, wondering if I ought to follow. Duke rose and gave me a reassuring smile before leaving too.

Fabian apologized and looked rather sheepish, but Chronos seemed to forget about Willie the moment she was out of sight.

"Speaking of Barratt," he said. "He told us of the difficulties he had with his printer. Forgive me, but I have to ask." He cleared his throat. "Was it you who threatened to expose the printer's illegal operation, Glass?"

Matt's gaze turned frosty. "No."

"You didn't *have* to ask," I said to Chronos. "Honestly, you're as subtle as...as Willie, sometimes. And I'm somewhat glad Oscar's book won't be printed. It's too soon. The world isn't ready."

"Ah, but it is ready, India. Look at the reception his articles produced." Chronos looked too smug for my liking.

"Has he found another printer already?" I asked.

"Perhaps," Fabian said. "We do not know Mr. Barratt's plans. They do not concern us. What does concern us, India, is your answer." He shifted forward on the chair and clasped his hands together. "May I be so bold as to ask if you will consider researching spells with me?"

I pressed my fingers to my temple. It was all a little too much, coming so soon after Hendry's arrest and release, especially with the wedding only days away.

"India," Matt said gently. "You don't need to give an answer yet."

"I say," Chronos spluttered. "Let *her* speak."

"Matt's right," I said. "I won't be considering your request until after the honeymoon, Fabian. Besides, I doubt whether I'm as powerful as everyone thinks I am. My new watch doesn't even chime when I'm in danger. It's likely the old one did as a result of the magic my father put into it, not me."

Chronos snorted. "Your father wasn't all that powerful."

"How do you know? You said yourself that you know

very little about him. Perhaps he kept the strength of his powers from you. Perhaps he kept a spell from you."

"And how would he have learned a spell to make a watch save someone's life? Either from me or your grandmother, that's who, but neither of us knew such a spell."

"She might have, but you wouldn't know, since you abandoned her. It's likely she kept certain things from you, considering the way you neglected her."

"I didn't neglect her." He sounded like a sulking child again. "I gave her everything she wanted, including leaving her."

I pushed to my feet. "Good day to you both. I have wedding preparations to see to."

"There is one way to know if you are powerful or not." Fabian's quietly confident words stopped me by the door. I didn't like that he knew such a statement would intrigue me, yet I couldn't deny that it did.

"Go on," I said.

He rose and approached me. "A powerful magician will be a spell caster. If you can create new spells, India, then you *are* powerful, and the magic in the watch will have come from you. If you cannot, then..." He shrugged. "We will work together to find out, if you like. After your honeymoon, of course."

"Of course," I murmured.

He took my hand and kissed the back of it. "My warmest congratulations to you both."

I watched him leave, my heart in my throat and my head feeling stuffed with wool. I thought I might have just agreed to work with him.

CHAPTER 18

"**I** don't like him," Matt said.

I tucked a strand of hair under my cap, adjusted my neckerchief, and hitched up my trousers. A thorough inspection of my reflection in the dressing table mirror brought a smile of satisfaction to my face. If I angled my head down, and pulled the cap low, I could pass as a man, thanks to my height. Although the overcoat would have to be large to adequately hide my breasts.

"So you've already told me, Matt. Several times."

He leaned against the closed door to my bedroom and crossed his arms, looking every bit the brooding Byronic hero. I tried not to smile. It would only make him self-conscious. "Not several," he mumbled. "Only three."

"It's understandable that Fabian wants to explore my magic with me. He has been studying the language for years, and now he has the opportunity to fill in some gaps in his knowledge. In theory, anyway. The reality might be quite different." I smiled at him in the reflection. "But we'll worry about it after our honeymoon. We have quite enough on our plate at the moment."

He responded with a grunt.

I turned and performed a bow. "How do I look?"

His gaze swept down my length and settled on my breasts, straining against the shirt and braces. He pushed off from the door and prowled toward me, a devilish smile curving his lips. "I like it."

"You're not supposed to like it."

He settled his hands on my hips and nuzzled my throat above the collar. "Ask Willie if you can keep the outfit."

I swatted his arm but succumbed to his kisses and roaming hands, only for a few minutes, before I pulled away. "We have to go. It's time."

He sighed and checked his watch. "Put on the coat. If the servants ask why we're dressed like this, tell them we're doing maintenance at the convent."

"In the evening? They won't believe us." I reached for the coat lying across the bed. "Anyway, it's not the servants you have to worry about. They're too discreet to ask questions. Your aunt, however, is a different story."

"Good point. I'll go first. If the coast is clear, I'll whistle."

THE CLANDESTINE EXERCISE promised to be thrilling—until we arrived at The Worshipful Company of Watchmakers' hall on Warwick Lane. My visits to the guild hall had not gone well in the past. Not a single one. Hopefully this time would be different—for all our sakes.

We'd passed the lamplighter, on our way into the lane, carrying a long pole on his shoulder. He'd touched his cap brim, paused his whistling long enough to wish us a good evening, and continued on.

"He didn't realize I was a woman," I whispered to Matt. "He thought we were both men."

"I'm still going to do all the talking," he said, pulling harder on the cart to outstrip me.

A man stood on the pavement, stretching his neck out of his collar as he peered up at the figures of Old Man Time and the emperor, represented in the guild's coat of arms, above the main entrance.

"There's Ronnie," I said. "He's nervous."

"Hopefully he'll change his mind and go home," Matt said, stopping at the service door.

"He'd better not. We're here now."

Ronnie nodded at us and knocked on the door. It opened and he was admitted. Matt waited a minute before he knocked on the service door. With my head bowed, I didn't see the face of the man who opened it, but his voice wasn't one I recognized. It was just as we'd hoped; the regular porter, who knew us all too well, worked only during the day. The night porter had taken over and, according to Ronnie, he wasn't the cleverest fellow. When Ronnie had requested his test be scheduled in the evening, to allow him to continue working for his father during the day, the guild had agreed.

Perhaps this visit would go smoothly after all.

"Delivery from Compton's Metalworks," Matt announced in a perfect Cockney accent. "Apologies for the lateness. One of the machines had a fault in the factory."

"There must be a mistake," the porter said. "We received a delivery from Compton's earlier."

"Aye, but only for half the order. This is the rest. Didn't the boys tell you?"

Willie's earlier reconnaissance, and subsequent questioning of the delivery men, had been fruitful. She'd learned of a delivery of parts from Compton's Metalworks factory. It had been Cyclops's idea to pretend the delivery hadn't been complete.

The porter stepped aside. "Take the boxes down to the storeroom."

"I know where it is," Matt said, picking a box off the cart. With the step up to the door, we couldn't wheel the cart inside.

"Even so, I'll take you."

Damnation. We needed to get rid of the porter.

I lifted a box too, pretending it weighed a lot when it was actually empty. We followed the porter through the building's service corridors to the storeroom out the back near the kitchen. Matt and I both deposited our boxes on the shelves and returned to the service entrance. The porter escorted us.

A resounding knock on the main door echoed through the building. "It's like Oxford Street here tonight," the porter muttered, heading off.

Once he was out of sight, Cyclops and Willie emerged from the shadows near the service door. With Willie dressed in the same outfit as me, she should pass for me unless the porter was particularly observant. Since he hadn't looked at my face, I hoped he wouldn't notice the switch. It was only our difference in heights that set us apart. We were counting on the fact that people rarely observed servants and workers such as deliverymen very closely.

Willie gave me a nod, and Matt pecked my forehead. Then they wordlessly returned to the cart to offload the fake delivery. I cracked open the door through which the porter had gone. Cyclops leaned over me and we both peered through the gap toward the main entrance, where Duke engaged the porter in discussion. With the false beard and thick European accent, I hardly recognized him.

"What's that then?" the porter asked, loudly and slowly. "I can't understand you. Speak English."

I opened the door wider and crept into the hall,

Cyclops at my heels. The regular *tick tock* of the long case clock helped settle my nerves a little, even though everything could still go wrong at this point. Not only could the porter turn around and see us, but we could meet someone on the stairs and be trapped. Despite the late hour, and the fact there were no meetings tonight, there would be at least one guild member present to supervise Ronnie's test. Hopefully that person wouldn't remain in the testing room with him.

"No, no, sir." Duke's voice rose high, warning us of the porter's growing restlessness with the nonsensical conversation. "You do not understand. Listen."

I picked up my pace and dared not look back. We reached the second floor without being seen from below or passing anyone on the stairs. It was darker here, the only light coming from the gaps around the door to the testing room at the end of the corridor. I'd never taken the test myself. My application hadn't even been considered. I used to believe that was because I was a woman. I now knew it was because I was a magician, although I expected the Court of Assistants were misogynists as well. It would be interesting to see if Catherine would ever be allowed to sit the test.

Cyclops took up position in the storeroom opposite the testing room. He kept the door open just enough to watch for anyone coming along the corridor. In the darkness, he was invisible.

I carefully twisted the handle of the testing room door and opened it a mere sliver. I could just make out Ronnie sitting at a desk, his face glowing in the lamplight. Beyond him stood another man, his back to me. I waited until he turned, and when I did, I reeled back.

Abercrombie.

I should have known he'd be the one to supervise

Ronnie, but it was still a shock. He'd be more suspicious and vigilant than other guild members.

I looked again, but Abercrombie had moved out of my line of sight. Ronnie bent over the workbench, an Oriental style clock in front of him with the housing open. I'd never seen anything quite like it, with its golden dragon decorations, filigree mounts, and open frieze panel. He removed a cog with tweezers, inspected it, and replaced it.

"Having trouble?" Abercrombie asked from somewhere to my left.

"No." Ronnie smiled at him. "Just getting started."

"Time's ticking. You might want to leave that if you're having trouble and take a look at the paper."

Ronnie dutifully turned his attention to the paper on the table. He read it and wrote something down in pencil.

I joined Cyclops in the storeroom and waited.

Nothing happened. No sounds came from further along the corridor or the staircase. I couldn't even hear a single clock ticking, even though the hall was full of them. The testing room was quite separate from the guild's dining hall, meeting rooms and service area.

Finally, the porter appeared, his strides long and fast. He muttered under his breath as he knocked on the testing room door.

Abercrombie opened it and scowled. "What is it?"

"There's a foreign watchmaker downstairs, sir, says he needs to speak to you." The porter leaned in and lowered his voice. "Something about magicians in his own country. He says he heard you're having similar problems here and wants to discuss a solution. At least, I think that's what he wants. His accent's real strong."

Abercrombie looked behind him to Ronnie. Then with a huff of breath, he opened the door wider. "Stay here. Make sure he doesn't cheat."

"I'm not going to cheat," came Ronnie's voice. "How can I?"

The porter and Abercrombie swapped places. I watched as Abercrombie pocketed his *pince-nez* and hurried off along the corridor, carrying a lantern.

Cyclops waited for him to leave before he slipped out of the storeroom. He gave me a small nod and headed the same way. Once he was near the end of the corridor, he banged his fist on the wall.

The porter poked his head around the door and glanced toward the sound, but Cyclops had disappeared into the dense darkness at the end of the hallway. Just as the porter was about to return inside the testing room, another bang echoed along the corridor, followed by a raven's caw.

The porter clicked his tongue, glanced back inside the room, and said, "Stay here." He emerged and hurried down the corridor, plunging into the darkness.

I slipped into the testing room.

Ronnie's face lit up. "Thank God. This clock is defeating me. And these questions... I've managed half, but the rest are impossible without my study books." Even as he spoke, he folded up the paper and handed it to me before removing another paper from his pocket. He spread that out on the desk while I tucked the real test into my coat pocket.

Then I went to work on the clock. It was an exquisite and quite rare triple fusee bracket clock with the loveliest detail. Internally, it was one of the more difficult mechanisms I'd seen, but most clockmakers could fix it if the right tools and parts had been supplied.

"He has given you the wrong sized cogs," I said.

"I knew something wasn't right! The bloody cheat."

"Tell him when he returns that—" I spotted some boxes stamped with Compton's Metalworks's mark on a shelf. I opened one, then another and another, until I found what I needed. I handed Ronnie the box. "Try these."

"Thanks, India. You'd better go before the porter gets back."

I patted the pocket with the test paper and made to leave, only to stop dead when I heard voices. Both Abercrombie and the porter were returning, and I was trapped in the room. My stomach dropped. There was nowhere to hide. If they entered, I would be seen.

Ronnie had heard the voices too. He stared at the door, frozen. The voices stopped just outside. The handle turned.

Hell.

"I don't care what you heard, you shouldn't have left your post," Abercrombie was saying.

The door opened wider and I slipped behind it, flattening myself to the wall.

"It's them ravens again, sir," the porter said. "They've been pecking away at the window frames. If we don't scare them off, they'll destroy the wood."

"Did you see them?"

"They must have flown off when I opened the window."

"I asked you to stay here," Abercrombie growled.

"He didn't cheat. Look, he's still here."

Long, fine fingers grasped the edge of the door. "Return to your station. If that foreigner comes back, tell him to go away. That's if he *is* a foreigner."

"What else would he be?"

"A friend to Mr. Mason, here."

Ronnie looked up from the desk, all smiles. "You've given me a real difficult task with this clock, sir. It's a fine piece, though. Real fine. I'm sure I'll fix it. I don't like to let things beat me."

"You only have fifteen more minutes."

Footsteps retreated along the corridor as the porter left.

Soon Abercrombie would be back inside and closing the door. I squeezed my eyes shut and wished I could disappear into the wall at my back. With my heart in my throat, I waited for the inevitable confrontation.

A series of knocks and raven calls sounded along the corridor. I opened my eyes just as Abercrombie swore.

"What the devil?" He must be standing just outside the door, too close for me to escape.

Ronnie shook his head at me. I was right; Abercrombie hadn't moved away.

I waited, my heart beating a warning in my throat, making it hard to breathe, hard to concentrate. I remained where I was, certain that my heartbeat could be heard as clearly as Cyclops's knocks.

"It's that bloody raven, sir!" the porter shouted. He sounded like he was far down the corridor. "I think it's inside! Christ, it just bloody swooped me. Where'd it go?"

"That's not a bird," Abercrombie said.

Ronnie waved at me from the desk and mouthed, "Go."

I hesitated. I hadn't heard Abercrombie's footsteps retreat. I emerged from behind the door and peered into the corridor.

Abercrombie stood a mere three feet away, his back to me. He held the lamp high but its circle of light didn't extend far. The end of the corridor was in darkness.

"What's going on?" he called out. Clearly he wasn't going to venture further to see for himself. He wasn't willing to risk leaving Ronnie alone.

I had to take this opportunity. If he turned around, he would see me, and I was certain he would turn any moment. The knocks, made by Cyclops, seemed to grow more distant.

I tiptoed out of the testing room and slipped into the storeroom. I closed the door but not all the way, stopping just as Abercrombie turned around. Thanks to the poor light, he didn't notice the door ajar, and he re-entered the testing room.

I breathed a sigh of relief and crumpled to the floor. My knees were suddenly too weak to hold me. I removed the test sheet from my pocket but it was too dark to see it. I'd spotted a lamp near the door and reached up to unhook it, but the door sprang open.

I fell back but was saved from toppling into the shelves by a strong arm circling my waist. Matt's familiar scent enveloped me as thoroughly as his arm.

"You scared me," I said on a breath. "Where's Cyclops?"

"Doing his best raven impersonation. Willie was right. They do have a raven problem here." He struck a match and lit a candle he must have brought with him. "We have to hurry. The test is due to end soon."

I read through the test paper, completing the questions Ronnie couldn't and checking his answers on the others. He'd got one wrong but I decided to leave it for authenticity.

"Do you know how he's faring with the practical part of the test?" Matt asked.

"He'll be fine. We have to get this back to him."

"Leave it to me. Ready?"

I kissed him on the lips then blew out the candle. "Ready."

Matt opened the storeroom door a fraction and knocked on it. Abercrombie emerged from the testing room and peered into the darkness. He frowned in our direction, and I had the sickening feeling he'd seen us.

"Sir," said Ronnie from within. "Sir, I've finished the clock. I was right. You'd given me the wrong parts, but these cogs fit. Think I'll just have a quick stretch of my legs while I read the rest of these questions. Mr. Abercrombie, sir, can you check the clock?

Abercrombie returned inside and closed the door.

Precisely ten seconds later, I slipped the corner of the test paper underneath it.

Ronnie yawned loudly on the other side. He sounded very close. Good. He'd timed it perfectly and followed the plan precisely. The rest of the paper suddenly disappeared, pulled through the gap between door and floor.

Matt took my hand and together we raced along the corridor. It was up to Ronnie now to swap one paper for the other without Abercrombie noticing. We could do nothing more.

We paused at the top of the stairs to listen. The guild hall was silent except for the ticking of the long case clock. Matt tugged on my hand and we hurried downstairs, stepping lightly.

The porter suddenly appeared in the entrance hall below. "Them bloody ravens," he muttered.

Matt and I stopped. The entrance hall was lit by two lamps but the light didn't reach us. It was dark enough on the stairs that the porter might not see us if we stayed very still. Of course, if he decided to climb the stairs, our ruse would be ruined, and all the planning and tonight's adventure would be for naught. We could pretend we'd become lost after our delivery, but if the porter mentioned the incident to Abercrombie, he'd know it was us and what we'd done.

"Now where could it have gone?" the porter said, scratching his head. "I'm sure I heard it down here."

I held my breath and squeezed Matt's hand. He squeezed back, but there was nothing more he could do. We were trapped on the stairs, utterly exposed.

CHAPTER 19

a raven cawed. It sounded like it came from the back of the building, near the kitchen.

"Bloody hell," the porter muttered. "The devil take you, wretched beast. Where are you?" His footsteps receded and the entrance was clear.

I breathed again.

Matt tugged on my hand, and together we crept down the rest of the stairs, tiptoed across the tiled floor, and exited the building. We ran. The task was much easier in men's clothing than women's and I was able to take long strides. I felt giddy and my heart beat wildly, not just because of the exertion. We had achieved what we'd set out to do, and Abercrombie was none the wiser.

We rounded the corner, almost colliding with Willie and Duke, who were waiting with the cart.

"Well?" Willie asked.

I beamed at her. "Success!"

"Here comes Cyclops," Matt said as he peered back down Warwick Lane.

"It was so thrilling!" I said. "Duke, you were marvelous. Your accent was...unique."

Duke grinned, causing the false beard to detach from the left side of his jaw and hang loosely.

Willie snorted. "It was unique because it didn't sound like anything. What were you supposed to be? Prussian? French?"

"Worldly," Duke said, smoothing the beard back in place.

Cyclops joined us, all smiles. "That was close. The porter almost walked right into me. I had to brush his cheek to make him think it was fluttering wings. He yelped like a puppy."

I threw my arms around him. "Thank goodness you're safe. We're all safe."

Cyclops chuckled. "Thank the lord for making that porter as stupid as a brick."

Matt cleared his throat. "Don't I get a hug?"

I propelled myself into his arms. He caught me, laughing.

"We better get going," Willie said. "Staying near the scene of a crime is a sure way to get caught. I learned that the hard way."

I took Matt's hand. "And tomorrow's the eve of our wedding. We have a lot of things to do."

"We do?" Matt asked. "I thought I just had to arrive at church on time on the appointed day."

"With the rings," I added. "And your suit pressed, shoes shined, and hair trimmed. Those are your tasks for tomorrow. Oh, and packing for your overnight stay at Brown's Hotel."

"Don't worry, India," Duke said. "Cyclops and me will see he looks presentable."

Matt placed his arm around my shoulders and drew me

in for a friendly hug, as I'd seen him do with Duke and Cyclops many times. "Don't worry, dearest fiancée. *I'll* be fine. *You're* the one spending all day with Willie and my aunt."

"Aye," Willie said on a groan. "And we'll be doing women's things. It's going to be hell."

"I'm looking forward to it," I said. "If nothing else, keeping you and Miss Glass from irritating one another will take my mind off my nerves."

Matt slowed his pace, allowing the others to walk ahead. "Are you nervous about marrying?"

"I'm nervous about the wedding. I'm not used to being the center of attention. But I'm not nervous about marrying you. Not in the least."

He scooped me tighter to his side and planted a breath-stealing kiss on my lips, though it ended all too quickly. "I admit to being nervous too," he said as we continued on, arm in arm.

"About being the center of attention?"

"About the wedding night."

Thank goodness for poor street lighting. I didn't want him to see my reddening cheeks. "I'm sure you'll be fine," I quipped.

"It's not my performance I'm worried about." His voice was light and full of humor. He wasn't taking this conversation at all seriously, which was just as well. I was anxious enough about the wedding night. I didn't want him being nervous too. "It's your reaction to seeing it that worries me. You'll be shocked."

I laughed but quickly swallowed it. Men probably didn't like women laughing about their manhood. "I promise not to act shocked."

"You say that now, but you might not be able to hide your reaction. It's quite ugly, really. You might be overwhelmed."

"I'll try not to faint at the sight of it. Besides, I'm sure ugly is too strong a word. I may not be an expert but I have seen them before. In diagrams, of course, not in real life."

"You've seen diagrams? Where?"

"Books about nature and that sort of thing." Good lord, were we really having this conversation? At least the others couldn't hear. They'd be in fits of laughter.

"They put diagrams of bullet wounds in books about nature? Clearly you've read different books to me."

Bullet wounds! Oh. The devil. I thumped his shoulder. "Very amusing."

"My, my, India Steele, what were *you* talking about?"

"You'd better stop now or I might find I have a headache on our wedding night. You'll have to wait before I see your... bullet wound."

He laughed softly. "You win."

* * *

AFTER THE WEDDING CEREMONY, I found I couldn't recall all of the details. I remembered our first kiss as man and wife but not the signing of the register. I remembered how Matt had looked when he first saw me, because I'd never seen him look overwhelmed, happy, and awed all at once. But the rest of the ceremony passed in a fog.

Had I spoken the vows clearly? Did all of our invited guests come? Did Cyclops and Catherine look at one another? Had the sun been shining as I entered the church? It was certainly sunny afterward as we stood on the steps, receiving congratulations as man and wife.

Man and wife. Not long ago, I thought I'd never use that phrase to refer to myself. Now, I couldn't imagine never having met Matt. How empty my life would have been, how dull, like a black and white sketch compared to a vibrant painting. There was no comparison, and a life without Matt didn't bear thinking about.

We didn't leave one another's side as our friends and family offered us congratulations. Our fingers wound together, entwined in a knot that neither of us cared to untangle. Not yet.

Even passing strangers stopped to congratulate us and, just as we were about to climb into our carriage, one unwelcome party burst onto the scene, his equine nose in the air.

Cyclops and Duke saw Abercrombie first and tried to stop him. They managed to keep him back but his voice traveled.

"You cheated, Ronald Mason! I know you did, and I know Miss Steele helped you."

Ronnie crossed his arms. "How could I have cheated?"

"What's all this about?" Mr. Mason asked. He went to approach Abercrombie, but his wife grasped his arm.

"Your son is a cheat!" Abercrombie wailed. I couldn't even see him with Duke and Cyclops blocking my view. "*She* helped him. That *witch* did his test for him!"

Matt tensed and stepped forward.

"Wait," I whispered, watching Mr. Mason. Like all good fathers, he looked indignant that his son's reputation had been called into question. His wife clung to his arm and spoke quietly to him, but he still held himself rigidly, his fists closed at his sides. I'd never seen the rather bland man look so furious.

"Do you have proof?" Mr. Mason barked.

Abercrombie stepped into sight, adjusting his tie, but Cyclops and Duke remained within arm's length. "No one could have passed that test except a magician. That's all the proof I need."

Mrs. Mason and Miss Glass gasped. Mr. Mason cocked

his head to the side, frowning. "Why could only a magician pass it?" he demanded.

"I, er...that's not what I meant."

"I never left that room, sir," Ronnie said. "I ask again, how could I have cheated?"

Abercrombie stabbed a finger in my direction "*She* must have given you the answers."

"Why couldn't he have simply passed on his own?" Catherine asked, blinking innocently at Abercrombie.

"Yes," Mr. Mason added. "You were about to tell us why only a magician could pass. Did *you* cheat, Abercrombie? Did you give my son an impossible test so he'd fail?"

Abercrombie's jaw worked, and a hiss of air wheezed from his nose. "Of course not!" he spluttered. "The test was difficult but not impossible. I merely question your son's ability. He's not intelligent enough to pass."

Ronnie merely laughed, but his parents' faces darkened. Mr. Mason's knuckles whitened. But it was Mrs. Mason who exploded. "If either of you lack brains, sir, it's you," she spat. "You've presented yourself at a function where you are not invited, and you have admitted to manipulating the test."

"What?" Abercrombie said. "No!"

"It seems *you* have failed. You've all but said that our son passed. He's now a full member of the Watchmaker's Guild. Tomorrow, he and our Catherine will re-open Steele's shop. And we couldn't be prouder."

If Mr. Mason was still reluctant to let Ronnie and Catherine set up shop together, he didn't show it, and nor would he now. There was nothing like a common enemy to bring people closer together.

"I will see that they're blocked at every turn," Abercrombie said through gritted teeth. "A friend to Miss Steele cannot be granted a license."

"Who will stop them?" Mr. Mason asked. "Not you. You

have admitted to making our Ronnie's test more difficult than usual. You have admitted to trying to block his application at every turn. You are dishonorable and have none of the qualities I want in my guild's master. I'm going to see that an extraordinary meeting is called for next week to elect a new leader."

Abercrombie scoffed, but he didn't look quite so cocksure. The glare he turned on me still managed to shred my nerves, however. "I know you helped him, Miss Steele. I know it."

"It's time to move on now, sir," Detective Inspector Brockwell said.

Matt broke away and stormed up to Abercrombie. I couldn't see his face but it must have been fierce, because Abercrombie paled. He backed up, almost tripping over his own feet, before turning and hurrying off.

"It's Mrs. Glass now!" I called after him. "Please try to remember in future."

I enveloped Matt's hand between both of mine and watched Abercrombie until he disappeared around the corner. Finally, I stopped shaking.

Matt circled me in his arms. "Are you all right, Mrs. Glass?"

"I am. Let's go home and enjoy Mrs. Potter's fine cooking with our family and friends. I think we deserve it for a job well done." I nodded at Ronnie as his father patted him on the back.

Beside him, Catherine sported a tentative smile, but it wasn't directed at her brother. It was directed at Cyclops. He, however, pretended not to notice, but if his shuffling feet were an indication, he could certainly sense her attention.

* * *

THE WEDDING FEAST was a marvelous affair with a delicious array of meats, seafood, salads, vegetables, cakes, jellies, ices and confections that necessitated the loosening of my corset laces. We managed to all fit in the dining room, although it was tight, and I was glad to move into the drawing room with just the women when the men removed themselves to the smoking room.

Willie looked uncertain of which way to go, and it was only because Miss Glass scooped her arm through Willie's and hauled her toward the drawing room that she ended up with us. We were not left alone for long, though. The gentlemen returned with an announcement.

"The photographer is here," Duke said.

"We're having our photograph taken?" I asked. "I don't recall organizing that."

"You didn't," Willie said. "We did. It's our gift to you. Come on, gather 'round."

We had to move into the entrance hall to allow space for everyone. I sat on a chair while Matt stood by my side. Our guests arranged themselves on the steps behind us, with Miss Glass closest to Matt. She wouldn't stay there, however, and while the photographer set up his equipment, she made a great fuss over my dress, settling the long silk train where it could be seen.

"You must try not to embrace everyone so much, India. You're crushing the skirt."

I looked down at the white satin skirt. It was indeed a little crushed. The bodice, however, was still in excellent condition, with its intricate lacework and glass beading creating a dense pattern of leaves and flowers. I hugged her as she went to move away.

"Thank you, Miss Glass," I murmured.

"It's quite appropriate for you to call me Aunt Letitia now," she said, hugging me back.

"Letty, sit down," Willie said. "The photographer's ready."

"But not Aunt Letty," Miss Glass added.

Matt and I had a photograph with all the guests, then another with just Aunt Letitia, and finally alone. I was exhausted by the end of the day and ready to farewell our guests. Mr. and Mrs. Mason and Gabe left mid-afternoon, but the rest lingered, including all of the Mason siblings. Ronnie was in good spirits, having attained his guild membership, and his brothers seemed determined to celebrate with him. Their sister didn't look quite so happy. The one time I saw her trying to engage Cyclops in conversation, he hardly even looked at her, let alone addressed her. She finally gave up and went home, leaving her brothers behind.

"That wasn't fair," I said to Cyclops. "You ought to give her a chance. You should give yourselves a chance."

"Don't lecture me today, India," he said and walked off.

I caught Matt's eye as he stood by the fireplace in the drawing room. He arched a brow. I shrugged. He jerked his head toward the door and winked. I smiled and rose to join him, only to be accosted by Chronos. I sat again with a sigh.

"Now that the wedding is over," he began, "have you decided—"

"I told you I'd decide after the honeymoon," I said hotly.

"I was only going to ask if you've decided to stay on in London or move to the countryside."

"Oh." I hadn't thought about moving. London was such a part of me that I wasn't sure I could live anywhere else. Although I did like the countryside with the fresh air and green as far as the eye could see. "We'll decide on that after the honeymoon too," I said.

"It's time to start thinking of the future."

"One step at a time, Chronos."

He looked to Matt. "You found a good one there. I like him."

"Even though he's artless?"

He closed his hand over mine. "It's a pity your children's powers will be diluted, but not even I'm selfish enough to want you to give up a rich and titled gentleman for magic."

"Thank you. But you do know I'm not marrying him for his money or his title, don't you?"

"Of course." His gaze wandered around the room, growing sadder by the second. "My wedding day was nothing like this. This is full of joy. Mine resembled a funeral. I saw your grandmother sobbing into her mother's apron in the kitchen." His grip tightened. "We weren't suited to one another, and if she were here, she'd agree. We weren't given a choice, though. We married because our families wanted to keep the magical lineage strong. They succeeded, but at what cost? Your grandmother and I grew to hate each other, and your father... What did our hate do to him? Maybe it forced him to hide his magic from the world. It definitely put a wedge between us, one neither of us knew how to repair. My only regret is not getting to know him better. But I can make up for that now, with you."

I hugged him. I was too full of tears to tell him what I wanted to tell him—that he surprised me sometimes, and that I loved him, despite everything.

He patted my shoulder. "You can still be happy with Glass and help Charbonneau at the same time. You can have both, India."

And sometimes he could ruin a wonderful moment with a few ill-chosen words.

"I knew you'd bring him into the conversation somehow." I kissed his forehead and rose. "If you don't mind, I'd like to talk to my husband now. I've hardly spoken to him all day."

I joined Matt by the fireplace. It was another full hour before our guests left, and another hour still before Cyclops,

Duke, Willie and Miss Glass—Aunt Letitia—all decamped to Brown's Hotel for the evening.

Mrs. Bristow had left a bowl of strawberries in Matt's bedroom—*our* bedroom—with a bottle of wine. I didn't notice them until the following morning.

"Hungry?" I asked, offering Matt the bowl at breakfast time. He lay sprawled on the bed, entirely naked, the sheets rumpled near his feet. He looked sleepy, sated, and more delicious than the strawberries. I set the bowl down before I dropped it. "Me either."

I joined him on the bed and snuggled into his side. My hair fell across his chest and my skin warmed at his touch. His hand skimmed over my thigh, my hip and dipped at my waist, finally settling over my breast. Heat banked in his eyes.

"I love seeing you like this," he murmured. "I love touching you, being with you. I love that you give yourself to me freely. I love *you*, India." He kissed me with renewed passion, proving that he wasn't entirely sated yet.

"It's seems I'm hungry, after all, but not for strawberries," I said as his kisses moved to my cheek, my jaw, the hollow of my throat. I moaned and arched into him.

I felt him smile against the swell of my breast. "I would never have guessed that behind the prim and proper façade lay a tigress."

"You mistake my intentions, sir." I caressed the contours of his muscular chest, stroked the light dusting of hair across his flat stomach, and continued down, down. "I merely want to inspect the scar again."

His breath hitched. "Inspect away."

The ragged scar on his upper thigh had been the result of a bullet shot by his own grandfather. It had almost killed Matt. If it hadn't been for Dr. Parsons and Chronos, he would have bled to death. If it hadn't been for magic, he would not be lying there, as healthy as any thirty year old. The scar itself looked ugly, and it had been caused by a cruel man, but I couldn't hate it. For one thing, it was a part of Matt, and for another, we would never have met without it.

I traced my finger around the scar's rough edges only to pause as warmth spread across my fingertip. Not ordinary body heat but magical warmth. Even after all these years, Dr. Parsons' magic was strong enough to be felt by me.

Matt touched my hair, stroking it off my forehead. "What is it?" he murmured. "What are you thinking about?"

"Magic."

He touched my chin, and I peered up to see him better. His hooded eyes watched me as intently as the first time we'd met. With his disheveled hair and a lazy tilt to his lips, he was an intoxicating combination of devil and hero. The effect sent a rush of heat through me that had nothing to do with magic and everything to do with basic nature.

"You have much to think about," he said quietly. "Charbonneau's request, your own power..."

"Yes." I climbed on top of him and leaned down to kiss him. "But not today. Today I want to enjoy being Mrs. Matthew Glass."

He grasped me around the waist and flipped me onto my back, reversing our positions. "Then allow me to introduce you to another benefit that comes with the title."

I giggled as he kissed me from head to toe. Then I was no longer giggling as he paused at my hips and did indeed show me one more benefit to being his wife.

AUTHOR'S NOTE: Buffalo Bill's Wild West show really did visit London with Annie Oakley, but not in 1890 as I have depicted here. I hope you'll forgive a little artistic license with the smudging of timelines.

Now Available:
THE PRISONER'S KEY
The 8th Glass and Steele novel

India and Matt investigate when a powerful magician accused of murder escapes from prison.

GET A FREE SHORT STORY

I wrote a short story for the Glass and Steele series that is set before THE WATCHMAKER'S DAUGHTER. Titled THE TRAITOR'S GAMBLE it features Matt and his friends in the Wild West town of Broken Creek. It contains spoilers from THE WATCHMAKER'S DAUGHTER, so you must read that first. The best part is, the short story is FREE, but only to my newsletter subscribers. So subscribe now via my website if you haven't already.

A MESSAGE FROM THE AUTHOR

I hope you enjoyed reading THE CHEATER'S GAME as much as I enjoyed writing it. As an independent author, getting the word out about my book is vital to its success, so if you liked this book please consider telling your friends and writing a review at the store where you purchased it. If you would like to be contacted when I release a new book, subscribe to my newsletter at http://cjarcher.com/contact-cj/newsletter/. You will only be contacted when I have a new book out.

ALSO BY C.J. ARCHER

SERIES WITH 2 OR MORE BOOKS

After The Rift

Glass and Steele

The Ministry of Curiosities Series

The Emily Chambers Spirit Medium Trilogy

The 1st Freak House Trilogy

The 2nd Freak House Trilogy

The 3rd Freak House Trilogy

The Assassins Guild Series

Lord Hawkesbury's Players Series

The Witchblade Chronicles

SINGLE TITLES NOT IN A SERIES

Courting His Countess

Surrender

Redemption

The Mercenary's Price

ABOUT THE AUTHOR

C.J. Archer has loved history and books for as long as she can remember and feels fortunate that she found a way to combine the two. She spent her early childhood in the dramatic beauty of outback Queensland, Australia, but now lives in suburban Melbourne with her husband, two children and a mischievous black & white cat named Coco.

Subscribe to C.J.'s newsletter through her website to be notified when she releases a new book, as well as get access to exclusive content and subscriber-only giveaways. Her website also contains up to date details on all her books: http://cjarcher.com She loves to hear from readers. You can contact her through email cj@cjarcher.com or follow her on social media to get the latest updates on her books:

Made in the USA
Coppell, TX
23 January 2020